No Room
at the
Little Cornish
Inn

ALSO BY NANCY BARONE

New Hope for the Little Cornish Farmhouse

No Room
at the
Little Cornish
Inn

Nancy Barone

HEAD
of
ZEUS

An Aria Book

First published in the United Kingdom in 2020 by Aria,
an imprint of Head of Zeus Ltd

This paperback edition first published in 2021 by Aria,
an imprint of Head of Zeus Ltd

A CIP catalogue record for this book is available from the
British Library.

9 7 5 3 1 2 4 6 8

ISBN (E): 9781838938048
ISBN (PB): 9781800245969

Typeset by Siliconchips Services Ltd UK

Cover design © Cherie Chapman

Printed and bound in Great Britain by
CPI Group (UK) Ltd, Croydon CRO 4YY

Aria
5–8 Hardwick Street
London EC1R 4RG
WWW.ARIAFICTION.COM

To Lidia with love

I

O'er Hill and Dale

'Mummy, why do you have to work over the Christmas holidays?' Danny, my almost eight-year-old son, wants to know as we speed down the M3 towards Cornwall instead of Birmingham. 'Can't we go see Nana and Grandpa like we planned?'

The answer, my friend, is, unlike the famous song, not blowing in the wind, but actually blasting from my mobile phone in the form of the infamous and ominous 'Ride of the Valkyries' tune. It's the ringtone I've assigned to the HR manager at Johnson Hotels Head Office, Susan Hearst – better known as Susan the Sacker.

I've lost count of the number of times she's called since we left London, so I'm entitled to ignore her at least this once. I can always use the excuse that Cornwall has an iffy signal. Even the county border sign I've just sped past advises to – and I'm quoting here – remove my face from my phone because I won't get a decent signal anyway.

I was hoping to have a lovely Christmas with my family

and some old friends. Some good food, stops at the local bakery, time for reading a quality book by the fire. All the things that I don't have time for in London and was really looking forward to this year. And thanks to her, none of it is going to happen.

Because, at the eleventh hour, she gave me an assignment without any alternative, implying that I could be up for promotion as manager if I sort out the Old Bell Inn in Cornwall. It has lost a star due to a cartload of bad reviews and recent cancellations, creating a big black splotch on the pristine reputation of Johnson Hotels who, in turn, are considering closing it.

I'm supposed to go in incognito, observe, find out what the problems are and report back. But if I don't, it is, as Susan so politely put it, my ass out on the street. And if working during the holidays isn't bad enough, the 24th of December, only three weeks away, is Danny's eighth birthday.

My little boy shouldn't have to spend his big day watching his mum work. He should be having a ginormous party with his friends and family in Birmingham. My parents are crushed we can't be there this year, but they won't show it so as not to make me feel bad. However, every now and then, they ask me to move back and work in their coach company. Taking care of Danny there would be a breeze, surrounded by my people. Aunt Milly alone would kill to have him to herself. So why do I keep saying 'Thanks, but no thanks'? Why is it so important to me to be independent, when being independent is making me so miserable?

I shouldn't be here at all. I'm not a hotel inspector. I'm simply an assistant manager slash single mum, trying to make a living. Which Susan the Sacker, on a daily basis, seems to enjoy making impossible. When am I going to find the guts to stand up to her and make her stop treating me like the fifth wheel? I may not shout at everyone like she does, and yes, I do fraternise with my staff, but I get the job done. All I have to do is ask.

But Susan? Just know this: when I came home from my only sick leave in years, all my things – including Danny's first scan – had been tossed into the bin: my Hello Kitty writing Post-its, pads, photos, my York Minster pen, my *Women – half the population, all the brains* mug, my yearly supply of Skittles and Reese's Pieces, my Canada mouse pad, and even my battery charger. All gone, and my desk completely rearranged at a forty-five-degree angle so she can see what I'm doing from her own office desk. Because, oh how lucky can I be, I work at the flagship hotel adjacent to Head Office, where we are watched like guinea pigs.

She monitors my toilet breaks, how many times I go for a cup of coffee, and even what I eat. I can't count the number of times I've returned from the printer room and found my doughnut on the floor while she hides behind her computer screen with a smirk. I swear this is beyond harassment. And this year will be the sixth time she has turned me down for a promotion. I would understand if I was a slacker, but I work very very hard for my crust of bread.

So why don't I do anything about it? Because I have everything to lose and she holds the dagger by the handle. Anything I claim will not be believed unless I can substantiate it. Besides, what am I going to say to the people on the top floor? Excuse me, but your Head of HR has just binned my Krispy Kreme?

Rumour has it no men are allowed anywhere near her

home, where she lives with her divorced sister who joined the Single and Furious Club. Apparently, they have a ground-to-air missile they use to fight off blokes. You'd think that, softened by her sister's plight, Susan would give a single mum like me a break. But no.

So here I am, on the M3, ass and all, because she couldn't bully anyone else into doing it. I have absolutely no choice. But perhaps, just perhaps, if I can get this mess sorted, I'll finally crack that promotion and get her off my back.

I turn and ruffle Danny's blond hair. 'It'll be *fun*, darling, you'll see.'

So I've been telling him, my poor kid. He needs a break more than I do. I wish I could give him so much more. Like a real, complete family, as opposed to the two of us. Mum and Dad are always trying to pair me off with sons of their friends whenever I'm up there, probably in the hope that I'll move back. And when they're not doing that, they're asking me if Mark has phoned recently, and when was the last time he saw his (my) son, etc. etc. And the answer is usually, 'A couple of years ago.'

I'm on my own, and it's fine. Sometimes, I'll admit, during my weaker moments, I start thinking that I should find someone new, and that maybe I should just take my parents up on their offer, enjoy the free babysitting and all that.

Because, seriously speaking, I have had enough of London, our tiny flat and our even tinier finances and would like nothing better than to settle down in a quaint little village like – I check my map again – Little Kettering. And maybe even forget the hotel career altogether to return to my love before Danny, i.e. pottery throwing. I used to have my own stall in Covent Garden, just fresh out of art school and way into my pregnant and abandoned state.

You should see *those* particular pieces. They're all lopsided because I couldn't stop crying, let alone stop my hands from shaking. I'd get up in the middle of the night, suddenly wired and worried, ease my huge belly behind the pottery wheel, and let my imagination run wild, conjuring up images of Mark. Headless Mark. Eyes-gouged-out Mark. Legless Mark, and yes! Mark Minus His Implement. It was the only thing that would make me giggle uncontrollably. Until I cried just as uncontrollably. For nights on end. I never want to go back to feeling like that again.

And once Danny was born and I was on my own, it rapidly became clear to me that I needed a stable income in order to take care of my son.

So I sold my pottery wheel and my kiln, and applied for this job. And I haven't thrown any pottery since. I don't even know if I'm still capable. I used to be quite good, actually, specialising in beach themes.

And now I can almost see my future self, with my own little shop and a makeshift sign reading, *Come in, we're open*. Prospective buyers or even passers-by could come in all the way to the back and watch. Scratch that – they'd better buy, otherwise we don't eat.

I try to calculate how many vases I'd have to sell to keep Danny and myself living in a dignified manner but give it up as the scenery has piqued my interest. Multi-coloured, quilt-patched hills gently kneel towards the sea, almost in respect of the beauty surrounding it. Oh, how I long to make a life change and move here!

Would Danny settle in a place so small, where everyone

knows everyone else? Back in London, it seems his life revolves solely around the people in his school and myself. He looks happy enough, but the confidence he still seems to be lacking, and which makes me worry every now and then, is it due to the fact that his father isn't around? Does he crave a complete family, or am I enough? And what about when he gets older? Will he not be needing a father figure? Will his stability depend on it? Will he resent me?

Maybe I should have left him with my parents for these holidays. Contact with his grandfather, the only man in our lives, would have been more beneficial. But I blame myself. I just can't let him out of my sight. I know I am too protective, and that I should maybe step back, just a little, every now and then.

Call me paranoid, but I am so terrified that if I'm not always super-alert, something horrible will happen to him. You read about nothing else in the news: parents take their eyes off their children for one moment, and that's it. Tragedy strikes. I'm one parent on double-shifts. All he has is me, so no, I can't take my eyes off him for one moment.

My mobile plays 'Ride of the Valkyries' once again and I salivate like Pavlov's puppy; only I've absolutely no appetite, because her bell means trouble. Four hours down the highway, and the screeching harridan *still* has this effect on me.

I'd love to tell her what I think of her attitude, but my unpaid bills currently sharing the glove compartment with my Adele CDs – alongside that letter that I haven't had the courage to open – tell a story of their own.

So I hit the speakerphone button, trying to sound confident. Project my voice and all that.

'Hello, Susan.'

'Rosie, are you there yet?'

'Twenty more miles, Susan,' I lie. Surely she'll give me the time necessary to check in and have a short break?

'Right. Remember you are incognito. No one must know you work for the company. Not housekeeping, not accounts, nor anyone else. Do you understand me?'

I slide Danny a glance. He's not used to hearing this kind of tone. We don't talk to people like that. But I let my boss do it to me. I grind my teeth in perfect silence, because she can hear a frown on the phone from three counties over. So I respond in perfect, textbook Susanese, just the way she demanded, as if she was our headmistress, from Day One.

'Yes, ma'am.'

'Good. I want an honest and fair preliminary report as soon as you get there. And I don't mean tonight, but this afternoon. Do you understand?'

Meaning that, when we get there after a four-and-a-half-hour drive, I won't even have time for dinner. And that I'll have to find something for Danny to do. I can see she wants this to be all about the company and absolutely nothing about Danny and his Christmas birthday, poor boy. But not if I can help it.

Susan knows I have a young son, and that I've no choice but to take him with me. The only reason she didn't veto Danny's presence was because of the Christmas holidays. Not even she would be that insensitive. And yet, I may still stand corrected.

'Another thing, Rosie.' She pronounces my name like it's a swear word. 'I want you to observe the manager closely. If, and I underline if, he seems dodgy and surly as they say, I want you to report to me and you can get rid of him. You'll hold the fort until we can send down a replacement.'

'Me? Get rid of him?' I whisper in horror. 'I thought I was just looking into the bad publicity. You never mentioned me firing anyone. Or even replacing them, for that matter.' It looks like she's bent on ruining not only our Christmas, but some other poor sod's as well.

'No, you're not fit to replace him, we all know *that*. But it's the holidays and people have a life. Except you, of course.'

I can't tell you how charmed I am. I can hear her smiling as she slurps mojitos on the beach. That's Susan for you. Instead of switching off when on holiday, like the rest of the planet, she likes to 'stay in touch'. Why doesn't she just get a life and leave me alone? I'm secretly hoping she'll meet someone in Spain, get laid and forget I even exist. At least for the holidays. But given her track record, I know I'm hoping in vain.

'Besides, you'll like Cornwall. I hear it's very relaxing, especially at Christmas.'

Relaxing? Possibly for the tourists, but not for me. Because how is firing someone considered *relaxing*? Of course it is in her twisted little world. But in my twisted little world, I wonder how the hell I got stuck with this task. I have been in this job for years, so I can safely say I know how to run a hotel. It's the self-confidence thing I need to work on. And I've no experience whatsoever in giving feedback, especially to a manager who is already above my position.

But I'm the loser whose name was drawn and I can't well refuse, can I? Or can I? Could I actually, right now, turn the car around and go back to London? I quickly weigh the pros and cons of this. If I do, nothing will change, except for the fact that I'll be jobless. The promotion bubble I've been working on for six years will burst once and for all and I'll end up with absolutely nothing. I will in effect be taking a step back in life.

But if I go forward, go to Cornwall and do what has been asked of me, maybe, just maybe, things might change for us. For Danny. So if I feel guilty about working over the Christmas holidays, ultimately I'm doing it for his future. He will benefit from it. And if that's the case, I'm doing it. I'm going to Cornwall. But before I can reply to Susan, she rings off. Which is no surprise, because she never says goodbye.

What The Sacker doesn't know is that any victim of hers is a pal of mine and I'm *already* on the guy's side. Unless he really is surly and rude and the place sucks as much as the reviews state. But if he's just having a tough time, I'm going to try and help save him and his inn. Because if he gets fired, he'll never be able to work in this field again.

The power to crush people's lives might make Susan's rotten heart sing, but thankfully, I'm not like that. I was raised like most of the human beings on this planet – with dignity, and a sense of respect for other people. Sometimes I actually feel sorry for her, because she might be feared by all, but she will never be respected, nor loved.

'Your boss is mean, Mum,' Danny whispers, yanking me out of my reverie.

I force a laugh for his benefit. 'Only because she's very lonely, Danny.'

'Because she's not married?' he asks.

I ruffle his hair, my heart spilling with joy at the mere

sight of my boy sitting next to me. I am so so lucky. 'No, my darling. Because she doesn't have *you*.'

'But, Mum, don't you want a boyfriend, too, like Auntie Liz?'

Is that what he worries about, my little boy, rather than thinking about having fun and enjoying his life? 'No, love, I don't want or need a boyfriend. You are everything Mummy needs to be happy.'

He grins, happy with the answer. For now.

'Can we listen to some music?' he asks.

'Of course, love. You choose.'

Not that there's much of a choice beyond Adele. Her songs about break-ups have been my best companion over the past few years, ever since Mark dumped me. I suspect that my being up the duff might have had something to do with it.

For months, I cried and sang her songs, sang her songs and cried. And often at the same time. It was not a pretty sight – nor a pretty sound; I can't carry a tune to save myself. It had got so bad (not just my singing) that I couldn't even wear any make-up, and my friends spent their Saturday nights lugging bags of cakes and chocolates over to my place and watching me scoff it all down in one evening, rather than going to the pub. You'd think I'd be huge, but I suspect the misery ate away the excess calories.

Eventually that stopped. Because, after a night of excruciating labour pains, when I looked down at Danny's little pruned face, he instantly became to me the most precious thing in the world. And life – finally – made sense. I had a goal. To protect my son, and teach him things and keep him happy and loved. And I knew that, even if it was going to be extremely difficult, I would be able to do it on my own.

And it doesn't matter that, every couple of years or so, Mark will still ring and want to see him. Just often enough to make sure Danny remembers him, but not enough for Mark to feel obligated. You know the game.

But now I've had enough. No more hoping, no more re-falling in love with him all over again. Now I'm determined to never look back and to make the best of it for Danny. I look at my beautiful blond-haired, blue-eyed boy who just has to grin at me, or slip his hand into mine, and I can conquer the world all over again.

Danny is now drumming his fingers on his thighs to the rhythm of 'Rolling in the Deep', which I feel I will soon be doing in this hotel mystery I am here to solve. Fingers crossed I can solve it in time for Christmas, although I've been told to book through to the New Year.

When we finally pull up in the ample parking lot (first box ticked, good start), I heave a huge sigh of relief. On the outside, the Old Bell Inn, just a few minutes beyond the village, is beautifully preserved, the way only love and respect can keep things together. Another brownie point.

This is just the kind of place I wish I could manage, as opposed to the London boutique-y hotels I've always worked in. My heart yearns for Olde World England, particularly the West Country, which is galaxies away from the rat race with its humongous shopping centres, its streets strewn with Dantesque, zombie-like figures trudging to and fro from work, the endless crush on the Tube and the strong odour of unhappiness.

I dream of an inn like this, with maybe ancient oak tables, dark beams, and an original hearth. And now, even if only for a few weeks, I'm here.

TripAdvisor has the Old Bell Inn as a pretty, quaint inn perched above the sea, with excellent food and clean rooms. There were a couple of negative – and long-winded – reviews, one by a Ms. Lorna Greene, and another by The Wanderer. But upon reading them, I gleaned the nature of the reviewers. Pedantic, trouble-making, t-crossing and i-dotting people who really have nothing better to do than comment on the not-deep-enough-hues of the wooden staircase, or that the armchairs in their rooms didn't have castor protection cups. Please.

According to various other blogs and articles, however, the Old Bell Inn is a den of vice, dirty, with surly staff, with an exception, and I quote: 'The only good thing the joint has going for it is the chef, Russell Jones, who should be in a five-star hotel, not that dump.' Hooray at least for that. I can only hope the situation is not as bad as it seems, and that the manager, one Mitchell Fitzpatrick, will be willing to make some changes. Otherwise it's his ass that will be hanging out to dry alongside mine. God, I hate my job.

'Oh, wow!' Danny swoons as we get out of the car, his eyes widening at the sight of the horses beyond the fence. His room at home is plastered with pictures of quadrupeds and farms, and I am hoping the horses will keep him busy and distracted from the fact that his mum is working her arse off round the clock.

Personally, I'm gobsmacked by the sea crashing against the rocky cliffs on my left, and the sunset that's about to take place. Oh, just *look* at the colour of this *sky*! It's… like a completely different country. The air is different, the colours are different, and my spirits lift immediately, like a mole (if you'll pardon the spy-pun) suddenly let loose after years of living in the dark. I feel ten years younger. Or better, ten years *happier*, and I've barely got out of the car.

'Mum! Look!' Danny cries, spotting a roebuck in the woods beyond the fencing behind the inn. It's such a beautiful creature, wide-eyed and innocent, caught in a slanting ray of golden light, almost like in a dream from your childhood. Danny breaks into a run to get a better look and, in his haste, trips and falls to the ground as the roebuck, startled, darts back into the woods.

'Danny!' I cry out, dropping my cases, but before I can reach him, an arriving guest puts down his own bag to help him up.

'You all right, lad?' he asks in a friendly Irish accent as he helps dust him off.

'Yes, thank you, sir...'

'Where's your mam?'

'Here, I'm here!' I cry, flapping my arms as if they could propel me faster to my son. 'Darling, are you all right?'

Danny rubs his knee. 'I'm fine, Mum...'

'Are you sure, love? Did you hurt yourself?' We've only been here two seconds and he's already injured. Is this a sign that this was probably not a good idea after all? Maybe not all change is good. Or maybe I'm just being my usual overprotective mum self.

'No, Mum, I'm okay.'

I turn to the man. 'Thank you so kindly. It's the animals, you see. He's absolutely mad about them, especially horses. He runs off whenever—'

But the man isn't listening to me. He is distracted by a gaggle of party hens who have just pulled up and are spilling out onto the parking space, decked in full celebratory gadgets such as flashing light necklaces and other accessories that exceed their actual clothing by far. He gives me the once-over, shakes his head, slings his black leather bag over his shoulder and turns to go inside, muttering something like: 'This is exactly what's wrong with the world.'

'I beg your pardon?' I say, but he's already halfway across the front garden. 'Sir,' I call after him, hands on my hips in what my friends define my Ooh, Are You In Trouble Now / Teapot stance. 'What's that supposed to mean?' I'm pretty thin-skinned and don't respond well to criticism without cause. Susan the Sacker is more than enough to put up with, thank you.

The Irish bloke stops and turns around, one dark eyebrow raised as he glares at me. 'Only that I'm sick and tired of seeing kids at the mercy of women like you.'

I gasp. 'Women like me?'

He puts his hands on his waist to mirror my stance, his travel bag dangling from one hand. 'Yes, women like you. Why the hell would you even bring him here?'

I blink. By the look in his eye it's almost like he knows I'm a single mum. 'What's wrong with wanting to spend Christmas with my son?' Granted, we might not have the best holiday ever, but still. I'm doing my best, here, and I don't need a perfect stranger reading me the Riot Act.

He snorts and moves off, mumbling, 'Forget it. Why do I even bother anymore?'

My cheeks are on fire now. 'Well, that's rather rude. If you don't like children—'

He stops and turns around again. 'I happen to love children. Only I would *never* bring my son along.'

'Good job he's not yours, then.'

'Whatever,' he shoots back over his shoulder as he leaves me standing in the parking lot.

I give his broad back a filthy look and grab Danny's hand, feeling the steam coming out of my ears as we hurry back to the car to retrieve our luggage so as to make it to the reception desk before the hen party. Arrogant sod. What exactly about me screams Bad Mother? Am I binge-drinking and fixing alongside my boyfriend/pimp while my son is home, neglected and starving? The bloody nerve of some people! I turn away and decide to block him out to concentrate on my task.

The entrance to the inn is surrounded by bountiful bushes laden with berries and there is a wrought-iron bench with cushions. The sign, which says Old Bell Inn, is an authentic slate slab, hanging from a wrought-iron pole. This is truly textbook, fairy-tale Cornwall. Five stars for the setting and the aspect.

But inside, the first thing that hits me is that there is no Christmas tree, nor any Christmas decorations. Nothing. It could be absolutely any day of the year, in fact, were it not for a blazing fire in the huge hearth taking up the entire wall to my right. Oh, dear, not a good sign at all when the establishment can't keep up with the calendar. People who go away at Christmas need the festive cheer. Unless they go to the Bahamas, maybe. But a Cornish inn with no Christmas decorations? Not flying.

Moving on. I cast a quick glance around and breathe deeply, partly because I'm still fuming from that arse's comments and partly because I'm a *judge by odour* person. Nice, clean smell of lemon polish. And a hint of cinnamon. Old-world furnishings. Classy, but not pretentious. Excellent.

This place is obviously loved, albeit a bit behind the times, and I immediately decide that although he may be a bit swamped, the manager can't be the incompetent scumbag the reviews are implying.

'Are you angry at that man, Mum?' Danny wants to know.

'Of course not, love. We won't let anyone spoil this Christmas for us,' I assure him as we reach Reception. 'It'll be the best we've ever had – that's a promise.' And I'll be damned if I'm not going to do my best to keep it.

The girl behind the desk is checking her screen and doesn't look up as we walk in. I silently will her to do so, so that I won't have to mention it in my bloody report and checklist that occupies most of *Part One: Upon Arrival* of the damned inspector's manual Susan is so in love with and which I absolutely loathe.

I clear my throat and smile. 'Hello – I'm Rosie Anderson. I've booked a family suite.'

The receptionist is a dead-ringer for Sporty Spice. Her name – Laura – is pinned to her tracksuit jacket. I take a surreptitious but thorough look. Yes, it most definitely is a tracksuit jacket. How do you mention that the attire is not quite proper for the front – or even back – office, for that matter, without sounding too patronising? And without giving myself away? Because, let's be honest, if I'm to stay in incognito, I have absolutely no weight here. And besides, I'm the one to talk, with my arsenal of jeans and sweaters. But at least I'm supposed to be playing the part of casual Christmas tourist, while she's supposed to be dressed professionally. I realise that I'm trapped. If she's wearing something similar tomorrow, I'm going to have to write this up, and if this is only the beginning, it's going to be an absolutely horrible stay.

'Hello and welcome,' she answers with a nervous smile. 'If I can just have your credit card for a swipe, please...'

I sigh inwardly at her *Let's just cut to the chase, we only want your money* attitude, and oblige, while Danny finds a spot on a huge brown leather sofa by a large bay window, already enthralled by a magazine on horses.

Laura taps away at her keyboard. She seems like a nice girl, but it is immediately obvious that she's a little green around the ears in hotel matters.

'Right, hmm, that's odd,' she says with a frown. She taps away again and hits Enter; then again.

'What is it?' I ask, but already I have a sinking suspicion. You get to learn a thing or two about human behaviour when you've been working in hotels as long as I have.

'I'm, uhm, so sorry, Ms Anderson. But it appears you've been double-booked. There are no rooms available.'

2

No Room at The Old Bell Inn

I stare at her, fully-fledged flames of panic now licking at my insides. No, no, no! How am I supposed to carry out an anonymous inspection without a room?

'What do you mean, double-booked?' I echo, as if I didn't know. It happens all the time, of course. But that it has happened now, of all times, is a disaster for the manager of the Old Bell Inn. I can already *hear* Susan the Sacker sharpening her knives. And to think I had made the booking and double-checked it myself.

Laura scrunches her mouth regretfully. 'There has been a mistake. All of our rooms are booked.'

Only five hours ago, when we started off, Danny and I were singing Christmas carols and making a list of things to do on our break-away holiday, as our car dashed *o'er hill and dale*, just like in the best of Christmas stories. And now we're roomless? And how can that even be possible? Part of the very problem of this establishment is due to the excessive amount of cancellations, and now suddenly they're overbooked?

As the herd of loud girls burst through the doors and shuffle up to the desk, demanding her attention, Laura turns her head and bites her lip, obviously torn between duty and sentiment. I'd been there myself, years ago, during training – wanting to do my duty, but not having a clue how to do so. It's not an easy job at the best of times. But when something like this happens? There should *always* be a spare room.

Laura jerks her head towards the girls. 'I really am sorry, Ms Anderson, but we've just filled the house with last-minute bookings. We were pretty much empty before that.'

You don't say? I rub my eyes. 'Never mind. Can you please get your manager, so we can sort it out?' I might as well grab the bull by the horns and get started here if I want to save his job.

She looks at me like a deer trapped in headlights. I dart my eyes to the crowd of cackling girls sporting sparkly pink tiaras, stopping to take selfies and screeching at the top of their lungs, looking like *Playboy* bunnies. The girls are already, by the looks of it, just one rum and Coke away from tearing the house down. It seems that the reviews weren't too much off the mark after all.

Laura's face falls. 'The manager? Oh, uhm... he's... not available at the moment, I'm afraid.'

Not available? What else could he possibly be doing instead of working, accepting a Nobel prize? 'What about the assistant manager?' I ask.

Laura bites her lip. 'She's... unavailable as well.'

Oh, shit, shit, shit. I can't write any of this in my report.

Head Office will shut them down immediately. 'Head of Reception?' I try, as a last resort.

She smiles apologetically. 'That's me for now, I'm afraid.'

For now? What the blooming heck is going on here?

Laura leans forward. 'You seem to have caught us at a busy time.'

I sigh inwardly. Despite myself, I like Laura already because she seems to have her heart in the right place, but she is totally, completely clueless, as if someone had parachuted her down and she'd landed smack-dab in the middle of all this mess. And Susan will be calling me any minute for an update. That woman's got me so by the throat, I wouldn't put it past her having a tracking device on my car and maybe even a listening device linking my mobile to hers or something as outrageous as that. I see that I'll have to report the truth or they'll be dead in the water before I even get a chance to start. *Think, Rosie, think!*

'Look,' I say. 'It doesn't matter about the family suite. I'll take anything you've got.'

Laura turns white. 'But... I haven't got *anything*...'

'Come on, Laura, it's company policy to always keep one room available.'

She blinks. 'It is?'

Uh-oh, almost gave myself away there. 'I'm assuming so. Lots of hotels do.'

'I'm sorry, but I just don't have anything left.'

I hate to resort to emotional blackmail, but I've no choice at this stage. How else to get what I need without blowing my cover and, consequently, their entire business? I turn to glance at Danny, who's still leafing quietly through his magazine, oblivious to everything around him. 'Laura, you see that little boy over there?'

'Yeah?'

'That's my son, Danny. His birthday is on Christmas Eve. And by the way, I'm a single mother.'

Laura glances at him regretfully, wringing her hands, at a loss for words, and, more importantly, a solution. 'I'm so sorry, Ms Anderson, but I honestly don't know how to help you...'

What am I going to do now?

To make a mock of our misery, yet another posse of girls traipses in, only these ones are wearing hairbands with red devil horns. Indeed, *two* wild hen parties at the same time. Ouch. Talk about giving the place some Christmas cheer, let alone some tone.

'Oh, I know! I could make some calls for you, to a nearby hotel?' Laura suggests.

What other choice have I got? We've been travelling for hours and I've got to get Danny settled in somewhere. 'Please do, Laura.'

She's realised that this problem isn't going to solve itself, and nods, grateful for a momentary breather.

Danny looks up from his magazine. 'Are we not getting a room, Mum?'

The resignation on his face, and the quiet acceptance in his voice make my heart ache. For years he's watched as his friends got absolutely everything and then some, as their fathers took them to football games, while I dashed home just in time to take him out to the local park for a measly kick-about. And when I say kick-about, I mean Danny kicking the ball at me and me chasing after it, much to his amusement.

It was all I could offer financially and time-wise, due to the double shifts I often pulled to make ends meet. And then there were all the holidays abroad I couldn't take him on. While his classmates were going to France and Spain, and a lucky few even to Disneyworld, I'd head up to Birmingham to my parents' place. And this Christmas, he doesn't even get to see them.

Of course, Mum's right when she says that moving back home would solve three-quarters of my problems. And if I don't accomplish this hotel miracle, I just might have to.

I take another look around, just as my old friend, *Mr Irish Charm*, saunters up to Reception, sheer arrogance clinging to him like a second skin. He plonks his bag down onto the counter and pulls out a pile of documents. You'd think he might be able to wait for his turn. Or acknowledge the fact that I was here first.

Just look at the arrogant bastard, so full of himself, standing around as if he owns the place. As much as it would serve him right, I hope he hasn't been double-booked as well. Because that would really dig a bigger hole for the inn and Susan would be all over the issue like a bloodhound.

When he doesn't find what he's looking for, he scratches his six o'clock beard with impatience and begins pushing everything to one side to start the search all over again. Finally, exasperated, he turns to Laura. 'I need the invoice for Master Clean Company. They say we haven't paid them yet, but I remember we did.'

Oh, good grief. I should've *guessed* he works here. It makes sense, in a twisted sort of way.

'Okay, I'll have a look,' Laura answers, then eyes me. 'We've, uhm, got a bit of a problem, Mitchell.'

Mitchell? As in Mitchell *Fitzpatrick*, the actual manager of this nuthouse? Good God, it's worse than I'd feared. Imagine if he spoke to all his guests the way he spoke to me. No wonder there's been such an issue with occupancy rates if that's the greeting everyone gets. With someone like him at the helm, the inn truly is doomed.

'What is it?' he asks, not looking up from the invoices, his dark brows knitted in concentration.

'We've overbooked a guest.'

'Send them to the Coach and Four.'

Gosh, how many of the golden rules of the trade have these two broken in the space of a few minutes? Never, *ever* discuss guests as if they aren't there. And never, ever... oh, never *mind*.

My mobile sings 'You're my Best Friend'. It's Liz, Head of Accounts at Head Office, and also, as the tune implies, my BFF, so I step outside for a moment, still able to see Danny through the window as he leafs through his magazine.

The first thing I hear when I answer is the tapping of her keyboard. It feels strange to be away from the office while most people haven't broken for Christmas yet. 'How's it going, doll?' she says.

'Ugh. Don't ask. Susan's already called me a dozen times. I still don't understand why she didn't send you. You're the Accounts Manager.'

'It's not a question of balancing so much as the guy's reputation. So, what's he like?'

'He's the rudest man I've ever met. He even said I was a horrible mother.'

'*What?*'

'Well, not literally, but that's what he intended.'

'Don't listen to him. He sounds like a real bastard.'

'And we've been double-booked. There are literally no rooms left.'

'Looks like the reviews weren't biased after all. Have you tried around in the area?'

'Laura – the receptionist – is trying, but so far nothing.'

'And you can't even pull rank or the whole operation blows.'

'Pull rank? He's a manager, I'm only an assistant manager.'

'Yes, but you're from the mother hotel.'

'As if that makes a difference. Not with someone like him.'

'Forget about him a minute. How's my boy?'

I eye Danny who is one of the only children I know who doesn't fidget. He is perfectly capable of sitting still and staying put if you ask him to. 'Danny is just happy to be out of the house.'

More typing. 'Yeah? Did you remember to pack my pressies for him?'

'Of course. I'll make sure he calls you on Christmas morning.'

'Okay, doll. You take care and keep me posted.'

'I will, Liz. Bye.'

I hang up and return to Reception to watch Laura and Mitchell faffing around. When I can't take it anymore, I clear my throat and approach them, resting my elbows on the counter to draw his attention. Because this is the only kind of behaviour that he understands, I can already tell. And in fact, it takes him a few lazy moments, but he finally looks up. And that's when his face falls.

'Uh, Mitchell,' Laura says, clearing her throat. 'This is Ms Rosie Anderson, the guest who was double-booked.'

'Oh,' he says, deflated. 'You.'

Yeah, I'm not that happy with you, either, I'm thinking, but I merely say, 'I'd like to speak to you, please.'

His right eyebrow shoots up, and his mouth twitches in an effort to not scowl at me again. But when he speaks, his voice – finally – is drenched with professionalism. 'Ms. Anderson, we're terribly sorry, and we're going to make it up to you.'

Now we're talking.

'So we're offering you and your son a complimentary weekend...'

Good, good...

'...in the New Year.'

The New Year? Is he taking the Mick? I know he'd give an arm and a leg not to have to deal with me – the feeling's mutual. His lovely inn may be actually perched on a breathtakingly beautiful cliff, but he has no idea that it's just about to take a dive straight into it, with him in the front seat. God, how I want to call Susan up and resign this very instant. And move to the Bermuda Triangle, which has seen fewer disasters than this place.

'I'm sorry, but I don't want a complimentary room in the New Year, or any other weekend. I've booked for a very merry Christmas.'

For a brief flash, his eyes crinkle in amusement, but he catches himself and turns to Laura. I can only hope he's going to do something to save his ass, because the ball's in his court now.

He's already got a very narrow margin to redeem himself, and what does he do?

'Call the youth hostel, see if they can give her a bed somewhere,' he suggests, once again, as if I'm not even there. Then he remembers I actually am, and turns to me. 'Sorry for the lad. More than you think. Maybe next time you'll think twice before bringing him.' And with that, he turns his back on me, leaving me definitely homeless – and pretty soon jobless.

What am I supposed to do, let him ruin himself, *and* my career, not to mention my son's Christmas-slash-birthday? It's too much, even for me.

'Hey! Mr Manners!' I call after him, scaring even myself. When have I ever, *ever* raised my voice at anyone, let alone on the job? But he seems to be bringing out the worst in me today. 'I've got a little boy whose Christmas will be ruined if you don't help me out here.'

He stops in his tracks, his back straightening, his arms tensing, and when he turns around, his dark eyebrows are lowered in an ominous scowl. Again, he slaps his invoices down onto the counter. Basil Fawlty couldn't have done it better. He takes a deep breath. 'I'm sorry, Ms, uhm…?'

I huff. He's even got the memory of a goldfish. 'Anderson. Rosie Anderson.'

The muscles of his jaw twitch and he opens his mouth to retort as if he doesn't even like my name, but then glances at Danny and then at Laura. 'You sure you've tried everywhere?'

Laura nods regretfully, sliding me a sympathetic look.

He runs a hand through his mop of dark curls. 'What about The Duck and Pig? Or some place in Penworth Ford or Wyllow Cove? Have you tried them?'

Laura bites her lip and nods. 'I've tried everywhere, Mitchell, but everything's booked.'

Now I finally understand how Joseph and Mary must have felt after being turned down by every inn in Bethlehem.

'Mum?' Danny is now at my side, tugging at my hand. 'I'm hungry. When can we eat?'

I curse myself. Not only does the bloke think I'm a distracted mother, now he'll think I'm a neglectful one as well.

He kneels down to Danny, instantly defrosted in his manner. 'Tell you what, mate,' he says. 'We'll offer you a lovely dinner tonight – with a special dessert – while we try to get you sorted. How does that sound?'

Danny grins and nods. 'Thank you, sir.'

Mitchell Fitzpatrick grins back. 'Good lad.'

I nod. 'Thank you. That will do – for a start.'

His head snaps up as our eyes meet. With the look he gives me, you'd think I was sent here to kill his first-born. Good thing he doesn't know who I really am, and that I've been sent to practically terminate him.

'Yeah, well that figures...' he grumbles, scoops up his papers once again and heads out into the hall, shaking his head with evident disdain.

And then my mobile rings. Susan. God, doesn't she have a life of her own?

'Susan, hi,' I say breezily.

'Are you settled in yet?' she barks.

'Just about,' I lie. How to tell her my little boy and I are still standing in the lobby, starved, exhausted and parched, without so much as a glass of water offered to us? And no bed in sight, unless we're willing to spend the night in a youth hostel?

'What does that mean?' she wants to know. 'Have you started your evaluation or not? Have you even *read* the Inspector's Manual?'

Jesus, her and her manual. Does this woman never chill?

'As a matter of fact, I have,' I lie again.

'Right. What's it looking like, then?'

'It's a beautiful place,' I defend.

'I know that,' she bites off. 'Otherwise it wouldn't be one of our hotels, would it?'

'No, of course not,' I say.

'Staff?'

Completely non-existent, although Laura has done her best, bless her. 'Very kind and helpful.'

'Manager?'

Better off without him. 'Very… professional.'

'Assistant manager?'

Yikes. 'In… transition.'

A tapping on her keyboard. Is she seriously doing this while on holiday? 'Oh, that's right. She left a year ago and hasn't been replaced yet. This is unacceptable.'

Ah, so that's the reason he's acting like an arse. He's one man down, and during the holidays, to boot. And Susan didn't know about it. Am I a horrible person if that makes me smile?

'They are in the process of hiring a new one,' I lie, trying to hide the relish of catching her out. I don't want her giving me payback one day.

'So who's doing her job then?'

Terrific question. My guess is Absolutely No One. Laura and Mitchell barely seem able to do their own jobs.

'The manager. I'm told he's always here.'

'By whom?'

'Staff.'

'Gossip?'

'None.' But I'm keeping my ears open.

'I don't believe that.'

'What do you mean?'

'All staff gossip.'

'Well, all I've seen so far is the utmost respect for him.'

'What's he like?'

'Like?'

'Yes, Rosie. I need to know more about him.'

Then why the hell doesn't she read his records? Or come out here instead of sending me? And beside the fact that he is a piece of work, and well, come to think of it, kind of easy on the eye, what else is there to know?

Mitchell Fitzpatrick has returned to the lobby, carrying an even larger sheaf of invoices, his head held high. Just the sight of him makes me want to smack him.

'Is he up to par?'

I stare at him as he shoves the disorderly sheaf of invoices into his jacket and strides past me without so much as a glance while giving Danny, for no reason at all, a high five. Is it his natural gift to be so unnerving, or is it just me?

I'm seriously thinking of leaving him to his own devices, and see how he likes it in shits-ville. It's just not worth it, lying to Susan, thus risking my job just to save someone who doesn't even deserve it.

'Up to par?' I echo. More like a jerk. 'Oh, extremely.'

'Good. Well, I expect regular reports from you about everything – the kitchen, the cleaning staff, et cetera.'

'Yes, ma'am.'

And she hangs up as usual without saying goodbye, just like they do in the movies.

3

Desperate Measures

'Don't mind him, Ms Anderson,' Laura whispers as I walk back to the desk. 'He's really a great guy. Only he's been going through a rough patch.'

And here comes the gossip, finally. My ears prick up at the smell of a bit of dirt. I wonder if it has anything to do with the assistant manager leaving. It can't be easy working in these conditions for sure. 'Oh? How so?'

She leans in. 'The assistant manager was his wife.'

'His *wife*?' Bingo.

'Yeah, she upped and left him. He's been fighting to save the inn, and hasn't been the same since. It's not his fault, though.'

If not for her professional discretion, you have to love Laura for her loyalty to her boss. And now I'm intrigued. If he hasn't hired someone else, is it because he's hoping she'll come back? He certainly doesn't look happy here. If he doesn't like staying in this job, as is so obvious, why doesn't he just quit? Says me, captive extraordinaire of my own finances.

'Why did she leave him?' I ask, although I know it's none of my business. I'm no expert in matters of the heart. On the contrary. Besides, if his personality is anything to go by, I don't wonder at it. But I do need to know for the sake of the business and my report. God, I'm starting to sound like Susan.

Laura shrugs. 'The nicest people are always unappreciated, you know? He'd do all sorts of lovely things for her and she'd just let him and not even say thank you. You could tell he loved her way more than she loved him.'

Just like Mark and myself. I was always the attentive one, never missing a chance to show him my love, while he just sat there, reading his paper, letting me shower him with my attention. Which had made me realise that if your partner loves you less than you love him, it's not really love at all.

Sometimes, in the middle of the night, without wanting to, I still let my mind wander to thoughts of Mark. I wonder about the oddest, most random things: if he still drinks straight from the milk carton, or reads the paper standing by the sink while waiting for his toast to pop up. I wonder if the plants I'd strewn around his flat have managed to live at least a little longer than our relationship. And then I remember how he dumped me, and then I become strong all over again. A bit like in Adele's songs.

Sure, once in a blue moon he will send a text to ask how Danny is, but they are so few and far between, it's like his son is just an acquaintance he checks on occasionally. I provide for us financially and make all the decisions. I'm his only parent. Danny barely knows his father.

And now he's actually written me a letter. To say what, exactly? There is nothing on the face of this earth that he can say or do to make me forgive him. So it's staying exactly where it is – in the glove compartment, unopened.

How it must hurt Danny to think he's not important to his own dad. I try to talk to him and to reassure him, but he can be like a clam when he wants, my little boy.

Laura sighs. 'She didn't deserve him at all, while all *he* did was make allowances for her.'

Of course, I don't know about their relationship, but on a professional level, I feel sorry for him. Without his assistant manager, or even an experienced receptionist, to face the juggernaut of Christmas, he has about the same chances of surviving the season as a snowman in hell. He needs someone who actually has hotel skills.

And that is when an almighty plan flashes before my eyes. So I leave Danny with Laura for a second to rack up my courage and knock on the open door of Mitchell's office.

'I'm *busy*,' he booms.

It's hard to imagine him ever having been nice, so I'll have to take Laura's word for it. I poke my head in. 'Mr, uhm, Fitzpatrick?'

He's leaning forward with both hands on his desk, still examining the same pile of invoices, his dark, curly head hanging so low between his shoulders I can see the label on the inside of his shirt collar. He looks up and straightens his back, rubbing his face with both hands. 'What, you again? What is it you want?' he prompts.

I bristle, but this time make allowances for his rudeness. 'Yes, me again. Just so you know, unsatisfied customers don't return.'

He scratches his beard, frowning at me, his dark eyes flashing. '*You* did.'

It's no wonder the reviews are crap, with this attitude. *Oh, please, please,* I silently beg him. *Stop digging your own grave.* And then I realise that if I want him to understand, I have to speak his own language, so I step over the threshold and walk all the way into his office, placing my hands on the desk opposite him, my eyes never leaving his. 'Ah, but there's a difference, Mr Fitzpatrick. I never *left*.'

'Yeah, I can see that. And?'

Calm down, Rosie, I urge myself. *Right now, you need each other like air, only you don't want him to know that.*

'I couldn't help but overhear that… you have a problem.'

Mitchell Fitzpatrick starts going through his invoices again, without so much as glancing at me. 'You eavesdrop as well, so?' he asks in his Irish lilt.

I shake my head. 'No, it wasn't like that. I—'

His eyes swing to mine. They are a dark brown, with long, long lashes. Intense. Sexy, even as he smirks. But the smirking is almost like admitting his predicament.

'You are in trouble,' I say. 'You have two hen parties running riot, and your poor friend at Reception is doing her best, but she's inexperienced. It's a recipe for disaster.'

He scowls at me, his nostrils literally flaring, and then looks away, sifting even more energetically through that bloody pile, like a dog trying to dig up a lost bone.

'You, of all people, should say that?' he added.

'I beg your pardon?' Shit. How can he possibly know who I am? It was a secret mission and I only just got here.

'You're part of one of them, are you not? The *hen* parties,' he prompts when I simply blink at him.

'What? Oh! No, of course not. I would never bring my son to a hen party,' I answer, annoyed. This is so rich – I'm here to help him – against all orders – and taking nothing for granted and assuming nothing, and he immediately slates me as a bad mother. How quickly people are ready to judge.

His face falls. 'Oh. I assumed you were.'

'So that's why you were cross with me out front?'

He runs his fingernails across his beard in what I can only assume and hope is embarrassment. 'Uhm, yes. Sorry. It's been a long day.'

Tell me about it. My own wasn't too clever either with my worries being interspersed by 'Ride of the Valkyries'.

'Sorry, we're in a bit of a mess here lately. We just double-booked you, so?' he repeats and I make an effort not to roll my eyes. 'I can't see how I can help you, though. You heard Laura – there's literally nothing available anywhere.'

I am definitely in trouble now, or rather, he is, but I can't tell him who I am. However, I can still help, if he'll only let me. No one needs to know. And yet, I can't believe I'm about to do this. It goes against all my professional knowledge, but my instinct is telling me it's the right thing to do. Well, maybe not the right thing, but the *kind* thing. It is Christmas, after all. So here I go.

'Look, I'm an assistant mana—' I bite my tongue. *Be less threatening.* 'I mean a receptionist at… a hotel in London.'

The utter disbelief in his eyes is so offensive it's almost comical. 'You?'

I huff, trying to ignore the hostility pouring out of him. 'I can get you out of this mess. In exchange for a room.'

I can see from the tiny wrinkles forming at the corners of his eyes that he's struggling not to laugh. 'I beg your pardon?'

'I have years of experience. I could train Laura for you and man the front office while you do your stuff in the back office.' Yikes. Why did I just say that? Working here will rob me of the already very little time I'll have with Danny. How am I going to manage now?

He gives me the once-over and I stand up straighter. I know what he's thinking. That as I'm already neglectful, it's not a problem for me to abandon my baby. Well, he's wrong. I'm a damn good mother. Strong. Competent. I know I don't look like much in my faded jeans, my oldest jumper and my *five-hours-on-the-M3* hair, but if anyone can save this bloke's ass, it's me, and he'll have to either take it or leave it. But I have to play my cards right. Because if I don't, we're all dead.

He puts down his papers, his face a combined mask of disbelief and annoyance as they roam over me. 'How did you even *get* here?' he groans.

'In my Kia.'

'No, I mean… how do I know you are a professional receptionist?'

I feel my body freezing. What an idiot I am. If he decides to check out my story and finds out we work for the same company, I'm screwed.

He rolls his eyes. 'Oh, for Christ's sake, you don't expect me to hire you on two feet, do you?'

I'm trapped. Either he believes me at face value, or two seconds on the Internet are going to blow my cover, the entire operation and my job. Susan would have a field day. *Quick, quick, think of something!*

'I don't want to be hired. I was just offering you my help, for free, while I was here, even though you have ruined my son's Christmas – and birthday. Anyway, whatever,' I say, and make to go, but turn back and, with my index finger, single out a sheet from under his pile. 'Here's the Master Clean Company invoice you were looking for.'

As his eyes scan it, his eyebrows shoot up. 'How... did you do that?'

I shrug. 'It's not rocket science. We use the same company. They've recently changed their logo, and lots of people don't know about it yet.' And with that, I turn and head for the door. If that doesn't do it, we're both on the dole.

4

Room 122

Dinner is already a huge improvement. While Danny has a hearty meal of steak and kidney pie, mushy peas and mash, followed by chocolate cake, I am enjoying what is probably the best beef wellington I've ever had in my life, bar none. No wonder the reviews always compliment the chef. I need to make a note to speak to him tomorrow, and see what he thinks about the bad reviews. Internal intel is essential at this stage.

Even our waitress is a gem: polite, quick and competent.

After dinner, I retrieve our bags from Reception where Laura had offered to store them, contemplating a long drive to find accommodation elsewhere, while trying to hide the issue from Susan the Slacker.

'Good news,' Laura says, producing a key. 'You've got a suite. Number 122.'

I exhale in relief. Mitchell must have found a solution, somehow. I hoped he'd come through, although I have to admit I didn't think he would. Maybe he really is worth helping after all.

'Thanks, Laura.'

'Mitchell told me you work in hotels, and that you're going to be helping us out?' she asks.

I eye her. 'If that's okay?' I certainly don't want her to begrudge me. It would be a bad start, as we will be working together a lot.

Laura takes my arm. 'Thank *God*. I don't know *what* I'm doing. I'm just passing by, you see.'

I do a double take. 'Passing by?'

She shrugs. 'I'm just a friend. Don't know the first thing about hotels. I've only been here a few days.'

Yikes. Is there no end to the bloke's troubles?

'So listen. Help yourself to Russell's kitchen at all hours – he won't mind – or anything else you need. Danny can potter about with any of us. I hear he likes horses?'

I grin as a shadow of a possibility opens up to me. If I can give Danny his horses, he'll forgive me anything, and not miss me as much. Thank you, God! 'He's obsessed.'

'Excellent. He can muck around in the stables with Jeremy, if that's okay? He knows all you need to know about horses, and he is the kindest man alive.'

I almost cry with relief. My little boy's holiday might not be that bad after all. 'That would be heaven, thank you.'

'All right, then. We really appreciate your help.'

'Thanks, Laura. See you tomorrow morning.'

'Nighty night.'

As tired as I am, who can sleep? I have a gazillion ideas to spruce up the place. My only limit is the manager, but he'll have to deal with it. *Oh, Mitchell Fitzpatrick*, I almost murmur aloud, *you're in for one hell of a Christmas...*

Room number 122 is none other than Mitchell's personal quarters I realise, as we step over the threshold. It is a small suite, with two bedrooms, a kitchenette with a breakfast bar and a tiny bathroom with a shower stall so minuscule I wonder how Mitchell could possibly fit inside it.

The main bedroom has a lovely old brass bed and dark furniture packed with books. I pull one out and am surprised to find *Jane Eyre*. Surely he's more into stuff like, I don't know, bloke movies, on big plasma TVs? But nothing in here is modern aside from the CD player. To give me his room means that there really wasn't another one to be found. So where's he going to sleep, I wonder?

As Danny throws his trolley onto the master bed and begins to unpack his toys, I imagine what it must have been like for Mitchell's ex-wife, living with him here, and waking up to these stunning views from her bed – and, well, *in* her bed as well.

Mitchell is the opposite of Mark. Where Mark was well-groomed and elegant, Mitchell, with that growing beard and those untamed curls that dig into his shirt collar, has a ruggedness to him that speaks of honesty and intensity. He looks more like a mountain climber than a corporate ladder climber. Despite his unbelievable arrogance, he looks... earnest. And I'm going to do everything I can to make sure he survives this bloody inspection. Correction: that we both do.

As Danny lines up his toy cars, I open the window and breathe in the crisp evening air, enjoying the whisper of the sea crashing against the rocks below. Absolute paradise. And, if only temporarily, Danny and I are going to be a part of it.

When 'Ride of the Valkyries' rings again, I sigh with pure exhaustion, the idea of her grilling me again making me queasy. My own *mother* doesn't even call me that often. I'm tempted to let it go to voicemail again, but twice in one day is too much even for Cornwall's broadband signal strength, and it would only make things between us worse, so I tap the green phone icon.

'Hello?'

'Talk to me, Rosie.'

If I wasn't shit-scared of her, I'd laugh. She uses American expressions she must've picked up on TV, only she doesn't use them like a native speaker, in other words, sparsely. No, sir. She speaks *mainly* in Hollywood quotes, much to everyone's mirth. Phrases like, 'Show me the money', 'Houston, we have a problem', 'Life is like a box of chocolates' pepper her speech, along with 'Shucks' and 'Golly', and believe me, it's actually very hard to keep a straight face because she sounds like a female version of John Wayne. I can almost see her in her spurred boots as she moseys on down to the saloon, sits at the bar, orders a tall class of castor oil and starts spitting fire at anyone who has the guts to look her way.

'Yes, things are going well,' I say. 'It's a lovely place.'

'And the manager?' she wants to know again. As if she already doesn't. She has pictures of all Johnson Hotels employees on file, and if she weren't so anti-man, she'd have his blown up to poster size in every room of her home. I know I would.

What's he like, she wants to know. Tall, dark and

handsome isn't the half of it – not even a millionth, actually. Did I mention the body of a Greek god? Not that I can see much beyond his clothes, but the width of his shoulders, and the narrow hips bode well. Not that I've been ogling him, of course. My senses have been closed down in that department for years now. Especially after the stunt that Mark, who was a real looker, pulled on me. These days, I'm afraid that good looks alone won't do much for me. Besides, who needs sex – or a relationship – when you are a single mother with a full-time job?

'Mr Fitzpatrick is very professional and amiable,' I hear myself saying. Why I'm putting my own neck on the line for someone so undeserving, I don't know. Probably because he's been dumped, and just needs a break. Remind you of anyone?

'You're not on first-name terms yet?' she asks.

Is that what I'm supposed to do? Chat him up, drag him to bed and when he has his pants down, shout, 'A-ha! You shouldn't be sleeping with your guests?' In that case: a) I know I've blown it already because he hates my guts, and b) I'm not, as I've already tried to tell her, suitable for this task. What the hell do I know about inspections, for Christ's sake? I'm just an assistant manager, not a HR person. With people, I go by my guts. But so far, it's not going very well at all.

'What, with Mitchell?' I say. 'Yes, a very nice man.' My nose is still growing, by the way.

Pause. 'Really?' she says.

'Absolutely.'

'Are you already flirting with him, Rosie?'

The question throws me completely. Have I exaggerated a bit in my praise? 'I beg your pardon?' And what does she mean by 'already'? I don't flirt.

'You sound like you're very chummy with him.'

Chummy? If she only knew. 'Uhm, no, you see, the receptionist and I got to talking…'

'Oh. Is she indiscreet?'

I slap my forehead. Can I not get *one* thing right? You can tell I'm not used to lying, can't you? 'No, of course not. She's very professional.' My nose has just hit the opposite wall.

'Has she got a crush on him?'

What kind of a question is that? 'I beg your pardon?'

Susan pauses. 'I'm looking at a picture of him as we speak. I suspect the staff are a bit distracted.'

Bingo. Told you she'd know. 'No, I don't think they are. I'll email you my preliminary report within the hour, bye,' I promise in one breath and hang up before she can answer.

Three weeks. Three weeks and I'm out of here. I call Liz, just to hear a friendly voice, and to erase the unpleasant effect of Susan's screeching.

'Hey, Rosie, how's it going? How's The Rudest Man Alive?'

'Well, actually, he's just given up his own suite for us.'

'Really? What a gent.'

Always sarcastic, my Liz. But to me, it is a big deal. Where's he going to go? From what I can see, I don't think he has his own place outside the inn. I just hope he doesn't end up sleeping in the broom cupboard because of us.

'And what's the joint like?'

'It's really, really nice, Liz. The dinner was superb, the place is spotless.' Apart from the lack of festive cheer. I understand that the bloke hasn't much to be cheery about, granted, but business is business and the show must go on and all that.

'Tomorrow I'm going to start my digging,' I tell her.

'Okay. Just make sure he doesn't find you out. I'd hate to come looking for your bones,' she says with a laugh.

'Ha, ha. I'll keep you posted.'

'Bye, love.'

It's already the end of Day One of my mission and, apart from the double booking, which every hotel does, and Mitchell's prickly personality, I've discovered absolutely nothing that warrants the bad reviews. Because, to be fair, against all odds, Mitchell did find a solution. All in all, I think he did a top-notch, proper job, as the Cornish say.

I reread my preliminary report once more and send it off. I'm so absolutely shattered that I barely manage to tuck Danny in before I'm out completely. Susan would be overjoyed to see me brought down by a twenty-two-bedroom inn in the middle of nowhere. I dig deep under the covers, enjoying the feeling of letting go, something I rarely do at home. It must be the fresh air, or the good food. Maybe even the physical distance from Susan.

'Mum?'

I bolt up into a sitting position, eyes wide, heart racing, instantly ready for combat. Mother's instinct, I guess. Danny is standing by my bed. He looks all in one piece, except for a worried expression on his adorable little face.

'What is it, darling?'

'This place is so quiet, I can't sleep. Can I sleep with you?'

I bite my lip. It took me ages to get him to sleep on his own, and I don't want to revert back to that. I want him strong and independent. But this is a new place for him and, well, maybe just for tonight. 'Of course, darling.'

5

Reviews and Déjà-Vus

When I open my eyes the next morning, Danny is already up and dressed, munching on some cereal, sitting at the breakfast counter, his little legs dangling from the high stool. 'Morning, Mum!'

'Morning, darling,' I manage and roll over for another five minutes of blissful oblivion, thinking how strange it is that I can see him eating breakfast from my bedroom. And then I remember where I am.

I shoot out of bed, raking my hands through my hair.

'Oh, God, oh God,' I moan, pulling my beauty case out of my trolley, digging for something to wear. 'What time is it?' I cry, trying to remember which door is the bathroom. 'Have I got time for a shower?'

Danny turns on his stool and grins. 'It's the last door at the end of the corridor, Mum. And relax, it's only eight thirty.'

I stop in horror. Is it *that* late? This isn't going to look good, to be late on my first day!

'Okay, uhm, sweetheart, you're going to have to come downstairs with me. Bring your toys or something to do and—' I stop, halfway to the loo, as realisation hits me.

This is not what I'd planned. We'd made a list of all sorts of activities he liked and that we'd never had a chance to do together: fishing, horse-riding, trail-walking, seal-watching. Granted, I'd never be able to cram it all into the space of a few weeks, but I at least wanted to give it a try. Perhaps after breakfast I can steal an hour or so to take Danny down to the stables to meet Jeremy and see a real, live horse. And then maybe I could take him down into the village for a Christmas treat of some kind? One thing is certain. I owe him big time.

I call to Danny as I make a dash for the loo. 'Give Mummy a shout in five minutes?'

'Okay, Mum.'

As it turns out, there's no time to shower. I sniff under my arms; not too bad, all things considered. As I brush my teeth with one hand, I try to pull off my nightie with the other, getting my hair caught in one of the buttons, so it hangs from my head like a huge turban as I'm already dragging on a pair of jeans and panicking at the sudden realisation that I don't have any work clothes with me. Still, a pair of jeans and a jumper is better than Laura's tracksuit – just about.

I check my hair out. It looks too limp, let down like this, and would benefit from a wash. But I'd planned to do that this morning, *after* waking up at my leisure and after I'd had a lovely, lengthy breakfast at a table by a window overlooking the sea. But thanks to my soft spot, my bright ideas, *and* Mr Manners downstairs waiting for me, I don't even have time for a bloody cup of coffee.

'Five minutes are up, Mum!' Danny calls, a little too enthusiastically, from behind the door.

'Oh, already?' I squeak at my frazzled face in the mirror. *Shit, shit, shit.*

I throw the bathroom door open, kick my feet into my ankle boots and reach for my favourite cornflower blue jumper, the one with the high neck.

'Got everything, love?'

Danny nods.

'Good boy,' I pant and kiss the top of his head as I grab a Kit Kat from one of the cupboards, making a mental note to buy a replacement. Taking a man's bed may be one thing, but his chocolate? Unforgivable.

Passing a mirror, I almost scare the crap out of myself. My face is haggard, smears of make-up are still clinging to my lower lashes so that I look like a junkie. I lick my index fingers and rub them under my eyes and, in practically the same breath, wind my hair into a haphazard bun and secure it with a pencil. I know – real class. But needs must.

Just before we reach the lobby, I pop the last stick of Kit Kat into my mouth. Only I shove it too far down my throat, and end up in Reception gagging, only to spit it out into a bin right in front of Laura and Mitchell, who are studying the computer screen.

Both look up in surprise as I wheeze, trying to come back from what I'd thought was certain Death by Kit Kat, and Mitchell's eyebrow shoots up as usual whenever he sees me. 'You all right?' he says, giving me a very cursory once-over.

I slap my hand to my mouth and nod for fear of gagging there and then, but his eyes won't leave my face, nor are his eyebrows going down.

'What is it?' he asks.

'Nothing. I'm fine,' I assure him as my air passages are restored to normality. That had definitely been a close call. I always knew that one day chocolate would kill me.

He studies me until I begin to feel twitchy under his gaze. 'All right. I've got to run some errands in town, but Laura here will show you our system and get you up to speed.'

'O-kay...' I turn to Danny with a stab of regret to my heart. 'Darling, would you like to—'

'He can come with me,' Mitchell offers. 'Would you like that, Danny?'

He remembers Danny's name?

My little boy's face lights up. 'Can I, Mum? Please?'

Can he go with a total stranger, who is under unofficial investigation, to boot? Not that he is a murderer or a child kidnapper suspect, but still, apart from my family, I'm not used to sending him off like a parcel. Besides, if Mitchell is really the culprit Head Office thinks, is he really the kind of person I want my only son hanging out with?

My eyes swing to Mitchell's. They're waiting for an answer and I've still got a tiny, gob of Kit Kat stuck to the roof of my mouth. I swallow it down. How to get out of this? 'I... Will he not get in your way?'

'We'll be fine,' Mitchell says. 'Won't we, Danny?'

'Absolutely! I'll be good, Mum! Promise! Thank you, Mitchell!'

'What is it now?' Mitchell asks at the look on my face. 'What's wrong?'

Wrong? Nothing's wrong, per se. It's just that... in eight years, no bloke has ever offered to take care of Danny for a whole morning. But, unlike any other male who had transited through my life (not that I'd had a boyfriend since Mark), Mitchell is actually coming *back*. Granted that's because he lives here, if not for anything else. But still, it's a certainty I've never had before. And he'll drive carefully, because, well, I can tell, he looks like he can take care of a kid, no sweat. And do many of the other things in life that require responsibility. He doesn't look like a 'leaver' like Mark. After all, he's been left by someone else. He's suffered abandonment, and he knows all about heartache. That much we have in common.

For years I have been too guarded, seeing bad things were there was nothing, and I am trying to ease up a little because I don't want to transfer any of my anxieties to Danny. I want him to grow up a normal, confident boy. But my own anxieties about his safety are difficult to dispel. I need to make an effort. For him.

And as far as Mitchell Fitzpatrick being an embezzler, I may be wrong, but he doesn't strike me as one. I get instincts now, post-Mark. And they tell me that Mitchell may have a few rough edges, but he doesn't strike me as dodgy. Otherwise I wouldn't even be thinking about doing this.

I flash a look at Mitchell, who is eyeing me expectantly, and then settle my gaze on the carpet. 'Nothing's wrong. He can go. Uhm…' I cough. 'Thank you.'

'Yoo-hoo!' Danny hollers, stabbing the air with his toy helicopter.

Mitchell grins at him, taking him by the shoulder, turning to go, but then stops again. 'I promise I'll hold his hand when we cross the road and all that. Right, mate?'

If he isn't too thrilled about that, Danny doesn't show it.

He nods, chomping at the bit, dying to go and explore the world with a male adult, for a change. My heart goes out to my little man. I open my mouth to tell them to be careful, but clamp it shut again.

'And when we get back, I'll take you both to meet Jeremy, our stable boy. He can spend as much time as he wants with him and the horses. Jeremy loves company.'

'Oh, wow!' Danny cries. 'Do I get to ride a horse? A real one?'

If I could slide 'n' hide under the floorboards, this would be the moment I'd choose to do so.

Mitchell looks at me with a 'You've never let your son ride a *horse*?' expression, but I stuff my hands in my pockets and stare at the carpet again.

'Right. Thanks. See you later, then,' I say, watching as Mr Irish Charm takes my entire world with him out the main entrance. I can only hope that he will be entertained and not feel abandoned. I promise to work as quickly as possible to spend all my free time with him.

'I'm so happy you're here to help,' Laura exclaims, taking my arm as if we'd been friends our entire lives, and studying her friendly face and open gestures, I can see that she is imbued with kindness – not something that I'm used to in a big city.

'I only hope I'll be useful to you,' I confess. As opposed to detrimental, which is going to be more likely, and I can't help feeling like a heel. I like Laura.

'Oh, you will, Rosie!' she assures me. 'And you'll love it here in Little Kettering. We're actually interwoven with two other villages as we're so close. You can actually walk down the coast to Penworth Ford and Wyllow Cove. We're like the Bermuda triangle, only instead of disappearing, people pop up from nowhere, especially celebrities!'

'Really? Who?'

'Well, we've got the famous novelist and scriptwriter Nina Conte in Penworth Ford. She now co-produces with that Hollywood actor Luke O'Hara – oh, isn't he a dish?! And then we've got Natalia Amore who writes for *Lady Magazine* over in Wyllow Cove. Her column's called *That's Amore!* and it's hilarious! And then there's her sister, Yolanda Amore, the celebrity chef. The Amore sisters were born here, but Nina Conte is a Londoner, just like you.'

'It sounds like a fairy-tale place to live in.'

'It is. But maybe you'll move down here, too,' Laura says.

I only wish. But I'm no Nina Conte, nor Natalia or Yolanda Amore. Those women have superpowers and are wickedly talented, while I'm just forced to be simply wicked on this horrible little mission I've been pushed into.

As Laura is showing me the ropes, I try to relax in the knowledge that all I really have to learn is where the various paper files and documents are stored. I can't tell her she should be storing documents and folders as per Head Office directives (so that any Johnson Hotels employee can work seamlessly in other branches) because officially I shouldn't know any of that.

The morning passes rather smoothly. Laura and I go over the list of our guests to see if anyone has any particular requests and/or needs, namely which of the hens might require a remedy for their hangover. The two hen parties have wiped out the twenty-two rooms, but I know for a fact that the first party is due to leave. Maybe I can get my hands on a room now. Apart from the occasional girly shriek down the corridor, all is going well and we seem to have everything under control.

And then, just as the red devil hen party is leaving, a coach containing a stag party pulls up, out of the blue, wanting rooms.

At first, they seem okay. Nothing too OTT. You know, the usual effing and blinding, the pulling off of T-shirts upon arriving at Reception and the spraying deodorant into their armpits. High-class manners and all that. But once we've checked them in and they are on their way to their rooms, the last one in sight turns and spits into one of the potted plants. I glance over at Laura, who bites her lip.

'Is it always like this?' I whisper.

'Only when Mitchell isn't around. Most blokes are scared of him.'

'But does he go out *every* morning?' I want to know, already beginning to see where the issues are. There needs to be someone authoritative but friendly on the premises, and Laura, who has been left in charge, wouldn't scare an ant.

She holds up her hand, counting on her fingers. 'He has to get supplies, take stuff to his accountant, keep an eye on stationery – it's never-ending and the poor guy tries to be everywhere, but…'

'What about the assistant manager?' I ask, remembering Mitchell's wife. 'What did she do?'

Laura lowers her eyes, then looks up at me, a doleful expression on her young face. 'Diane wasn't exactly… hands on.'

I sigh inwardly. 'Meaning?'

'Well, she… normally received the bookings…'

Without vetting them, I conclude in silence. 'And then what?'

'She basically… hung around in the back office.'

'Did she communicate with Mitchell?'

Laura frowns. 'What do you mean? They were married.'

'I mean, did front and back office communicate on a daily basis? You know, liaise and such?'

Laura slowly shakes her head, and it doesn't take rocket science to understand all of the problems here. Firstly, there's no one really manning the place. Mitchell had put his wife in charge, while refusing to delegate the million errands that he ran. Mitchell's delegating issues mean that he has *trust* issues. And as a Johnson employee, his wife was required to give notice, not just up and go.

Other than that, where to start? The Old Bell Inn is stunning, but its present guests are the real problem. Laura should've seen beyond the red devil hen party's booking form, reading F.U.K.C, i.e. Female United Kingdom Choir, which sounds so much more respectable than Wild Hen Junket. A trick as old as dirt, but the inexperienced always fall for it.

There's nothing wrong with stag and hen parties, of course; they're a healthy part of a hotel's income. But this is the wrong time of the year, as the place should be full of families celebrating Christmas, not yobbos of both the male and female gender having *How far can you flick your knickers* contests. I'll have to talk to Mitchell.

I have no idea what his reaction will be. The idea is that I'm here to help relieve the pressure, but when I start giving him all sorts of pointers, won't he get a little suspicious? After all, I told him I was only a receptionist. I just hope he'll be reasonable and not take it the wrong way, because I don't know him, apart from the fact that he's irascible, irritable, quick-tempered, quick to judge and hard as stone and steel combined.

Unless he, like I sometimes still do, puts on a brave face during the day and then cries himself to sleep every night? However, I very much doubt that, judging by that sardonic grin he seems to have permanently pasted on his face. Some men have no chinks in their armour.

'Hey, love of my life,' comes a drawl from over the counter.

I look up at a blondish young man in his late twenties who looks like a member of one of those boy bands, wheeling in a huge baker's rack covered with a sheet of muslin.

'Oh, you again, Alex,' Laura says flatly and busies herself with her keyboard, but the blush seeping into her cheeks does not escape my notice.

'Who's the blonde dreamboat?' he continues as Laura theatrically rolls her eyes.

'Alex, meet Rosie. Rosie, meet Alex, the baker and village fool.'

To which he waggles his eyebrows and whispers confidentially, 'Only for you, Laura.'

'Yeah, yeah.'

'Where's Mitchell?' he wants to know. 'I need his signature.'

'Out,' she answers. 'You're going to have to wait or come back.'

Another time-consuming issue. This boat is springing more and more leaks by the second. 'Can't we sign for it?' I ask.

Laura's eyes widen. 'I don't know. It was always Diane who signed for everything.'

'Well, we need to have at least one person per shift available to take similar responsibilities,' I say in textbook Johnson Hotels lingo.

Laura nods. 'Makes sense.'

'Know what else makes sense?' Alex asks her.

'No, Alex, what's that?' Laura drawls, now blatantly concentrating on reading an old, dog-eared office furniture catalogue.

He smiles. 'You and me, going for a coffee.'

'As if.' Laura rolls her eyes, but at the same time slides me a quick glance.

I wave her off. 'Go, go. I'm pretty much set up here, and if the royal family arrives, I'll just wing it.'

Laura puts on a show of being completely bored with him. 'Five minutes,' she sighs, following him to the dining room.

Finally. Now I can stick my nose everywhere without arousing suspicion and catch up on my little investigation.

Just as I'm getting stuck in, Susan calls. 'Good morning, Susan,' I say in my most pleasant voice.

'You call this a preliminary report?' she barks.

My heart lurches. 'Why, what's wrong with it?'

'It wasn't even passable. All you did was describe the hotel and staff.'

What does she want, a psychiatric evaluation? 'It's only a preliminary report,' I defend. 'I'm in the office investigating, but so far there doesn't seem to be anything untoward.'

She smirks. 'We're not paying you to take your time, Rosie. Get on with it and send me a revision. And find me some facts.'

And she's gone again.

Facts. It's going to take time, because on the surface, the place is great: beautiful and clean. The food is delicious and the staff is, if inexperienced, friendly. The facilities may be a bit limited, but it is only a small inn meant for quiet getaways.

I need to understand why it has all these bad reviews, so I sit down at my laptop to reread the ones on TripAdvisor, which are pretty much all four or five star, minus the usual super-picky people, i.e. Professional Moaners. There are mentions of the picturesque setting, the breath-taking sea views, the olde-worlde feeling, the quality of the building and furnishings, the cleanliness, and even the superb food. It's a genuine but classy place. So far, so good. The last review dates back to a year or so ago. After that, Nothingness reigns. A complete void, like the inn's been sucked into a vacuum, a big black hotel hole.

I search the net for other references of any sort to the Old Bell Inn. Around fifty bloggers have given a thumbs up. But the problem I've got is that at least another sixty are chock-full with viciously derogatory articles about the staff, the manager, and everything under the sun. The only saving grace is that the place is gorgeous and that is how it manages to lure its victims. Why they leave and post such mean reviews is a mystery.

And then something catches my eye. Could it possibly be a coincidence? But I don't believe in coincidences and never have, so I pull up all the negative articles mentioning the Old Bell Inn and jot down the date that each site mentioned the inn for the first time. They all date back to a year ago. It's as if someone's suddenly started spreading the rumour that the inn is a shite-hole and everyone has since then been avoiding it. As a matter of fact, the rumours start immediately after the good reviews ended.

This looks a bit suspicious to me, so I save these particular sites on my Favourites and read them all over again. Something is bothering me. I can't quite put my finger on what it is, and by the end of the day my vision is blurred and I'm in a foul mood for all the ugliness I've had to plough through. People really can be so horrible sometimes.

6

Flowers from Judas

The state of the Old Bell Inn's records – I've never seen anything like it. Half of them are still in ledger form, each year running into the next, depending on how many pages were left in that particular ledger, rather than starting a new one in the new year. And the way they're filed? Almost haphazardly. I know I'm a control freak when it comes to filing, but who actually works like that today? No wonder I can't make heads or tails of it. Unless... someone has done all this on purpose, to cover their tracks? Because someone is subtracting funds, no doubt about it. But who?

I am treating my mission, i.e. pretending to be on holiday and offering to work for free, as such. Every morning I come down, spend three to four hours giving Laura tips on how to deal with difficult guests, how to input data in a much quicker, complete and efficient way, how to place calls to suppliers, where to jot down personal comments that will help her improve her service, and most importantly, how to deal with Head Office calls (my first tip was to chuck her gum out).

After a quick lunch, I go straight back to reception and start all over again. Sometimes Mitchell is there, so I can't be too nosy.

I spend the rest of my time covertly interviewing staff, trying to get to the bottom of why the occupancy rate and reviews are killing the establishment. Because, for the life of me, I don't understand what is going on.

Unless... is it all a façade? Has it all been done to scam the franchise, so that occupancy numbers only *appear* to be at their lowest in the mainframe system, while, under the counter, he's actually raking it in? Everything, from expenses to balancing, is off-kilter. It's so bad it almost looks... doctored. But it would take one hell of a mind to do that. A cold, calculating, dishonest mind.

Nah. As obnoxious as he is, I can't see Mitchell doing that. And yet, based on his personal lifestyle, questions must be asked. Laura has mentioned in passing that his daughter's schooling is expensive. He must be paying his divorce lawyers through the nose. Not to mention the artwork in his room and... *stop*. There must be some logical, plausible explanation. Granted, he looks like the devil on a bad day sometimes, and has the temper of a volcano. But deep down, he's got to be a good guy. I can just feel it in my waters. Otherwise I wouldn't be trying to save his ass, right?

So I set that thought aside, lest my suspicious nature takes me on an endless journey, and I spend the rest of the morning doing mundane, monkey-job stuff, such as handing out brochures, giving the stag and hen parties directions to the nearest pubs (let them puke on someone else's bar) and drumming up ways to bring in a better clientele. I just know that if this inn was mine, I could put it back on the map in less than a month. I make a note to meet every single person working here within the week and type up a spreadsheet with questions to ask them, which will help me assess the situation better.

I know Susan's manual has plenty of those in the appendix chapter, but I prefer to approach people in a natural way. No one likes being grilled.

When Mitchell brings back Danny, his baby cheeks are red with excitement. 'Mum! Mitchell's got the coolest car ever! It has seats that warm up and slide back and forth at the touch of a button!'

The evidence is piling up against Mitchell, and I don't like the look of it, but I manage to stifle it with a 'Really? That sounds so cool!'

'Maybe next time I can take him out on a pony ride?' Mitchell suggests, and I stare at him. 'What?' he says. 'The coastal path is a must-see, you know.'

You see? It doesn't tally – he's just spent the entire morning with my son, so he's got to be a good guy, and *could* I feel any guiltier about going through his private life? He didn't make the best first impression on me, granted, and I still don't know what he thinks of me, but the more I come to interact with Mitchell, the more I see that he is a decent, caring human being. How could he be otherwise, when he is so kind and patient with my son? Danny hasn't smiled this much in ages, and as much as it hurts me to admit my best isn't good enough, I am grateful to Mitchell.

But I have to have a word with him about the business. Particularly the financial mystery that enshrouds it, without him thinking he is even remotely suspected. If Susan were here, she'd sack him in a heartbeat. But, luckily for him, I'm not my boss.

'Are you excited, Danny?' I ask, wrapping my arm around his little shoulder as we exit the lobby a little later and turn onto the path leading to the stables.

He looks up at me and grins. 'Over the moon, Mum!'

I caress his cheek and squeeze his shoulder. He's all decked out in some borrowed riding gear and I can only wonder how much it will cost to kit him out. When we get back, I'm enrolling him in the nearest lessons because I've never seen him so happy, so fulfilled. If I'd known that that was all it would take, I'd have signed him up ages ago, even at the cost of doing overtime. Anything for my baby.

'Mitchell says I'll love Jeremy,' he informs me. 'He's the head stable boy.'

As we swing the gate open, a man comes out to greet us. The stable boy, Jeremy Gabriel, is anything but a boy. He's at least sixty, and just looking at him, with his checked shirt, leather cover-ups and quiet, kind manners relaxes me. I know they are going to get on like a house on fire.

'Mr Gabriel, I'm so grateful to you for agreeing to keep an eye on my son. Are you sure you don't mind?' I ask as Danny stares in awe at the real, live horses in the stalls sticking their heads out to study us.

'Name's Jeremy, ma'am. I'd be glad of the help.'

'He won't be a nuisance, I promise you. He's a quick learner, a hard worker and has read everything there is on horses. But he's...' I bite my lip. 'Never had the chance to actually ride one except for pony rides at village fairs.'

'We'll be all right, ma'am,' he says with a shy smile.

'It's Rosie.'

His smile broadens. 'Well, Rosie, don't worry about a thing. We'll start d'rectly with a few lessons. Then Mitchell's coming to take him out.'

I can't help but smile and I'd hug the man if I didn't want to keep it together. 'Thank you so much, Jeremy. I have to get back to the office,' I say with some regret. 'But I'll be back later.'

And that's when this country gentleman dips his head. God, I'm going to miss this corner of the world, with its genuine ways. No frills here, but definitely good, salt-of-the-earth people.

An hour later, there is a flower delivery to the inn. The courier saunters into the lobby carrying a long box, so I sign for it and leave it on the counter.

'Ooh, flowers,' Laura says as she comes back from her break on the heels of the flower man. 'Who for?'

I look up from my screen. 'The bride, I assume.'

'Shouldn't we check, in case they aren't?' Laura suggests.

'You're absolutely right. I just thought—'

'Ooh, Rosie! They're for you!'

I sit up, confused. 'Me?'

'Here, read the card!'

I lean forward. *I'm sorry. Give me another chance. Mark xxx*

Mark. First a letter, and now flowers. On what planet does he think it's actually going to happen? And by the way, how did he even manage to find out I was in Cornwall?

If I'd known they were from him, I'd have tossed them straight away without a thought. The same way I can't bring myself to open the letter in my glove compartment. I already know what it says. That he's a roamer, and wasn't born to be a father, to please forgive him, but it's better that way. Years of that codswallop. And now I'm done.

I shove the box into the bin without a thought.

'Aren't you at least going to have a look?' Laura asks, surprised.

'I don't need to look. There are twenty-four long-stemmed red roses in there.'

'Wow, no expenses spared,' she says with a whistle.

I look around the lobby to check no one has heard her and she covers her mouth. 'Sorry.'

'No worries. You can still look if you like,' I say.

Eyeing me, she pulls off the lid and oohs and aahs. 'They're gorgeous.' She swoons. 'I've never had anyone send me flowers.'

Flowers devoid of any sentiment. Besides a one-liner, he never feels the need to express any emotions. Not once has he ever asked for my forgiveness in person, nor had the grown-up conversation. And he keeps taunting me with flowers. I know him. He's saying that I'll never be able to forget him. In fact, never has anyone so absent left a mark so difficult to erase.

It had nearly killed me. I had loved him so much that I actually thought I would die of heartbreak. The injustice of it all. I had relived our relationship over and over in my mind, trying to understand what I'd done so wrong that he couldn't love me like I loved him.

Sometimes I wonder what I'd say if he ever called my mobile. He still has my number. I never changed it, just in case... never mind. It's done, he's gone and I've moved on. But why does it still bloody hurt even to think about him?

'Mum, it was fantastic! I got to ride Fletcher, the coolest horse ever!' Danny cries when he gets in a couple of hours later, all dirty and as happy as Larry.

'Did you?' I say, bending down to kiss him on the cheek just as Mitchell comes in, eyeing the box of roses. I wonder where he goes every day.

'Can I have lunch in the dining room with Sally?' Danny asks.

'Shower first,' I say.

'But I'm hungry now, Mum.'

'You can go with him,' Mitchell says to me. 'I'll watch the desk.'

'Thank you, Mitchell,' I say, and then I turn to Danny. 'Who is Sally, darling?'

'Head of housekeeping.'

Of course. I'm meeting her tomorrow.

'We bumped into her in L.K.'

He's going way too fast for me. 'L.K.?'

'Mitchell's name for Little Kettering. It's supposed to be like L.A., only it's not. It's a joke. Right, Mitchell?' Danny looks at him for approval, which he readily gets, along with another one of their high fives. It's become a private joke between them. Anything they agree on, they high-five each other.

'Right you are, mate.'

Mate? Ah, well. I certainly hope I haven't made a mistake, letting Danny hang with him. After all, there is still a very slim chance that I may be wrong and that Mitchell Fitzpatrick is doing something he shouldn't be doing. But my instincts are never wrong. Well, except about Mark, that is.

'So can I go?' Danny asks. 'Mitchell said I can, if it's okay with you?'

My eyes swing to Mitchell, who nods reassuringly. And, for some reason, I can't help but trust him. I caress Danny's cheek. 'Okay, love. I'll be in in a minute – you go.'

We both watch as he scurries off happily.

Mitchell grins. 'You've got yourself a little gent there, Rosie.'

I feel myself blushing like Laura when Alex is around. 'Thanks. He really is a good boy. He's my blessing.'

'He wouldn't stop talking about you all morning.'

'Oh?'

Mitchell laughs. It's a nice, hearty laugh that makes his eyes twinkle and crinkle at the corners. How can anyone resist the rugged looks, the captivating, sexy grin, and oh... that voice, so deep that it vibrates in your stomach? I touch my stomach instinctively, and Mitchell's eyes flicker to my hand, but he says nothing.

'Nothing embarrassing, I assure you. Which reminds me. I have to apologise to you. For our rocky start...'

I shrug. 'That's okay, I know you're – I mean I imagine you're under a lot of pressure.'

He nods. 'Well, yes, but that's not it. I misjudged you completely. I see that, and once again, I'm sorry.'

This must have been one monumental effort for someone as proud as him. 'It's all water under the bridge,' I concede.

'Thanks. And in case you hadn't forgiven me at this point, here,' he says, producing a bag containing coffee and doughnuts. 'I know, I know, we have all this here, but sometimes you just need a little contact with the outside world, don't you?'

'Yeah.' Which is something I think he has a bit too much of. 'Got a minute?'

'Sure.' He passes me a coffee and a doughnut. Caffeine might just give me the courage to start the List of What's Wrong With The Joint conversation. I'm dreading it, and I'm not even the one on the receiving end.

I take a deep breath. Here we go. 'This is a gorgeous place, Mitchell...'

He takes a sip, purses his lips, swallows, and then turns to me, his dark eyes probing. 'But...?'

'It could be better,' I say as kindly as possible.

'I know. I've had a few blips along the way.' He dips his head and looks up at me with an apologetic expression I'm not expecting. I didn't think he could do spaniel eyes, and yet, in the space of a few hours, I am learning things about him that make him much more human and kinder than I thought. I'm actually seeing a side of him that I didn't know existed, so different from his Arrogant Superman attitude.

'Blips? You mean your wife... quitting?' I say before I can stop myself. You see? I'm a natural disaster. I should stick to my own job. Honestly, I tried telling Susan that I'm not the right person for this mission. Mitchell, who is bringing his cup to his lips again, does a double take at the boldness of my question, his dark eyes wide with surprise.

And then he becomes guarded again. Like I'm trying to penetrate his deepest secrets and poking at his open wounds. It's not what I mean to do. I'm on his side, of course.

'Sorry. I didn't mean to pry...'

'Diane had nothing to do with the problems here. It's all my fault.'

Well, if he's in a *mea culpa* mood, he might just take some things on board all the more easily. 'How so...?' I ask.

He puts his cup down on the counter and rubs his face with both hands and then turns to grin at me, but I can tell he's unhappy. 'Bloody hell, where do I begin? My heart just isn't in this place anymore. Do you have any idea how many hotels belong to this franchise?'

I seriously hope he doesn't expect me to answer that.

'Fifty-three. It's become part of a faceless corporation now.'

Faceless corporation. If he only knew it did have a face, and that, for the next few weeks, it's mine.

'My dream is to open my own holiday cottages,' he informs me, and we're back to being friends again, hopefully.

'Wow, that would be a stroke of genius. And one day, I'm sure you will.' *Hopefully, before HO sacks you.*

'Thank you.'

'Well, for now, your biggest problem is sitting right in front of you. And I don't mean me.' Which, actually, I do, but we can't tell him that, can we? And after the evaluation, when he's found out about my role in it, I'll be out of this place before he can say *Merry Christmas and a Happy New Year*.

He looks around at his two-storey problem. 'I'm listening...'

'Well… the clientele, for instance.'

He rolls his eyes, dragging a hand through his loose, ebony curls. I can't help but notice his hair looks very healthy, and I become conscious of my own limp blonde hair and want to cry with envy. 'I know,' he concedes. 'I hate hen and stag parties.'

'Well, you shouldn't, because they are important, and not all parties are like these ones. There are also so many nice people. You just need to keep them away from the holiday season and concentrate on families.'

'I'm in no position to refuse business, Rosie.'

'No, but make it more family-friendly. Kit out the park and put in some kiddie stuff. Get some more horses. Open up the equestrian side of it.'

His dark eyes swing to mine. 'You think?'

'Yes, look at Danny. Lots of kids love horses. You could even have an equestrian school here. Or, you could make it available as a set location.'

'What?'

Oh my word, the man is completely clueless about the important things in life. Like absolutely great TV. 'This is Cornwall! Hello? *Poldark?* Rosamunde Pilcher? Agatha Christie?'

He makes a face. 'Aren't Agatha Christie's stories set in Devon?'

A-ha. So he's not a complete philistine. I laugh. 'A lot has been shot in Cornwall. Don't you know anything about your own county?'

He grins. 'I'm not English, in case you didn't notice.'

As if I hadn't noticed how he can switch on the Irish charm when he wants. 'So what brought you here?' I ask.

He lifts his eyebrows as if to say 'I'd like to know that, too' and turns to look at me, resigned to telling me the truth. 'I came for love.'

'Diane?'

He nods and takes another sip of his coffee, but I think he's just trying to hide his face in his cup. Strangely, he doesn't strike me anymore as the arrogant twat he acted like only yesterday.

And I can't seem to stay off this subject. It's like I need to know everything, even if it's not my business. They should call me Nosy Rosie. 'I'm sorry about how that ended, by the way,' I say. Which is true. No one should be abandoned like that. I should know, right?

Again, that quizzical smile. 'Boy, does my staff gossip, or what?'

'Oh, no. They love you, you know?'

He smiles. 'And I don't know where I'd be without them.'

Silence. How do you fill the awkward pauses?

He grins and leans in confidentially, like he's telling me a secret. 'In answer to your question about Di, I'm doing all right. Better than I'd thought. Thanks to Lola.'

I blink, my smile freezing on my face like instant icicles. 'Lola?'

'My little girl.'

'Oh!'

'She keeps me going with her cute face and adoring eyes. No matter what I do, she thinks I'm the best thing since pasties.'

Just like Danny. It was marvellous how blind love can make kids. 'Awh. Do you not see her often?'

'Mostly when she's home for the holidays. She prefers to spend them here, rather than with her mother.'

'That must be hard on Diane,' I concede.

'I wish it was. Diane only loves herself. And you? Any skeletons in the closet?'

I think about my secret mission, and the unopened letter in my glove compartment. I'm not letting anything spoil this Christmas, no matter what.

A gaggle of party hens clops by to distract us, high heels and heaving breasts. We watch them in silence as I try to figure out which one of them attracts his attention the most, but he turns to me.

'I've always wondered why people choose Christmas for the A-list things. Getting married...' he murmurs.

'Going abroad...' I add, then silently: *Sacking employees...*

Mitchell raises an eyebrow in a sardonic grin. 'Dumping their partners...'

At the question on my face, he shrugs. 'It was Christmas Eve, when I found out she had someone else. We had a fight and she left.'

'Nice...' I whistle, meaning exactly the opposite. 'Was it out of the blue?'

He purses his lips and shrugs his shoulders in a sign of helplessness. 'Was it? Dunno? I kind of had a feeling that things weren't going very well. But I thought it was just one of those moments, you know, where you sit tight and wait for the storm to pass. But it never did. And then, she went.'

'Did you miss her a lot?' God, can I *ask* dumber questions?

'If I did, I quickly changed my mind. You know, she always hated Cornwall. When we got these jobs together,

I thought it was going to be the start of something great. But then the company grew overnight, and it's not the same place it used to be. And she wanted to leave.'

'How can you hate Cornwall?' I ask in surprise.

He chuckles, draining the last of his coffee. 'I know, right? She said she wanted to get as far away from here as possible.'

'And go where?'

'London. She's a city gal.'

The opposite of me. I'd give ten years of my life to be able to escape the Big Smoke, and Susan, for that matter.

We sit there in amiable silence. I've still got a gazillion pointers to give him, but for now, it's nice just to shoot the breeze. Susan would have a heart attack if she saw me fraternising with the plebs, as she calls us, sitting shoulder to shoulder, with (apparently) no care in the world.

'Giving birth to babies,' I suddenly say, and his brow furrows in confusion as he looks over at me. I laugh. 'Another favourite Christmas activity. Danny was born on Christmas Eve.'

He chuckles. 'Makes you wonder what people do the rest of the year.'

I search his face, and upon spotting the now familiar, endearing twinkle in his eye, I grin back. 'Yeah. Makes you wonder.'

'So… will we pass muster, do you think?' he wants to know.

'I'm not here to judge,' I lie.

'Of course you are,' he says.

For a moment, I panic, searching his face, but then he smiles. It's a cheeky grin, complete with tongue-licking lips. It's very distracting and unnerving, considering that a) he's sitting a breath away from me, looking right into my eyes, b) I haven't flirted in years, and c) I have absolutely no right to do so with a future-ex-employee.

Good thing I'll be gone in a few weeks' time.

'Are these roses for the bride?' Mitchell asks, nodding to the box.

'No,' I answer sheepishly. 'They're for me.'

His face freezes in a smile. 'Ah. Danny's father? Or maybe some other bloke?'

My, he's a bit nosy, though, isn't he? I eye him. 'There is no other bloke.' Which sounds like I only have eyes for Mark, but if I hurry to correct myself and say that I'm actually single, it'll sound like I'm on the prowl, which I'm not. I mean, I wouldn't mind finding love again one day, but I'm not all that certain that I would be able to trust someone completely with my heart – and Danny's. Heartbreak is not on the menu.

And speaking of which. I clear my throat. 'If there's nothing else, Mitchell, I need to prepare for tomorrow's meeting with your chef, if you don't mind.'

He is still watching me with an undefinable look, and then he straightens. 'Yes. No, there's nothing else, Rosie. Thank you.'

And we are back on uneasy terrain again, I can sense it. Why can't we just have a normal conversation without ending up in these dead ends?

At the end of the day, Danny and I are exhausted. Or rather, I'm exhausted, while he's elated. All through dinner in the dining room, he's been talking about all the new horse-related – sorry, *equestrian*-related words he's learnt. Even as he's brushing his teeth, he's telling me about how Jeremy did this or did that, and how Mitchell promised to let him hang out.

'He's so cool, Mitchell. Isn't he, Mum?'

'Yes, darling, he certainly is,' I echo, and, happy with my answer, he spits and rinses.

I sit on my bed and toe off my shoes, waiting for him to free the bathroom where a nice hot shower awaits. What I wouldn't give for a proper bath right now. That would make Cornwall absolute perfection.

'I can't wait for tomorrow,' Danny enthuses as I tuck him in. Usually, he's content going to bed early, but now he seems too excited, too wired to fall asleep.

'Neither can I,' I assure him. But it's a lie. I don't want it to be tomorrow so soon. I want to stay here, tuck him in and read him a fairy tale and sleep with him in my arms. Because that's the only way I can spend time with him. Tomorrow he will be another day older, and another day wiser, and another day less my boy and more a boy discovering the world around him. I swipe at a tear, but not before turning off his bedside light. What the hell is wrong with me? I should be elated he has finally found his niche. And I am.

'Mum?' he whispers in the sudden darkness.

'Yes, darling?' I whisper back.

'Be happy, Mum, while we're here.'

I swallow and grope for his hand, which I gently squeeze. 'I am happy, Danny. I am happy when you are happy, love.'

He squeezes back. 'I am happy, Mum.'

'I love you, Danny,' I barely whisper, not wanting my voice to crack. Sentimental, yes. Pathetic, no.

'I love you too, Mum,' he says with a yawn and I kiss him on the cheek. My little man.

Content that all is well in our little world, I grab a towel and head for the shower, hoping I won't fall asleep in there, and wondering at the same time where Mitchell is right now.

But I can't sleep, still jittery from the roses. Mark knows I'm here. He's called Head Office where he used to work – that's how we'd met – and some old buddy of his gave him the tip. That's the only explanation I can think of. And now, after years of silence, he's suddenly interested in talking to me again?

My first visit of the next day is to the chef, Russell Jones, who is a cross between Schwarzenegger and Mr Clean, only with more swagger. His muscles are straining his T-shirt that threatens to burst at the seams. He gives me a flirty double-raise of the eyebrow as I knock on the door of his domain, the kitchen.

'Come if you want,' he warns me with a double-entendre tone.

'Hi, uhm, my name's Rosie Anderson? I'm helping Mitchell with a few things around here, so I thought I'd come and congratulate you for all the amazing reviews on your food.'

At that, his chest puffs up even more, and he pulls up a stool for me. 'Sit yer lovely bottom on this,' he says, and then turns away to lift a lid off a casserole. He dips a wooden spoon in it and promptly rests it before my mouth. 'Taste.'

'Oh? Oh, okay.' It is a sort of pink cream. I scrape my index along the bottom of the spoon and pop it into my mouth, realising too late that he probably sees it as an open invitation of sexual nature. At least it looks like that by the way he's watching me. 'Strawberry?' I venture.

'Passionfruit…' he swoons. 'Orgasmic, isn't it?'

'Uhm, if you mean good, then yes. Very good.'

He puts his wooden spoon down and grins at me expectantly. 'Food is like sex,' he instructs me. 'If you're going to bother at all, make it special.'

'I guess so,' I say, completely at a loss. What do I know about sex?

'Do you like food?' he asks.

I'm not so sure we're still speaking literally now. 'Uhm, yeah, sure.'

'Excellent. Now try my desserts. I have crème brûlée, baked Alaska and tiramisu, all with a twist.'

'Ooh, yes, please,' I say, my mouth beginning to water already, when my mobile rings. It's Laura.

'Rosie, I've confirmed you and Sally having a sit-down. She's ready now, if you are.'

That's the head of housekeeping. From what I've seen, she's got all her ducks in a row and her work is flawless. But her timing isn't.

'Sure, tell her I'll be right there.'

With great sadness, and eyeing the tiramisu in particular, I slide off my stool. 'Thank you, Russell. By the way, that beef wellington the other night was the best thing I've ever had.'

'That's because you haven't tried my other things,' he says, waggling his eyebrows again.

How do you answer that? 'I'll see you soon, then. Thank you.'

'I'll be here,' he promises with a wink.

Just before I sit down with Sally, Danny comes back from the stables for a quick hello. I haven't seen him all morning, but from his flushed cheeks and confident stride, I realise he is truly in his element, and I'm delighted. In a way, it sort of makes up for me not being able to see as much of him. I might be missing him like crazy, but at least I know he is happy, safe, and learning about things he loves.

'Your boy is lovely,' Sally says as he skips off again.

'Thank you.'

'I miss mine being that young.'

'How old is yours?'

'My youngest was three only yesterday. Now he's preparing for his GCSEs.'

I laugh. 'It does go by quickly, doesn't it?'

She smiles. 'You enjoy him, Rosie. Before you know it, he'll be bringing The One home. And then you'll be babysitting.'

I can't imagine what that would be like, but I know what she means. 'Yesterday I was changing his diaper. And today he's riding horses for the very first time. I confess I'm a little emotional.'

'Jeremy's a good man. Competent and kind. You can trust him.'

'I do. I feel that Danny is protected. I knew Cornwall was a completely different world, but this goes beyond all my highest expectations.'

She smiles. 'We are a close-knit community in Little Kettering. Besides, Mitchell would have our heads.'

'He would?'

She winks. 'Oh, yeah.'

Again, I have to admit to myself that I haven't captured the essence of this man yet and how he came to be investigated. It still doesn't make sense. One moment he'll be a complete, arrogant ass, and then the next he'll just take you by surprise with the kindest of gestures. Go figure.

Sally and I then discuss staff, shifts, whether there are any issues, and I offer her my complete availability if she is uncomfortable with anything.

'You're very good at your job, Rosie. You should take Diane's place,' she says with a smile.

'I've got a job to get back to in London,' I say, more to myself than to her. Because despite the fact that I didn't want to be in this position, this place is really starting to grow on me.

That night, I crawl into bed with Danny, who rests his head on my chest while telling me about his day in the stables with Jeremy and his favourite horse, Mabel, that he hasn't been able to ride yet.

'I rode all of them, but haven't managed to mount her yet,' he says with regret. 'She's a sweet old mare, but has trust issues.'

I stifle a laugh. I've never heard my kid use that phrase before. Sally is right. Time does go by quickly, and I want to cherish every single moment now.

'Jeremy says that if I insist and show my face every day and help brush her down, that eventually I'll be able to ride her.'

'Of course you will, darling,' I assure him. 'You can do anything you set your mind to.'

'Do you really think so, Mum?'

I lift my head to look him in the face. 'When have I ever been wrong about you?'

'Never.'

'And you will never be wrong about yourself as long as you believe you can do it.'

'Thanks, Mum. I know. Even Mitchell says so.'

Mitchell says so? Huh.

He seems so happy already after two full days here. My fear of him feeling abandoned was altogether my usual exaggeration. But I also have the feeling I've missed him more than he's missed me.

This room feels like home, the bed is amazingly comfy and welcoming, and I'm just about to drop off when Susan calls, scaring the crap out of me. I must change her tune to something a bit more relaxing. I groan as I fish my mobile from somewhere below Mitchell's nightstand.

'H'llo?'

'Rosie!'

I sit up, ramrod straight. I hadn't been dreaming after all. I clear my throat. 'Yes, hi.'

'You weren't asleep, were you?'

I eye the clock on the nightstand. Midnight. 'No, I was just, ehm, rereading some notes,' I lie.

'Good idea. Because the revision of the preliminary report you sent me is crap.'

I shift onto my side, trying to knock the sleep out of my brain. 'I'm sorry?'

'You should be – I've never read such drivel. Your report insists that there is nothing wrong with the place or the staff.'

'That's right, as far as I can see.'

'Then you need to delve deeper. I didn't send you there for a three-week holiday, Rosie.'

'No, of course not.'

'From now on, I want regular updates. I want theories, suspicions, and evidence to back up your suspicions.'

In other words, she wants to hang the bloke. 'I'll see what can be done,' I promise, crossing my fingers.

'You do that.'

'Goodnight, Susan,' I say, but she's already hung up. I'd love to meet her parents one day and ask them a lot of questions about her childhood, because she is one messed-up woman.

7

The Manager Who Stole Christmas

The next morning after breakfast, I walk through reception to the back office for another, real proper snoop before Laura gets in. There, I stop, frozen.

Mitchell is lying on the sofa in the corner, on his back, his arm thrown over his eyes. Wearing only a pair of boxers.

Without uttering a word, I backtrack out of the room, hoping he hasn't heard me, but I bash my elbow against the doorframe and he's instantly alert.

'Jesus, it's not seven o'clock already, is it?' he groans, jumping up and pulling on his jeans. He grabs his old shirt, balling it up and stuffing it into his back pocket.

'Not yet,' I answer, turning away. But, in one embarrassed glance, I've noticed a great deal. He's achingly handsome, with a body to die for. A body that he hides very well under large sweaters and—boy, I shouldn't be thinking these things. I'm here to work.

But his shoulders are wider than I'd thought, and his chest is covered with a good dose of dark hair that looks incredibly soft, leading to a six-pack that simply can't be improved on.

Not that I'm here to catch myself a man, mind you. Besides, in a few weeks I'll be gone. I'm not quite sure *where* I'll be going, if I keep my shenanigans up. I know I'll come to regret my lies to my boss, but Susan has the power to pulverise him if she chooses to, and she most definitely will, if I don't protect him. Maybe it's my strong sense of justice, or that I just don't like seeing people getting fired, but my instinct is to help him.

'Sorry, I, uhm, just wanted to get some photocopying done before the start of the day,' I lie. 'I had no idea you slept here. I'm so sorry, I feel so bad…' He can't live like this, like a refugee with no real bed. It's bad enough he doesn't have, as far as I know, a real home in the area. Goodness, what have I done? I've literally kicked a man out of his home. The least I can do is try to save him from losing his job.

Mitchell zips up his jeans.

'Look,' I say, 'Danny and I will move out—'

'Don't be silly. It won't be forever.'

That much is true. In less than three weeks' time I'll be out of here. I only hope *he* will be staying, though.

He slides past me, a sleepy grin on his face as he winks, and I can smell the wonderful smell of what can only be described as *bed* on him. Male. Cosy. Sexy. I inhale, like a dog sniffing a pot roast, and my senses, which have been turned off for the last eight years, are instantly alert, back in the saddle.

'Shower time…' he whispers as his arm touches mine in salute.

Huh? Shower? It's not an invitation, you daft, daft girl.

Now, normally, I'm not one to ogle men – I never do, ever. But, as he's leaving, I get a view of his bare, broad but lean back, and am particularly enticed by the tendons on either side of his spine. I have to make an effort to shut it all out of my mind. He's slim but muscled. Which would all be bearable, were it not for his gravelly bed-voice that stirs all sorts of thoughts I'd buried a lifetime ago.

In the past years, I've had a bit of office flirting banter here and there, but haven't been out on one single date. There's simply no one I've fancied enough to say yes to. But Mitchell... he's taken me completely by surprise. And, oddly enough, it's all come at the worst of times. If there is one man I shouldn't be having anything to do with – ever – it's Mitchell Fitzpatrick.

What the heck is happening to me? Three days in and I'm already thinking about a stranger's scent? I'm not like that. I just don't behave that way at all.

Mark's dumping me had changed my ways forever. I had not only lost my young girl's self-confidence, but I'd also lost, at a very young age, my faith in the opposite sex. So, no – this is definitely not the way I normally behave around men. I never have, never could. So, what's all this sniffing Mitchell all about?

When Laura comes in a few minutes later, she looks at me and cocks her head. 'You look... frazzled. Are you hot?'

Hot? I'm literally self-combusting. And I have a headache and a half. 'I'm fine.'

Laura puts her bag down. 'You don't look fine to me. Did you not sleep well?'

Sleep? How could I, sick with worry about this bloody evaluation and Susan calling at all hours? I just know I'm going to get another call from her today wanting an update, and I still have to get my nose into the bowels of the secrets of the Old Bell Inn. Because something is still bothering me. 'I'm fine, thanks,' I say as I take my place at my desk and look up my favourites on my laptop with the goal of rereading the reviews for the umpteenth time. Apart from the timing, and the viciousness, something else is staring me in the face. I can feel it, but I just can't figure out what it is.

In order to keep abreast of any new reviews, I log on with an alias (am I getting good at this sneaky business or not?) and sign up for alerts from each and every one of the sixty-three negative bloggers, in the hope that I may discover any clues as to what is happening.

About an hour later, as I have made no progress whatsoever all morning, I look about me, at the beautiful but bare stone walls and decide to start fixing the things I actually can.

'Sally, have we got a Christmas tree?' I ask as she wheels past me with her cart full of cleaning products.

She stares at me as if I am barking mad. 'Christmas tree?'

'And decorations. And lights,' I add. 'Surely you have some stuff lying around from last year?'

'Don't get your hopes up too high. When Diane left, she took most of her stuff with her.'

Diane. Why did she really leave him? Was it really because she hated Cornwall? I find that alone impossible to believe. What kind of couple were they? And then I remind myself why I'm here, and that none of this is any of my business.

'If you want, I'll have a look for you,' Sally offers.

'Thanks, Sally. I'd really appreciate it.' I smile at her. With her tired face and hands worked down to the bone, I have a feeling that she bears the weight of not only the inn, but the entire world on her slim shoulders as well. And yet she always finds the time to smile, to ruffle Danny's hair, to say something cheerful to anyone walking past her, and to even bring me a croissant. She is truly a rare gem of a woman whose whole existence is built on her own hard labour and sacrifices.

'You are a star, lady,' I say as I wink at her just as Mitchell is walking by.

'Awh, thanks, luv, so are you…' she returns.

He stops to watch the exchange as Sally, who is now blowing me kisses, steps back against him.

'Oh-oh,' she says with mock fear. 'I hit a brick wall. Please don't tell me it's the boss.'

'I'm afraid it is,' he whispers back.

She chuckles and moves away.

'Hi, can I have a word?' I ask.

Mitchell turns to look at me. 'About?'

'Christmas.'

'What about it?'

'Well, haven't you noticed anything?'

'What?'

'It's completely missing. There is not one sign of Christmas here in this inn.'

'We don't need a sign. Everyone knows it's Christmas.'

I sigh inwardly. Why am I not surprised, I wonder? I know he's having a tough time at the moment. I know last Christmas he was dumped by his wife and is not particularly keen on celebrating this time of year. No one knows it better than I do, but right now, I need him to shine more than ever, just as much as I need his lobby to sparkle with bright Christmas lights.

Besides, shouldn't he be happy I'm making the inn all the more festive for Lola to enjoy? All children love Christmas, and even with a father like Mitchell, I'm sure she does as well.

'I'm going to put up a tree,' I announce.

He groans. 'What for?'

'To spread Christmas cheer and make guests feel all the more welcome and at home.'

'If they wanted to feel like they were staying home, they would've stayed home,' he snaps as he marches to his office.

'Maybe it would be preferable, rather than hang around this mausoleum!' I snap back, rising out of my seat, only to duck back down when I spot a couple of hens sashaying past Reception, an amused smile on their faces. Sybil Fawlty couldn't have done it better. Are Mitchell and I becoming the Fawltys, without even being a couple? Everything I want to do, he simply turns around and vetoes.

From my station, I can see him through the open door, rubbing his face in exasperation. What the hell is his problem? And whatever it is, for the good of his business, he should be trying to get over it. And I'm going to help him do that. I'll make this place so festive, the poor man won't know what hit him. He'll be so cheerful he won't even recognise himself when I'm done with him.

When Sally returns half an hour later with a stack of boxes full of decorations, I can hardly contain my glee.

'Oh, goody, thank you, Sally!' I chime, and Mitchell looks up from his desk to see what the commotion is all about, only to frown when he sees the cause.

'Be right back!' I call to him as I hike my turtle neck

around my ears and brace myself for the cold temperatures outside to go and look for Danny in the stables.

We always decorate our Christmas tree together back home, and just because we're not home this year doesn't mean that we should be forgoing Christmas altogether. It has always been special to me, and more so after Danny's birthday on Christmas Eve. I have a lot to be thankful for. And, even if Mitchell can't see it, so does he. I'm assuming he'll be seeing his daughter either for Christmas or the New Year. Maybe that's it. Maybe he won't see her until the New Year and maybe that's another reason why he's so bloody miserable. If that's the case, I'll make sure Danny cheers him up.

I find him and Jeremy in the stables, caressing what is possibly the most derelict horse I've ever seen. She's way past her prime, even I can tell.

'Hi, Mum! Look, this is Mabel!' he whispers so as not to spook the poor animal. 'She's Mitchell's favourite. But we have to retire her for her own good.'

I come close to her and softly caress her nose. 'Hello, Mabel. Hello, beautiful. Is she sick?'

'No, just old,' Jeremy answers. 'It's time for her to rest.'

'Mabel's going to be put out to pasture,' Danny informs me. 'And Jeremy said I can take care of her all on my own.'

I look at my son and see how quickly he's changed in only a few days. He is more confident, more responsible. He even looks wiser. And certainly he is happier here. It's almost as if by travelling out here, Danny has become more in touch with himself. Because that's what Cornwall does. It lets you get back into a relationship with yourself and your loved ones. It gives you time to feel. There is no soul-destroying routine of fighting your way through the mad crowd to take the Tube. No faceless city that will swallow you if you only let it. Here, all is calm, all is silent. All is love. Just like Christmas should be.

I look up at Jeremy who has a strange expression on his kind, withered face. And I understand that he has complete faith in Danny. 'Thank you, Jeremy, for trusting Danny with such an important horse.'

He smiles. 'Thank Mitchell. He asked specifically for Danny to take care of her.'

'Oh? That's great,' I answer through a tight throat. Just when you think that Mitchell Fitzscrooge is hopeless. I swallow back a strange emotion that I can't quite place. It's a mixture between pride for my son, and gratitude to Mitchell. He and I might not see eye to eye on business, granted, but he keeps finding ways to tell me that he isn't actually half bad at all.

'Uhm, darling, would you like to help me decorate the Christmas tree?'

Danny's eyes swing to Jeremy's. 'Do you mind?'

'Go on, son. Mabel is in for the night now. You've done a great job.'

Danny gets to his feet and strokes Mabel's nose. 'Okay, then. Goodnight, beautiful Mabel,' he whispers into her ear. 'I'll see you tomorrow. Thank you, Jeremy,' he says without me having to prompt him. Back home, he hardly ever spoke to adults other than his teachers. Even in shops, he was always so shy. But here, it's different. He's found a friend with common interests, and it's helping him open up.

He dusts himself off and comes to my side, searching

for my hand. He may be growing up, but part of him will always be my little boy.

'Thanks, Jeremy,' I say, smiling, when really all I want to do is give the old man a great big hug.

Back in the lobby, Danny runs to the boxes and starts pulling out the sections of a fake Christmas tree. It would have been nice to have a real one, but this is the best we can do on such short notice.

'Mum, look at the size of this tree!' Danny exclaims after we have connected all the pieces together and stood it just to the right of the main entrance, by a window so that it will be enjoyed from outdoors as well.

He is right. It stands at least ten feet tall, which is how I feel every time my son smiles up at me. It's not a real tree, but with a little TLC it will look more than good.

'Shall we decorate it now, darling?' I suggest and he immediately dives into the stack of boxes containing the decorations.

There are countless choices as there is a mismatch of everything. 'We can have a silver and red theme, or blue, or—'

'Let's do all of the colours!' Danny exclaims. 'Let's make it really colourful and bright! And let's put up as many lights as possible!'

'Okay,' I say with a laugh. I swear I've never seen him this excited about a Christmas tree. Or Christmas, for that matter. What looked like a blue Christmas without the family is shaping up to be quite pleasing indeed.

As I reach into one of the boxes for a bauble, my hands touch a bit of bubble wrap. I carefully unwrap the round object. It is a silvery-blue baby ornament, with a baby in onesies depicted on one side. I turn it over and gasp when I read: 'To Mitchell on his first Christmas, with love from Mum and Dad'.

'Rosie, would it be possible for you to… Rosie…?'

I turn around at the sound of Mitchell's deep voice. And the panicked look on his face at the sight of our colourful mess of decorations on the floor is simply to die for.

'Hi, Mitchell!' Danny and I chime in unison.

'What's all this?'

'Christmas cheer. Remember that?'

He opens his mouth to retort, but due to Danny's presence, thinks better of it. Without a word, he takes off in the opposite direction. I knew he didn't want to celebrate Christmas because it's the time of year his wife left him. But he's done such a good job of looking as if he was over it that I actually believed it. The question is, now, is it his pride that hurts, or is his heart still aching?

8

Up Close and Personal

The next morning, when we get downstairs, there's no sign of Mitchell having been at the breakfast table. Annie, the waiter, shakes her head at my enquiry. No, he hasn't been at all, this morning. I must have really done it, if he doesn't even want to come down to eat. I only hope I can find a way to apologise without seeming to be meddling in his private affairs, which he is very jealous of. And rightfully so.

As Danny eats his sausages and eggs, I watch him lovingly. He's done a magnificent job with both Mabel and the Christmas tree decorations. He puts so much love into what he does. A wave of guilt washes over me. I'm spending so little time with him. How the hell did I get myself cornered like this? Me and my bloody habit of offering time I simply don't have. I should've booked a family suite so Mum and Dad could've come down and stayed with us. But then there would have been the four of us without a room, even if at

NANCY BARONE

the time I didn't know that. I know he misses them, and is making the best of things.

'You don't mind, darling, that I'm working so much?' I ask, gently pushing the hair back from his face.

'Mum, it's okay. I know you're busy helping Mitchell and that's good.'

I beam at him. 'You are a lovely boy, you know that?'

Danny rolls his eyes and grins at me. 'Yes, I know, Mum – you tell me every day.'

'And I love you to the moon and back.'

'Me too, Mum. But take a break now, okay? Stop worrying about me.'

My little man. 'Okay, my darling. I'll try.' I leave him to finish his breakfast and take two coffees, one for me and one for Laura, to Reception.

'Morning, Rosie, that's a gorgeous tree you and Danny put up.'

'Thanks, Laura. Has Alex been? I need to discuss the contract we have with his mum's bakery.'

'Oh?'

'We need to bring the costs down. Do you think you can get them to give us a better deal?'

I sit down at my desk and take a sip, but it tastes like metal to me. How odd. I read somewhere that that's what people can taste before a stroke. I wouldn't be surprised, what with all the stress I've had these past few years.

'I'll try,' she says with a shrug.

And now just as I'm hoping to finally nail that promotion, Susan drags me through this gauntlet of uncertainty, suspicion and frustration, just so she can sack someone over

90

the holidays for the sake of calling herself the HR Manager. No wonder my job is making me ill.

Why is it that all my other friends can chill? Look at Liz. She's so cool and calm and… almost, dare I say it, happy?

'Rosie, are you okay?'

'Of course,' I answer.

'Are you sure? You look… tired.'

'I'm fine. Now let's get down to business. What's up?'

She shrugs. 'The usual. The hens had a pool fight over who gets dibs on the boys in the stag party, breaking a few chairs.'

'Pool? We have a pool?' How could I have not known this?

'Pool *table*.'

'Ah.' That's the first thing that should go, I think. Along with the card table. In fact, there is too much attention on that kind of stuff and age bracket. What we need is, I decide, something completely different and useful.

'You want to put in a kiddie park and a crèche?' Mitchell sits back in his chair as if I'd struck him, pure annoyance seeping into his dark features.

I nod. 'Just a private one, for staff and guests.'

'Oh, good. For a minute I thought you wanted to open a public one…'

I can't help but roll my eyes at his sarcasm.

'And you want to do this because…?'

'To give staff – and guests – peace of mind.'

At that, he sits back, linking his fingers behind his head,

a look of mock wonder on his face. 'Did you know, Rosie, that there is such a thing as babysitters?'

'Yes,' I say, like you say to idiots, without wanting them to know what you think of them. 'But this would be an extra service that would put you a cut above the rest.'

He lowers his eyes, thinking. So I strike the iron while it's hot. 'Plus it would be great for staff. Look at Mary, the sous-chef. She's had to run home twice already to her youngest because her babysitter wasn't available, giving Russell a heart attack. Staff will appreciate their workplace more, and be happier and more productive if they know they can nip down on their coffee break to see their babies, rather than slash their family budgets on help, or spend the whole time on WhatsApp talking to their babysitters and asking them to send them pictures or videos, thus being only half as productive.'

Mitchell's brow creases in surprise as I catch my breath. I hope my fast-talking is also convincing.

He looks at me in surprise. 'They do that?'

I shrug. 'I know it's not right, but if your kid was running a high fever, wouldn't you want an update as often as possible?'

His face softens at the idea of his own kid, I can see it clearly. But alongside the tenderness, there is also doubt. 'Er... I don't know that it's a good idea, Rosie. This isn't London where people don't have time for family, you know.'

He means me. But I don't have time for my kid because of him, and instead of thanking me, he offends me. Just when I think he may be warming up to having some genuine help on hand. Oh, the cheek of him!

'Mitchell, you are losing patrons hand over fist because

of the management. I understand it's not entirely your fault, but perhaps, if you trusted someone else's opinion, you might be able to make some good decisions instead of all the bad ones that have led to your hotel bleeding to death.' There. That should put him in his place. Why am I even bothering to save this guy's unappreciative ass? He's really such hard work, so why don't I just turn him over to the Johnson Hotels grinding machine?

'Now, if you'll excuse me, I've got an inn to save.' And I leave him sitting there, gawping at me. End of Round Two.

'So how did a lovely Scottish lass like you end up on the opposite side of the Kingdom?' I ask Sally when she stops at the desk to say good morning with a mug of steaming coffee for me.

She shrugs, studying the contents of her own brew. 'I followed a guy here.'

'Oh, wow.'

She looks up with a half-smile. 'It didn't work out.'

'Oh. Sorry.'

'Don't be. I have my kid. He's everything I need.'

I nod. We're on the same wavelength, Sally and I.

'But I'm going to night school. No offence, but I don't want to clean the Old Bell Inn forever.'

I lean in, lowering my voice. 'What would you like to do?'

She grins. 'My dream? I'd like to open my own beauty spa.'

'Yes, I can see you running something like that.'

'Yeah? With my plain looks?'

Poor girl. She can't see how beautiful she truly is, and how her coarse hands and tired face are the signs of how much she loves and cares for her son. It's thanks to the hard work of women like her that the world doesn't go to pot.

'There's absolutely nothing wrong with your looks, Sally. We're all just stressed because we don't like our jobs. But you have an eye for detail. I noticed you like perfection and have a flair for beautiful things.'

She smiles. 'I do like pretty things. But who can afford them?'

'You and me both,' I agree.

'And you, Rosie? Where's Danny's dad, if I may?'

I dismiss her delicate approach with a wave of my hand. 'Oh, he's… gone.'

'Oh, I'm so sorry.'

'Not dead gone, just… AWOL. He's just in and out of our lives every few years and…' I stop and laugh. 'That sounds sad, doesn't it? This uncertainty is no good for Danny. Either in or out.'

'No, of course not,' she agrees.

'It's no good for me, either. It's taken me years to get over him, and still, every time I see him, a stab of pain rushes through me, and I always think of how we could have had it all.' I know those are Adele's words, but it's like she's in my head. Sometimes I want to ring him up and sing one of her lyrics to him, because nothing I could possibly say to him would convey all the pain he's caused me. I had never loved anyone as much as I did him.

'I hear you,' Sally agrees. 'Martin never cared for babies.

If he ever showed up, I'd kick his sorry ass all the way to Penzance!'

'Well, it's not an issue for me as Mark is never coming back, but I would sure think of a thousand things he could try and do to obtain our forgiveness.' The idea of him cooking and cleaning just to win me back makes me chuckle and when I share with Sally my thoughts of Mark in chains and an apron, we break into a fully-fledged laugh, Sally cackling, wiping the tears from her eyes.

And that's when Mitchell walks by and comes to a halt, his eyebrow raised. I swear if he tells Sally to get back to work, I'm going to sock him. But he simply stares, open-mouthed, then when we wave at him, he turns on his heels and disappears into his office.

'That one needs a kick up the ass, too,' she says, and I snort coffee through my nose, laughing.

'What...?'

'The boss. He needs someone to bring him back from the dead. You interested?'

'Me?' I squeak. 'My life is complicated enough as it is.'

She waggles her index at me. 'I don't know, I've seen the way you two look at each other.'

'Sally...'

'Just saying, love. It's tough out there on your own.'

As if I didn't know. More than eight years of loneliness, day in, day out, and having to leave my son to go to work, cursing Mark for leaving me all alone to fend for our child while he'd gone God knew where, but mostly for depriving Danny of his father.

So now I'd like to see Sally, and women like her, happy. I'd like something good to happen to her. So later that evening, I pull out my laptop and start looking into company policy on opening a business within the business. Sally would be over the moon.

'How would you like a go at your own beauty corner here?' I ask her the next morning. Her eyes pop open.

'Don't get too excited, just a tiny thing to start with.'

Sally looks around. 'Here? Is that even possible?'

'I'll, er, ask Mitchell to check the company policy. I'm sure chains like this would welcome a chance to earn more money. And it would give you some practice until you were ready to open your own, not to mention a higher salary.'

Sally's eyes glaze over with tears as she reaches out and takes my hands. 'Would you really ask him? Would you really do that for me?'

'Of course,' I answer. How I am actually going to broach the subject with Mr Tradition, is another story. 'Just leave it with me.'

'Are you nuts?' Mitchell says, drumming his fingers on his desk, which to me indicates he's actually considering it, even if he doesn't want to admit it.

'Do you know how much that would cost? I'm already down on my numbers as it is. Head Office would have my head. Where the hell do you get all these crazy ideas?'

I shrug. 'I just think that it would be a great idea. Most hotel chains welcome the chance to make an extra quid.

Why wouldn't ours? I mean yours?' Oh, if he only knew what HO was up to!

But he's just glaring at me, oblivious of my mistake.

'Why don't you at least ask them?'

'Because the answer will be no.'

'How can you be so sure?'

'Because I know the company policy. They're not exactly innovative.'

That's the understatement of the decade. 'That may be. But could I at least try and talk to them?'

'You? You think they'd listen? You're not even an employee.'

Ah, this man is killing me. 'Well, maybe I could suggest it. They have a suggestions box or something, don't they?'

He sits back and stares at me, and I can't tell if it's wonder for my enterprise or if he's pissed off at my nerve. 'They do.'

'So, what do you say?'

'Why are you doing this?' he wants to know.

'What do you mean?'

'All these ideas – the crèche, the Christmas tree, and now a bloody spa.'

I shrug. 'I'm just trying to make your inn a little more successful. I owe it to you, in exchange for your suite, remember?'

He's studying me, not quite convinced.

'Plus, Sally is going to night school to be a beautician. She'd be perfect for the job.'

'Then who's going to clean the rooms?'

I shrug. 'You could get someone else in.' Someone less exhausted. Someone whose heart hasn't been broken yet.

Someone willing to put up with people's lack of respect. 'So will you call Head Office?' I ask as sweetly as possible. 'For Sally?'

He sighs. More of a groan, really. 'I'll call Head Office.'

Bingo. At least he'll seem proactive and maybe they will get off his back for a while. Although I highly doubt it. Still, it's a step in the right direction. 'Thank you!' I cry. 'Oh, thank you so, so much!'

'Rosie,' he says in a deep, gruff voice. The voice of someone not used to apologising, lest he chokes on kind words.

He lowers his eyes, embarrassed. Oh my God, is he actually *blushing*? He licks his lips and then, the incredible happens. He grins, and it's as if the sun has come out on a stormy night, just to tease me with its warmth. 'Thank you. You're already making a huge difference to everyone here.'

And then, I can't help but smile back. Maybe, if we can get along, we do have a shot at keeping this boat afloat after all.

He's still watching me, his fingers caressing his chin, and I get another glimpse of his tongue as it absently caresses his bottom lip again. His lashes, no joke, are longer than mine when I'm wearing tons of mascara (I'm a natural blonde so need the extra help). He also has wickedly winged eyebrows that are very mobile. He can go from a demonic scowl to a boyish smile in half a nanosecond. Jesus, does he even know how dishy he is, with that square jaw, and the piercing dark eyes?

And then, another sexy grin lights up his face, complete with twinkling eyes – a far cry from the arrogant bastard I'd met in the parking lot.

'I'm glad,' I answer, about to reach out and shake his hand, but I'm still not quite sure about him. One moment he'll be all nicey nicey and the next he'll turn on me. He's like the Cornish sky – extremely unpredictable. Not an easy man to please or get along with, to say the least. Because, say what you will, Mitchell is a complicated man.

'Hey, Rosie?' he calls after me.

I turn to make a funny face, which dies when I spot the tender expression on his face.

'The tree looks beautiful, by the way.'

I could say 'I told you so, Scrooge'. But I don't. Instead, I smile despite myself. 'You're very welcome, Mitchell.'

And then I skip off, before he changes his mind and I say something snarky. Mum always told me you can catch more bees with honey.

Later that day, I give my best friend a ring to see what I can do for Sally's beauty corner. 'Liz? Can you check the feasibility of having a tiny spa room at the inn?'

'You need a proper licence, I can tell you that straight away.'

'Whatever happened to cottage industries?'

'You still need a licence.'

'Does the person with the licence have to be the same person running the spa?'

'Of course,' she says.

'Okay, I'll get her onto it, but can you pave the way for her by sending me the paperwork necessary to apply? I'll do the rest here on my end.'

'You really do care, don't you?' she asks.

'I told you I did.'

'Now I know why I love you so much,' she says.

'Thanks, Liz. Me too, you know that. Talk later.'

'Bye.'

I scribble a note to Sally telling her she needs to apply for a licence when she's done with her course in the spring and I put it in her pigeonhole. There must be something more I can do to help in the meantime. But I guess the most important thing is to make sure HO doesn't close them down in the first place.

So I go back to the reviews and reread all the offensive articles and look at my list of the sixty-three bloggers, among which, the corniest-looking, Cummings And Goings: 'To think that I actually slept their (he sure knows his grammar) makes my skin crawl. If you want to get food poisoning, lice and an STD all in one night, then the Old Bell Inn is you're (sic) number one choice.'

Jesus. And I thought it couldn't get any meaner, but then there's Wanderlust, Jack Kerouac (ha), Lily of the Valleys, The Globe-Trotter (seriously?), Come Sail Away and of course, Come Fly With Me. And that's when I have a thought, so I pull out my mobile phone and dial Liz's number again.

'Miss me already?' she chirps. 'It's only been a couple minutes.'

'Are you still in contact with that IT guy?'

'Who, James?'

'No, not our colleague, the guy you slept with last month.'

'John?'

'That's him,' I say.

'FYI, I slept with James as well.'

'You did? Blimey.'

'Judge much?'

'Of course not. Listen, I need you to contact him, not anyone connected to the company.'

'What for?'

'If I send you some links to some blogs, can you get him to find the IP addresses for me?'

'Sure, no problem. I'll get back to you ASAP.'

'Thanks, Liz,' I say and we ring off.

I certainly hope to come to grips with all this, but I have been here for a few days now, and as yet I haven't managed to find anything, despite the enormous pressure Susan manages to put on me.

So, I decide to look into the inn's accounts a little deeper. And each time I get the same result. There is some money undoubtedly missing. Has Mitchell bought something somewhere? A house, a yacht? Gold bullion? Has he gambled it away?

I call my go-to girl again. We might as well have a live feed. 'Liz, can you do an in-depth search on the inn's accounts for me?'

'You think he's skimming off the top?'

'I don't think so, but I just can't explain the fact that there is money missing. I need to dig into his life if I'm going to help him. I can't ask him directly if I don't want to blow my cover.'

'Why don't you sleep with him?'

'What?'

'That's how I get my info when I need it,' she says and I can almost see her winking at me. 'Besides, I've seen his picture. I think you are about to have yourself some good old-fashioned fun, my dear.'

'Liz, really…'

'I'm serious. He's really good-looking, if you like that lumber-jack kind of thing, with the light beard and all.'

'Liz,' I say in exasperation. 'Will you please help me?'

'Sure, I'll get back to you asap.'

'Thanks.'

'Yeah, yeah. And stop calling me, you're distracting me from my glamorous life at Head Office,' she mock-groans as she hangs up.

But she is right about one thing. I need to get up close and personal if I am going to make any inroads into my investigation. God, I hate the sound of that word. But personal research is what I need to do. With someone like Mitchell, in a village like Little Kettering, there's only one way to do this.

'Laura, you mentioned that Mitchell's wife walked out on him.'

Laura looks at me, thrown by my question, but eventually she nods. I'm glad she thinks she can trust me, but at the same time I feel awful. God, I hate my job. Have I mentioned that before?

'Yeah. She was a real piece of work.'

'What do you mean?'

Laura rolls her eyes. 'She was temperamental. And she had grand designs.'

She also had excellent taste in men. 'Which were?'

'She wanted to live in London, but they had just started this job and Mitchell didn't want to leave. He convinced her to stay, but she hated it. And last Christmas things fell apart and eventually she moved to London on her own.'

Last Christmas, when things started going awry. Of course it was my very first thought. My only solution, really. Is it a coincidence that the money started to disappear when things started to go pear-shaped between them? Could it be that she was taking the money in preparation for leaving him? Was she building her very own nest egg?

My cousin's wife did that to him a few years ago. No one could believe what she'd done, all the while smiling and inviting us to dinner parties. And then, one day, she just went. She'd been pretending to pay their bills, meanwhile squirrelling everything away into her own accounts. Could Diane have done the same? I don't know her, but on paper, it sure looks like it. Which would be great, because it would get Mitchell out of Dodge.

'Does Mitchell give her alimony?' That can be the only explanation, at this point.

'God knows. Mitchell never talks about her. If it weren't for their daughter, they'd never have spoken again. As a matter of fact, I think he manages to ignore her most of the time.'

'Ah.'

'Diane was all about money and lifestyle, whereas Mitchell likes to chill out and spend time with his kid. Take her for walks on the beach, rock pooling. Limits her computer time and encourages her to read books. He values a simple lifestyle. It's never about the money for Mitchell.'

Never about the money. How glad am I Laura has said that? Enormously. Because, the more I learn about this bloke, the more I convince myself of his integrity. I should've figured Mitchell was a great dad, what with being so good with Danny.

As I'm musing on this, my mobile shrieks 'Ride of the Valkyries' and I hold up a finger to silently excuse myself from Laura.

'Talk to me, Rosie,' Susan barks as I'm seeking privacy around the corner. The thought of me working my ass off delights her to no end; I can hear it in her pauses.

'All is well at the moment, Susan.'

'Hmmm. No complaints? What about Health and Hygiene?'

'We have an amazing chef whose food is Michelin quality.'

'We?'

Shit. 'I mean "they".'

'You sound mighty familiar with those people, Rosie. Remember that an inspector isn't supposed to fraternise with the management. Read the manual, Rosie.'

Again with the blooming manual. 'There is nothing untoward here, Susan.' How in hell will she believe me? Even *I* don't believe me. Everything indicates that Mitchell is stealing from the company. His car, his divorce costs, his child's private education, and even the artwork hanging in his quarters all tell the story of money. But it clashes with his persona. I just can't see him lying, cheating and squirrelling it away. It's just not him. Not that I know the bloke, but it's something I feel in my bones. Can I prove his innocence? Not yet. But I'll be damned if I don't try.

'Did you email me your new report yet?' Susan asks.

'Uhm… it's not ready yet.' And here comes the shite-storm. Three… two… one…

'What do you mean, it's not ready yet?' she barks with

sheer joy. 'Did I not ask for bi-weekly reports? That's not very professional now, is it, Rosie?'

This time her pause takes on a menacing tone. With Susan, it's more what she doesn't say that should scare you, rather than what she says.

'Yes, but ongoing—'

'Do I need to send someone *else* out there, Rosie?' she says, the threat in her voice palpable. Now *that* scares me. I begin to sweat profusely. If she fires me, I'm dead for this industry. I will never be able to work in this field again, even if I'm damn good at it.

'Haven't you found the problem yet?'

Meaning, am I ready to fire him? 'Not yet, but I've got a few leads.'

'Being?'

How can I tell her my suspicions without backing them up? 'I'm... waiting for—'

'Okay, so you don't have any idea what's going on, then,' she concludes.

No, I don't, truth be told, but I sure as hell am not telling *her* that. I want to get to the bottom of this without anyone losing their job – not Mitchell, nor Sally, nor Jeremy, nor anyone who depends on this establishment for their livelihood.

'He seems perfectly competent to me,' I argue. 'And so does everyone else here. The staff is like family down here. And they all work together so well.'

She snorts. 'Head Office doesn't agree. We believe that he has also been stashing money into his own coffers. I want you to unmask him and sack him.'

Again with the sacking. Does this woman have no

sympathy whatsoever? I understand this is a business, but whatever happened to human solidarity? I look at Sally, how hard she works to keep a roof over her boy's head and I want to cry. I also think of Jeremy, whose only dream is to work with his beloved horses. And Laura, who is just about to take a course in hotel management. They'll all be fired. What are they going to do? Good God, if Susan unleashes her temper and lets them all go, how are they going to survive?

After another few threats, Susan slams the phone down and a small huff of frustration escapes me. These are good people who work hard. They don't deserve to be sacked. I absolutely have to do something for them. If she fires these people, they won't have anything else to live on. I just can't bear the thought. How could Head Office agree to something so horrible? It just isn't right. When will the world stop belonging to the arrogant people who take advantage of their position?

Laura turns in her chair to look at me. 'Rosie... what's wrong?' she asks.

I surreptitiously dash a hand across my eyes and blow my nose. 'Catching a cold,' I mutter.

9

The Dream Job

'Uh, Liz? We have a bit of a problem,' I say to my friend after a night of tossing and turning due to the inn's financial books, and praying that the balance sheets would sort themselves miraculously on their own somehow, and that I'd made a mistake. But no. Things hadn't added up last night and still don't this morning.

'Yeah?'

'There are regular withdrawals here. At least twice a month. Can you account for them your end?'

'Not yet, but I'll get back to you, Rosie. How's he behaving?'

'Oh, not too bad, really. I think I misjudged him.'

'Then why all those bad reviews?'

'It doesn't make sense, Liz. The place is a gem, and yet there are a gazillion blogs warning guests not to stay here.'

'Well, there must be *some* reason,' she offers, but it isn't enough. I need facts.

'I'm going to do some research on him. See if he's on social media or anything.'

She snorts. 'A guy like him? I doubt it. Sounds anything but social.'

Liz has a point. I looked him up before I left London, and there was no mention of him anywhere. This is not turning out to be easy in the least. Still, I'm not one for giving up. 'Any news on the IP addresses yet?'

'Not yet. I'll have to chase it up. Maybe with a bottle of wine this evening.' She chuckles.

'Thanks, Liz.'

'Yeah, yeah. This'll cost you a dinner when you get back.'

When Liz calls back less than an hour later, I pick up, jamming my mobile between my cheek and shoulder, as I can't use speakerphone for obvious reasons.

'What's up, any news?'

'Your IP addresses? They're all the same. The author of all those blogs is actually one person writing under different names. Well done, girl.'

Just as I thought. 'Can you ask your guy if there's a way to access the name of the owner of the IP address?'

'No, not precisely. IP addresses don't work like that.'

'Oh.'

'Rosie?'

'Yeah?'

'I understand what you're doing and why, but sweetie, don't kill yourself over it.'

'What do you mean?'

'Even if he's the great guy that you say, no one can be

worth all this trouble. And we both know you don't need trouble. So save yourself and your job.'

I know she's right, of course. But I can't. These are all hard-working people who are risking their workplace closing down.

'If I don't get to the bottom of this, a lot of people will be jobless.'

'This is really important to you, isn't it, Rosie?'

'Of course it is.'

'Someone should sack Susan instead.'

'Now *that* would be the best Christmas present ever.'

She chuckles. 'I'll have a word with Santa for you.'

For my lunch break I grab Danny (or rather, the other way around) and pack a quick picnic as he wants to show me his favourite part of the South West Coastal Path that Jeremy took him on the day before. And boy, even as we're slowly hiking over hillocks and stiles – nothing major – I swear my lungs are leaking out of my nose because I'm wheezing like an old geezer on ten packs a day. And I don't even smoke.

If I lived here, I'd get fit in no time. If I lived here, I'd be *happy* in no time.

But there's no way I could live anywhere near this gorgeous area, not after Mitchell finds out who I am and why I'm really here, because after that, I'd become, rightfully, a social pariah around here. Because I'm slowly gaining his confidence, and every time he smiles at me, I feel like a heel. When he finds out – and he will – he'll hate me. Forever.

I have Susan the Sacker to thank for sending me down here, and as I sit here munching on a pasty, I feast on the views of Mullion Cove on this amazingly bright day. So I commit every single detail of this moment to memory. Because when we get back to London, no picture or high-gloss calendar will be able to live up to what is at my feet.

The rough-hewn cliffs jutting out of the water are majestic, and the emerald blanket of grass placed atop it is almost like a loving, protective afterthought; the sea that looks like liquid topaz today, and the sun-shot spray, a shower of tiny diamonds. Never, anywhere, not even in travel magazines, have I seen so beautiful a place. There is nowhere like Cornwall. *Nowhere.*

Danny is happy, prattling along, shooting his arm out to throw bits of bread to the seagulls that are giving us the beady eye, just waiting for the next offering. He is flushed and excited about just being outdoors. It takes so little to make him happy. Cornwall makes him happy.

'It's nice, isn't it?' I sigh and he looks back at me and grins. He's lost that city pallor and, in its stead, there is a rosy hue to his cheeks. Even his eyes are brighter. He looks healthier and stronger, and all in the shortest of time.

'It is,' he agrees. 'We never get to do this in London.'

'Would you rather be here than playing football?'

'Yes,' he says simply, coming to sit closer to me, and I kiss the top of his head. 'I love it here, Mum. I'm just sorry that you can't go out as much as I do.'

I shrug, but on the inside I am touched. 'No worries, Danny. I'm happy to help around here. I'm just sorry I see so little of you. But you are enjoying yourself, aren't you, darling?'

'I have everything I've ever wanted, Mum. Horses,

friends, freedom. And I can come see you at work whenever I want.'

It's true that in the city, I see so little of him, and only in the evenings and on weekends. I'm ashamed to say that it's only during the holidays that I get to know my son more. But I like what I see.

I hug myself and breathe deeply, and feel a sudden, unfamiliar rush of what I soon realise must be joy. I didn't know happiness could have its own fragrance. But I know I won't be here forever. Everything comes to an end, and soon I'll be back in London in my cubicle under Susan's vitriolic stare, with the artificial lights and the buzzing of the coffee machine and the disappearing doughnuts, not to mention the tediousness that accompanies me throughout my shift, wondering how Danny is and if he's missing his mummy and what I can do to make his life better. I need to find a solution to save our souls. Could it be Cornwall after all?

'And you, Mum? You look happier here, too.'

'Oh, I am, Danny. I'm very happy to be able to pop out and come and find you whenever I can.'

'It's a shame we have to go back in the new year,' he says with a heavy sigh.

I can only agree. It's a shame to have to put an end to this bliss.

When we get back to the inn, Danny heads for the stables and I get busy, trying to make up for the time away from my desk, and I hardly notice Mitchell coming in.

'Hey,' he says as he puts his documents down on the counter without taking his eyes off me. I'm getting so used to his presence, it's like a drug almost. A part of me is always wondering when he'll make an appearance, where he is and what he's doing. And it's not only in a professional interest sort of way, either. 'How's it going, Rosie?'

'Quiet for now. Everyone is out and about.'

He leans on the desk with his elbows in his usual fashion, letting me know that in this particular and rare moment, I have his undivided attention. Or rather, the business does. 'Guests happy?'

In response, one of the girls from the hen party – the pink one, saunters by, slowing down when she sees him. 'He-ey…' she says, openly eyeing him from top to bottom.

'Good afternoon,' he replies politely.

'You're not with the stag party, are you? I'd have noticed you.'

He looks at me and coughs. 'No. I'm the manager.'

She smiles up at him, putting her hand on the counter, near his, and smiles. 'Yeah? I'm Sandy.'

'Mitchell. Nice to meet you. And this is Rosie. My girlfriend.'

Sandy and I both stare at him, and then she shrugs. 'Yeah? Awh, well. Worth trying. See ya.'

Mitchell gives me a sheepish grin as the girl walks off. 'Sorry. She caught me off guard. It was the first thing that came to mind.'

Surely he can do better at keeping a woman at bay? All he has to do is treat her like he treats me – with complete indifference. Which is more than I deserve anyway.

'Uhm, Mitchell? We need to talk.'

His smile disappears as he stands to attention. 'Uh-oh. What is it?'

'I've done some sums.' I can't yet tell him I know the money is missing. I want to, but I have to make absolutely sure he's not the one skimming off the top.

'And?'

'Well, those scathing reviews have done you no favours.'

'I know...'

'And there's not enough money coming in this season.'

'So what's your idea?'

'What makes you think I have one?'

He grins. 'Because you are all about ideas, Rosie.'

'Well, seeing as the reviews are online, we have no control over them whatsoever. But you can drum up interest through word of mouth, meaning the family and friends of the people of Little Kettering who live elsewhere.'

He grins. 'Good thinking.'

'We'll prepare some e-banners or flyers for them to send out, along with a friends and family discount brochure. I'll leave you some notes that might come in handy in the future.'

He puts down his documents again and leans across the counter, peering into my eyes. 'This job of yours in London...'

Oh God, so he really is sussing me out after all.

'Is it... something you enjoy?' he asks.

'Oh. Uhm... not as much as I should, no. In fact, I wish I could change a lot of things about it.'

'Like what?'

I shrug. 'I'd like to deal more with the people than the bureaucracy, for instance. Help people out with their problems.'

His expression is unreadable. 'Ah.' He's sounding me out all right. I only wonder what *Ah* is supposed to mean? 'So… do you see yourself working there for long?'

I laugh off the uneasiness. I never was good under torture. 'Why, are you thinking of offering me a job?' I quip in the hope of throwing him off course.

He stuffs his hands into his pockets. 'If there were to be a vacancy, would you consider it?'

Is he serious? Is he seriously offering me a job? Why? If he doesn't trust me, why is he doing it? Unless it's all my imagination and he suspects nothing. But if that's the case:

a) How can I ever accept, knowing why I came here in the first place?

b) Can I leave London for Cornwall, and work in this hotel? Take Danny away from his school and his friends?

And c): I don't have a *c* at the moment, but I thought I'd slip it in there, just in case. You never know.

'It depends on the position,' I answer cautiously.

He studies me. 'Right. How does *Manager* sound?'

Manager? Meaning his own job. Oh God. He knows, all right. He's got me. Ooh, he is infinitely smarter than I could ever be. He's smelt the rat and smoked me out, and now I – the rat – am gasping for breath. Drowning in corporate deviousness. I always knew I would never rise to the top. It's just not where I want to be. I want to have my own, small business, just enough to tide Danny and myself over. No Susans, no performance goals, no inspection manuals, nothing.

'M-manager…? Isn't that your job?'

'Wouldn't you like to manage this place? From what I

can see, you'd be perfect for the job. Much better than me, no doubt. Head Office would agree.'

He's looking at me closely, gauging my response to see how much of a fibber I am. Is it me, or is the ground rushing up, moving to swallow me whole? I sure hope so, because I have never felt so humiliated in my whole life. And I have no alternative, but to run.

'I-I have to... to...' I falter, and dart out of there as fast as a bat out of hell and run up to my room. I mean Mitchell's room.

I'm such a mess. Maybe all this *trolloping* (that's my new word for this holiday season, meaning me being a lying hussy) around is for someone like Susan, but not for one the likes of me. I just don't do subterfuge. I never have and just can't handle the pressure. Oh, why don't I just throw in the towel, for once in my life, confess, and take the easy way out?

For two very good reasons. One is almost eight years old. I simply can't disappoint Danny like that and give him the complete, unabridged and illustrated version of *Mummy's A Quitter*.

And the other reason? Glad you asked. It's in its mid-thirties, has a dark mop of curls, a heart of gold under a thick crust of rust, and is presently being wronged for no apparent reason.

Someone has it in for him and I can't leave Mitchell to his own devices. He has no idea of the pooh-storm that is about to be released if I don't find some evidence discharging him pronto. Because if I give up and go home, Susan will only send someone else who doesn't give a crap about the fact that Mitchell – and everyone else here – have families to support and can't do it if thrown out onto the streets.

Later, when the coast is clear, I slink back to my desk. It's a good thing I'm volunteering, because if I'd run out on one of my real managers like that, they'd have my ass. What's happening to me? There's not a day that goes by now when I don't think of quitting and opening my own pottery shop again, which is looking more and more appealing every day.

'Hey, y'orrite?' Mitchell asks as I try to hide behind some files. 'You took off like you were on fire.'

Only my conscience, I want to say, but offer him a lame smile instead. Okay, so maybe he doesn't know after all. So why, then, is he offering me the job, if not to mock me?

'Didn't you like my offer at all?'

'You… were really offering me a job?'

'I'd be crazy not to. You're the best I've ever had.'

Oh, this is so rich. And so… *not*. 'No, I *know* that.' I can't help but grin at him. For many reasons. 'That's not what I meant.'

His tongue licks his top lip in the usual endearing fashion, his eyes smiling into mine. 'You cheeky little thing. What, then?'

'I… just didn't think… I thought…'

Mitchell grins. 'What did you think?'

I shrug helplessly, and he puts his hand on my shoulder.

'Listen, Rosie. I know I'm a handful and I've got a temper and a half. But I have my good moments too, you know? I'm not always a dickhead.'

I roll my eyes as if to say, *You could have fooled me*.

'Mitchell, I need— Oops!' Laura says, her voice dying as she comes out from the back office and whirls right around upon seeing us standing there so close to each other. 'Never mind… laters!'

Mitchell raises his eyebrow at me, that grin still there. 'Laura, it's all right. Rosie's just giving me shit again, telling me off for everything I'm doing wrong.'

She comes back to lean on the doorframe, a knowing smile on her face. 'Well then she should be quite a while…'

Mitchell leans back against the counter. 'What's up, Laura?'

Laura huffs. 'You have to talk to the guys from the stag party.'

His eyebrows shoot up. 'What's wrong?'

'What's wrong? One of the *gentlemen* was seen weeing down the drainpipe in the back garden.'

Mitchell sighs, running his hand through his thick, dark and, I can just tell, soft curls. But seriously. It's good that he's here to hear this.

Laura huffs. 'I swear it's like kids on an overnight school trip. Next thing you know some bloke is going to fall off one of the balconies and—'

'Do not even go there,' I say. 'That's the last thing we need right now.'

'Right, let me go sort him out,' Mitchell says, pushing up his sleeves. I sure hope it won't come to anything physical, but with that kind of guest, you never know. But one thing is sure – physically, Mitchell can more than take care of himself. Job-wise, I only hope he doesn't dig himself a deeper grave.

That evening, as Danny comes up for his cuddle, I play with his hair as he tells me about his day. And I wonder… could I accept Mitchell's offer? I know it would benefit

Danny no end. Look at how happy he is already. But a definitive move? What if he doesn't like his new school? What if something goes wrong? I can't broach the subject directly with Danny yet, in case Mitchell changes his mind. If he gives me his job, where will he go? Not far enough to dissipate all the hatred he'll have for me when he finds out who I really am, in any case.

10

It's a Wonderful Life

The following afternoon, I have a thought. If the Master Clean Company bills haven't been paid, I wonder how many others haven't. How many others have got lost in the financial fog that hangs like the Iron Curtain in this establishment? So, I retrieve the folder containing all the physical invoices and pull up the corresponding spreadsheet from the inn's bank details onto my screen. And check every single sheet against every item.

About an hour into my task, I begin to find some discrepancies. Items listed on the bank's outgoings have no physical invoice. Now, one lost invoice or two, I can understand, but so far I've counted seven, all in the space of the last three months. And there are even more going back for an entire year.

Why would Mitchell want to hide purchases for the hotel? And, judging by the amounts spent, they weren't small sums. Unless… they weren't for the hotel and he'd… borrowed the money from his business? Oh God, please don't let it be so. He's already in enough trouble as it is. I need to give him a chance to explain. So I pick up the desk phone and dial his mobile.

'Laura,' he answers.

'It's Rosie…'

'Hey… What's up?'

He sounds more than pleased to hear from me. Dare I believe he'd forgive me if he knew about my secret mission? If I'd come clean upon arrival, it'd have been easier. But now? Not that easy.

'Just a quick question. Do you use your business account for large purchases?'

Pregnant pause. 'Define large.'

'Five hundred pounds at a time. Every month for a year.'

I hear him whistle. 'Jesus. No, but check the invoices in case.'

'You don't remember, offhand?' That's not good. How can he not keep such large expenses in mind?

'Uh, no. Unless Diane bought stuff she forgot to itemise.'

Of course. It makes sense, being Mitchell's wife and assistant manager. But that doesn't account for the current withdrawals from the business account.

'Is there any way you can check for sure?' I ask. I don't want to force him to have an uncomfortable conversation with the ex, but I'm determined to solve this.

Another pause. He's not happy with the idea. 'I'm heading back now anyway, so I'll give you a hand.'

I hang up, the edginess of having made a faux pas regarding Diane compensated by the fact that I'll see him shortly. It's a nice, warm, fuzzy feeling I haven't had in years.

And I wonder: is there absolutely no way I can tell him who I am, without him hating me?

'Mum, Mitchell wants to go to the Christmas movie in the village hall tonight, can we go?' Danny says, bouncing into the back office, Mitchell on his heels.

I look up at the two, noticing the expectant, hopeful looks on their faces. Mitchell, who, contrary to Danny's biological father, goes out of his way to spend time with him, is becoming more and more attached to him with every day that goes by. And I just know it's going to be hard on Danny when we leave. All the harder, because Danny, like his mum, isn't one to give his heart away so easily.

'So can I, Mum? Please?'

Mitchell half-sits on my desk, leaning forward, his hands joined in a silent plea, working his huge spaniel eyes better than a four-year-old. 'Come on. I'll have a quick look at your papers while you two get ready. Plus there's always tomorrow. We all need a break, don't you think?'

As if I could deny either of them anything. In a short space of time, Mitchell alone has done wonders for my son's confidence with the way he treats him, asking him for his opinion as if he was the most important person in the world to him. I am so grateful to the bloke, and conversely, I feel so guilty because of what I'm doing to him, that I have to literally fight the tears back down.

'Oh, all right,' I say in my fake grouchy-mum voice, keeping my head low so they won't see my moist eyes.

'Yay!' Danny cheers, throwing his arms around me. 'Thanks, Mum!'

Mitchell places a huge hand on my shoulder and suddenly I'm flooded with warmth. 'Pick you up at seven? I mean, see you in the lobby at seven?'

I sit back, open-mouthed. 'Me?'

Mitchell rolls his chocolate eyes. 'You didn't think we would go without you, did you?'

It's twenty to seven and Danny is champing at the bit, while I'm having my umpteenth coronary crisis. I haven't got anything decent to wear and I look like absolute crap. My hair has suddenly gone limper than usual and I look... pasty. With a rising sense of panic, I throw some make-up on, and just as I think I might actually get away with it, I poke my eye with the mascara wand, which brings tears to my eyes and guess what? I have to start all over again. Knowing I'll *never* be ready in time now, I remove the whole shebang and settle for the faint traces of mascara that make my lashes look naturally dark rather than sophisticated. Fine by me – every time I make an effort, I end up looking like I'm trying too hard. I simply don't know how to wear make-up. End of.

I pull on my best jeans and slip into a white shirt. I'd look pretty plain if it wasn't for my super-cool silver belt that rests on my hips. But hey, shouldn't I relax? It's not a date. It's just two adults taking a child to the movies. Nothing too involving, no promises being made, no questions asked. Right? Right. So why is my heart still hammering away?

'Can I go downstairs, Mum?'

'Not yet, darling, Mitchell's finishing up some work and I don't want you rushing him.'

Fifteen minutes still to go and I'm already sweating buckets. I remove my shirt and check the thermostat, flapping my arms to keep cool, but I'm only making it worse. I'm an absolute wreck.

'Mum.' Danny laughs. 'Don't worry, you look beautiful.'

'Awh, thank you...' See why I love my little man so much? At almost eight years of age, he's my anchor, my solution to everything in life. He has this gift of tuning in to my feelings and thoughts and knows me inside out. But I have to be more careful round him. Mums are supposed to be the source of stability, not basket cases, right?

'Anyway, Mitchell likes you, too,' he adds.

I stop in the middle of the kitchenette. Now he's really got my attention. 'What? How do you know that?'

'He said so.'

'What? When?'

'Yesterday, when we saw a woman in the street who looked like you. He said you were much prettier and much more ruinous than her. I looked it up, but it doesn't make any sense.'

Ruinous? Oh, my *God*! Is that what he really thinks of me? Surely I deserve more than 'ruinous', for Christ's sake? Danny has no idea of the turmoil he's just thrown me into with his innocent comment. What does Mitchell mean by saying I'm ruinous? I came here to help.

'Oh, Danny, don't trouble yourself with that. He was only joking.'

He shrugs. 'Okay, Mum. Can we go now?' Danny says, pointing to his watch. 'It's seven o'clock.'

'Oh, already?'

My heart would be in my mouth if it were in one piece, but

shreds of it are dashing around inside me, in my ears, nose and throat. I can't do this. I can't be with Mitchell outside the frame of work, without a desk between us, or without work to talk about. Danny's presence is going to offer me the last shred of dignity that I have, and stop me from continuously eyeing Mitchell as if he was the last man on earth.

As it turns out, I can relax, because Danny and Mitchell are entertaining each other with all sorts of stories and anecdotes, and all I have to do is offer a smile every now and then at the appropriate moments. But even that is proving to be difficult, when all I can see is Mitchell's thick, corded forearms and hands caressing his thighs. I know that gesture. He's nervous about something.

'Right, Mum?' Danny says.

I'm so absorbed by Mitchell's presence that I have absolutely no idea what my own son has just said.

Mitchell lets out a hearty belly laugh, joined by Danny. I don't get the joke, but I find this man's laughter utterly sexy. I think at this stage I'd find him brushing his *teeth* sexy. Which means that the time has come for me to get a grip. I'm not a love-struck teenager anymore, and if I want to be precise, it's behaviour like this that got me pregnant the first time. I'm an adult now, so it's time I started acting like one.

As we climb into Mitchell's jeep, he looks at me appreciatively. 'You look nice, Rosie,' he says simply, which throws me completely.

All I can think of to say is a measly, 'Thank you.'

He looks good, too, actually. His beard keeps growing every day because he doesn't bother to shave, but he's made an effort to put on a proper jumper and not one of his old tatty fuzzy sweaters that irritate the crap out of me. Plus, he's pulled back his hair into a man bun, which reveals features I'd never seen before. Finally, I can see that his forehead is broad and straight, and that his cheekbones are vertiginously high. He looks almost as if he's actually trying.

And that's when I realise we are staring at each other. Proper staring, like you see in the movies. And I can't move or speak, I'm so enthralled. Luckily Danny is with us.

'Mitchell, can you turn the engine on?' Danny says, pulling me out of my reverie. 'We're going to be late.'

'Oh. Yeah, of course, mate, of course. Seatbelt fastened?'

'Yes,' he answers.

Mitchell turns to me to acknowledge the black nylon slash across my coat, nods in satisfaction and we finally set off.

Along the way, Danny does all the talking, bless his soul. A week ago I'd have to have bribed him to speak in public but luckily he's now enjoying partaking in the village activities. As we drive into town, many faces turn to wave at him and he waves back, his eager face stuck to the glass like an excited puppy's, and a wave of tenderness mixed with guilt washes over me. This is mainly due to Jeremy and Mitchell taking him out around town. Everyone now knows the pale and quiet boy from London. Only he's not that anymore. Now he's a happy boy, coming out of his shell. And I have all these people to thank. People I must get to know. But what with my work schedule, how am I going to manage that? It's important for me to know all of Danny's new friends, young and old. I'll have to think of a way.

The village hall has been decked out to the nines with

Christmas decorations, the walls plastered in tinsel and posters made by the children from the Little Doves Primary School. I swear they can draw better than most artists I've seen, with a flair for the Christmas spirit that makes your heart want to sing Christmas carols from morning to night.

And that's when I get my idea of how I'm going to become acquainted with everyone – all in one night. I decide to organise a carolling evening for the villagers. It'll be on December 22nd. We'll be leaving from the lobby at six p.m., when it's dark enough to enjoy all the Christmas lights dotting the road into the village, picking up the villagers living on the outskirts, touring the hotspots and ending up back in the hotel dining room where we'll be serving hot stew, freshly baked ciabatta and Christmas desserts. As Russell is averse to that kind of stuff – he calls cheesy because he only does 'proper, gourmet meals' – I'll ask Laura and Alex to help me pull it off. Mitchell, on the other hand, will probably leave me to it, as he is, I know by now, not a very Christmassy kind of guy. Shame. I personally wish it was Christmas every day.

'Can we get popcorn before the movie starts, Mum?' Danny asks and I nod, pulling out my purse.

'I'll take care of it,' Mitchell says, putting his hand on mine, and my skin literally fizzes at his touch. 'You are my guests. Just sit back and relax.'

I look at him in surprise. 'Oh? Okay. Thank you.'

How different he is from Mark, or what I remember of Mark. Who had always been selfish.

The relationship had always been about him, and never about us. When I used to go to the movies with him, on the rare occasion that he agreed to, I was the one who always paid for everything, from the tickets to the candy to the parking. And I was the one who would be queuing for it all. Sometimes I'd get in when the movie had already started, and when I asked what had happened, he would simply take the snacks off me and say, 'Shush.' No thank you, nothing. Not even a promise to do any of it himself the next time.

Our entire relationship, now that I think of it, was just like going to the movies – it rarely happened, I did all the legwork, paid for most of it and never got to enjoy any of it.

Mitchell smiles. 'Coming, Danny?'

Does he even need to ask? My boy is so gaga over him it makes me worry. Is it right for Danny to fall for someone who won't be in his life in a couple of weeks' time? Isn't it cruel to let him build a bond if he'll be taken back home soon? I argue with myself that it is healthy for Danny to have male figures around him without necessarily looking for a father figure, but then I realise that he is *of course* searching for a father. And he literally adores the ground Mitchell walks on.

The sight of him slipping his hand into his, the way he looks up into Mitchell's face, and the way Mitchell grins back at him makes me hate Mark even more than I already do. The man who should love me and Danny, as a matter of fact, doesn't. And I'm so so grateful that Danny has never asked him to stay on his brief visits. On the contrary, he seems much happier the moment Mark leaves. If Danny misses having a father, I'm positive he doesn't miss Mark per se. Which is a huge relief.

I wish that Danny could have what he deserves. He needs more than just me in his life. It's not the poor kid's fault that his father was an irresponsible jerk who knocked me up and left me like I was a huge mistake. Because that's what Mark made me feel like. A mistake. And I never want my son to feel that he isn't worthy of love. It makes me angry that Mark has put us in this position of tiptoeing through life when instead we should be strutting through it, because we, too, have a right to be here, whether we're rich or not, whether there's a man in our lives or not.

I'd cut out my heart for my son if I had to. And as I watch him and Mitchell head off for the food counter, I dash a hand across my eyes and wipe it on my jeans while no one's looking. Besides, it's not like I'm wearing any make-up.

The movie on schedule is *It's a Wonderful Life*. Danny and I have seen it about a gazillion times, and it's our absolute favourite. It always makes us grateful for everything we have, and I am especially appreciative of the fact that Danny really gets it, when instead he could simply look around and see that his friends wear designer clothes, have expensive sports equipment, and disappear to exotic countries for weeks on end, when he's excited to spend a day at Chatsworth, picnicking by the river on mini Scotch eggs and sandwiches and cheese, feeding half of his lunch to the ducks and the sheep.

And even now, he's happy, munching away on his popcorn, sitting between Mitchell and me. Every now and then he glances up at me, and I wonder what's going inside that darling little head of his. Is he making up romantic movies about Mitchell and myself? He is if he's my son, and if I know him at all. He's asked me several times in the past why I didn't have a boyfriend, when his friends' mums were already on their third this year.

Mitchell, on the other hand, seems immersed in the movie,

but every now and then, he'll glance at Danny, and then his eyes will furtively dart to mine, as if to make sure I'm still there. He's not a talker during movies, that's for sure, but I can feel he appreciates our presence. I'd like to say something funny, but then I remember the way Mark used to shush me, even when we were sitting on our own in front of the telly, so I change my mind and huddle inside my coat, glad for my thick scarf. It's not exactly the tropics in here.

When all is well again, Clarence earns his wings, and the curtains are drawn, everyone begins to file out of the town hall, anxious to get home to their own home fires. All except one.

'Well, hello, Mitchell, who's your little friend?' comes a shrill voice from behind us. Mitchell turns around and grins. 'Abby, hi! Please meet my buddy Danny, and this here is his mum, Rosie.'

'Well!' she chimes again, bending to Danny, but completely ignoring me. 'Hello, little man!'

I make to proffer my hand, but she is oblivious as she straightens and gazes up into Mitchell's eyes. She is older than me, maybe early forties, but she looks... confident. She is undoubtedly able to get any guy she wants, with her long black tresses and full, pomegranate mouth. Her dark eyes miss nothing, it seems, the way they size me up, and dismiss me altogether as innocuous.

'How have you been, Abby?' Mitchell says. 'London seems to be doing you well.'

'Not too bad, Mitchell. I just heard about Diane. I'm so sorry, love!'

Mitchell eyes me, and then shrugs. 'It's been a year. But I'm quite happy now, thanks, Abby.'

'Well, when you want a real, home-cooked dinner, love, come on over, and we'll see if we can't get you sorted, hmm?'

'Awh, thanks, Abby, that's awfully kind of you, but I'm really busy this season.'

Abby shrugs. 'Maybe I can swing by the inn, then. We can have a cup of coffee and catch up.'

'Sure, why not? It was good seeing you. Night, Abby.' And then he turns back to us. 'Ready to go home?'

Danny and I nod in unison. Anything to get away from Abby who is now further away but still staring me down as if I was a repelling insect.

During the drive home, Danny and Mitchell comment on the movie and the wide variety of snacks available, while I sit in silence. Why do all women act like that around me when there's a male in the vicinity? It's not like I'm some sex bomb who will steal their man away from them. I am the furthest thing away from it, with my faded jeans and ponytail. Or maybe they detect my loneliness instead, and think what a loser I am. Which is most likely.

I don't realise we're home until I feel the crunch of gravel under the tyres, and as we walk to the entrance of the inn, Danny and Mitchell still prattling away about George Bailey's luck, I suddenly become overwhelmed by the fact that we don't belong here after all, and that this is not our home. It's all temporary. For now, and a few more nights, we will call it that, but really, it isn't. And the thought makes me miserable.

'See you tomorrow, Mitchell,' Danny says yawning when we reach the lobby. 'And thanks for such a great night!'

'Awh, bless you, mate, you too,' Mitchell says, high-fiving him, and then stuffing his hands in his pockets to look at me.

I turn to Danny and give him the key to our room. 'Here, love, go on. I'll be right up.'

'Okay,' Danny says with a happy bounce as he bounds through the doors, not without turning to give us a quick glance. I swear that boy is tuned in to my feelings. I can only hope that he can't read my insecurities. Imagine having to explain all of them to an almost eight-year-old boy.

And then it strikes me that that was the equivalent of saying, 'Go on up, I want to be alone with Mitchell in case he decides to kiss me.' Which is ridiculous. He has not indicated any real interest in me in a boy meets girl way. It's just my imagination again, driven by eight years of loneliness. Well, almost nine, actually. Because now, having met Mitchell, I've started thinking about things like that again, and it's like being on another planet.

Mitchell hovers, playing with his own keys. Textbook 'I want to hang' language. 'Well, Rosie, thanks for the lovely evening.'

'Thank you, Mitchell.'

He shrugs and chuckles to himself. 'I guess that if this had been a date, I'd be giving you a goodnight kiss by now...'

I look up. His face is visibly much softer than it is during the day when we are tackling problems in the office. There is no furrow between his eyebrows and his mouth is upturned into an almost smile.

Is he asking to kiss me? What do I do? 'I guess...' Arrgh. Seriously? What does that mean: Yes, kiss me or... what am I, a teenager? Although, right now, I actually feel like one, with all the relative uncertainty. I've completely blown it, I know. But he doesn't budge.

'Danny had a good time, though…' he offers, studying his feet.

'Meaning you didn't?' I blurt out.

His eyes dart to mine. 'What? No, of course not. I mean… I did. I had a great time. Danny is a true joy.'

'Yes, he is.' Can I think of nothing else to say? 'Well, I'm glad you enjoyed his company.'

His face falls and he looks into my face. 'Oh, I enjoyed yours, too, Rosie.'

'You did?'

'Of course. And I'd like to do it again.'

'Danny would love that,' I agree, and then curse myself. If ever Mitchell wanted to say something to me, he won't do it with my son standing between us. Which is probably for the best, seeing as I still am The Spy.

But he grins. 'Great. We'll do it again, then. See you tomorrow, Rosie.'

That's it? No doorstep, first kiss? Of course not. It wasn't a date. Maybe that Abby woman is more his type? How am I supposed to know? I don't know anything about him, really. I don't know what he likes to do in his spare time, nor the kind of girl he likes. Because I can't bring myself to make light conversation outside the topic of work.

I open the door to my suite to see Danny already in bed, reading another one of his horse magazines. He looks up and grins. 'Did you have a good time, Mum?'

I put my bag down to sit on the edge of his bed and kiss his soft cheek. 'I had a fantastic time, darling. And you?'

'Mitchell is fun, isn't he?'

'Yes, he is. He wants to take us out again, soon.'

Danny closes his magazine. 'Mum, you guys go on your own next time.'

I eye him. 'Nonsense. Mitchell wants you to come.'

He grins. 'Mum. You and Mitchell need some time alone.'

I do a double take. 'Why do you say that?'

'Because when we went to get our snacks he asked me if it was okay if he asked you out to dinner one night.'

Dinner! 'And… would you be okay with that?'

He tilts his head and looks at me. I swear, sometimes he acts like he's eighteen, and not nearly eight. 'Of course. You can't spend all your time worrying about me. You've got to get yourself a life. I'm not a baby anymore, you know?'

Not a baby? Of course he is, and he'll always be my baby. I want to sweep him up into a desperate embrace and cry into his hair, and beg him to never lose this childhood sweetness. But instead I smile. He needs his mama to be strong, not an absolute, teary-eyed mess.

'Of course you're not, love. You're growing up quickly! But you still have a curfew. Now turn out your light, and get a good night's sleep.'

'You too, Mum.'

I kiss him again and pad into my own bedroom next door, leaving the door open as usual in case he needs me in the middle of the night.

But in Mitchell's bed, I toss and turn. Dinner. He was going to ask me out to dinner, but then I blew it. The one time that he and I are alone together, and not talking about work, I decide to panic and push him away. Leaving him to the likes of the Abbys of this world. Sometimes I can be so stupid. I deserve to be alone.

Just as I'm drifting off to sleep, thinking of Mitchell's lovely smile and large hands, my mobile pings with a missed call. Mark. I'd recognise that number anywhere, because I've spent years trying to forget it.

11

Drowning Unsinkable Sorrows

The next morning, Mitchell saunters in as Laura and I are deep in the accounts. I'm getting worse than Susan now, as far as dogs with bones go. Only my goal is to save him.

'Another request for payment has arrived from Master Clean Company,' I inform him without looking up. I need to keep it together. I can't be bawling every time I see Danny beaming at him. Nor can I be shaking every time he comes near me. When did this start? I always knew he was handsome, but when did he start having such an effect on me?

'Oh, not again?' Mitchell groans. 'We sent them payment at least ten days ago.'

Laura shakes her head. 'This refers to the months of October and November. It's from the same period as the other invoices.'

He leans in and reads it, then looks up at me with a strange expression on his face. 'Keep looking,' he says. 'I'll check the back office.'

The three of us spend most of the morning rifling through all the drawers. Mitchell even gets on his hands and knees and pulls out the bottom ones. In the end, he kneels back and runs a hand through his dark curls, his mouth twisted in concentration.

'Nothing?' I ask.

He shakes his head. 'Nothing.'

I bite my lip. The last thing I want is to arouse undue suspicion, but my instinct is never wrong. How to mention it again without angering him?

'Why don't I call Diane?' Laura suggests, reading my mind. 'She might have an idea.'

Mitchell raises an eyebrow at her. 'And let her know I'm having trouble now that she's gone? Never.' And with that, he stands up and strides out of the office.

Laura looks at me and shakes her head. 'Men and their pride.'

That may well be, but we have a situation here. I have a feeling that Head Office is not going to relent, and that maybe I should find out more about Mitchell's future Plan B. And maybe get him to bring it forward, if even just a smidgen.

So I grab two steaming mugs of coffee from the dining room and find him sitting, slumped, in his personal office. He is facing the wall, chin on his knuckles, one foot on top of the opposite ankle and in deep thought. I knock on the doorjamb.

'Mitchell...?' I call softly.

He swivels around in his chair, sitting up straight when he sees me. 'Come in, Rosie,' he says, his voice rough. He is truly upset and my own throat tightens at the sight of his distress.

I clear my throat. 'I brought you a coffee.'

'Thanks,' he says, nodding to the chair opposite. 'Have a seat.'

I slide his mug over the surface of his desk and his eyes swing to mine.

'It'll get better,' I assure him.

He suppresses a snort.

'Can I ask you something?'

He looks at me, tired, but the anger seems gone, which is what worries me more. 'This, uhm, dream you have, of working for yourself?' It's like the roles are reversed now, but I can't help but remember him saying that. It's his only saving grace from where I'm sitting. Head Office are bent on sacking him, even if the reviews are unfair. Better prepare him for the worst.

When some bosses have the upper hand, there's no peace for us underdogs. But Mitchell is so not an underdog. He's just going through a rough patch, is all. He needs time to heal, and to get on with his own life. A failed relationship is a guarantee for a false start in life. Don't we all deserve another chance?

He takes a swig of his coffee. 'What about it?'

'How... far along is it?'

He lets out a hearty laugh, but I can tell it's a forced one. There is pain and disappointment behind those dark eyes. Pain he is trying to hide. His wife left him just before Christmas, and with all probability has done him over five hundred pounds every month for a year. That's already six thousand, without counting all the unpaid bills for which he'll have to fork out more money.

Being kindred spirits, I recognise the look on his face,

recognise the attitude. He'd rather die than give her the satisfaction of letting her know he's in difficulty. Nor does he want anyone else to know. He sits up and suddenly smiles. The smile of someone trying very hard.

'Ah, you lookin' out for me, are ya? You're such a sweetheart.'

I can actually feel my face going red. Oh, I so am *not* a sweetheart. And when he finds out, he will positively hate me. But for now, he doesn't know, and I'll do my best to help him.

'I'm just wondering how long it'll be before it comes to fruition,' I say. 'In case you get sick of your job and want to quit sooner rather than later.' There. That should give me some info and a timeframe to work with.

But he just reaches across the desk and pats my hand. 'I'll be all right until then, I think, Rosie.'

No, you won't, I want to scream. *Head Office does not like its hotels losing stars and getting bad reviews. And even if you aren't to blame, you're the only scapegoat they've got. And I have no idea how to defend you.*

I desperately want to tell him who I am, and that even if he kicks me out, there will be more like me, more qualified and more heartless. What I'm willing to forgo, others won't. This drop in reputation is unexplained, and they want to know why. You just need to look into his eyes to know he's a good, hard-working man. He has to be, because I could never fall for another jerk like Mark. Not that I am falling for Mitchell, of course. I just care, that's all.

'Hey...' he says, sliding his hands across the desk again. I watch them, fascinated as he takes my fingers with his. I look up at him and he smiles. A genuine smile this time. Sad, but tender. 'I'll be fine, don't you worry, Rosie.'

I bite my lip. What can I say? It's a miracle that Susan hasn't called me in two days. I wonder if she's died or something.

His hand reaches up to caress my cheek and, for a split second, my heart stops beating. Literally. I'm waiting for my next beat, but it's not coming. It should be jack-hammering its way up into my ears, but it's stopped completely. And then I remember to breathe.

Call it his Irish charm, his stubbornness, his kindness towards Danny, or his deep voice, but Mitchell... with all his faults and quirks and problems and complicated life... melts my heart. I don't know what it is. Maybe it's the mischief mixed with his utter dependability. He may be a complex man, Mitchell, but he's a *complete* man, no doubt.

And his sex appeal is also largely due to the fact that he is completely clueless of the effect he has on women – me included. If he had an inkling, he wouldn't be sitting so close to me. Because if I can no longer deny my attraction to Mitchell, it's embarrassing to admit that I can't *hide* it, either.

He leans closer, squeezing my fingers gently. Is he going to finally kiss me this time? I swallow.

'You really are a sweet soul, aren't ya?' he whispers, his face oh-so-close to mine. So close, in fact, that I notice his eyes are not chocolate brown as I'd thought. They are a dark, golden hazel bordering on... dark *honey*. It's a bit like his personality. From afar, he looks all rocky and granite-like. Impervious. Flinty. But get closer, and you begin to see the human underneath, complete with sinews and blood and muscle. And heart. Yes, he's got a good heart. No one else would have given up his own home for a stranger and her child.

'Ah, before I forget, Rosie, I'm planning a surprise for you.'

'A surprise?'

'Uh-huh…' His eyes roam over my face at length until I realise he's not going to kiss me after all. *Damn.*

'What kind of surprise?'

He grins. 'You'll have to wait.'

'When?'

He lets go of my hands all too quickly, stuffs his hands in his pockets, and as he turns to go, he winks. 'You'll see soon enough.'

Now you try concentrating on your mission, after that.

When I get back from my break, Laura is smugly tapping away.

'What's with the face?' I ask as I slide into my chair at Reception.

'Nothing, only you've received a present,' she says.

'Me? From whom?'

'Why don't you open it?' she says, sliding me a brown paper parcel.

I sit and stare at it. There's a card. *To the sexiest woman in Cornwall.* I wonder who he'd bribed to know my whereabouts. He doesn't work for Johnson Hotels anymore.

'Awh, that's so hot!' Laura swoons, reading over my shoulder. 'I'll bet it's lingerie!' she almost squeals and I have to remind her of where we are.

Hot? If she only knew how not hot he was. If she only knew what Mark had put me through.

With trembling hands, I rip the box open. It is full of Reese's Pieces peanut butter cups in every form, shape and size – the mini-cups, the giant cups and even the bars. There must be over a hundred pieces in there. The pieces of my broken heart.

'I'll have to get a better job just to keep you in your chocolate,' Mark had once joked as he put his arm around my shoulder. I had been happy, over the moon. We had just started dating and I had not been uncomfortable around him in the least. We had been at the beginning, when everything seemed possible. Even the dream of an eternal love.

'First the flowers, and now the chocolates. Who is it that is courting you like there's no tomorrow, Rosie?' Laura wants to know.

'No one of consequence,' I say with a shrug.

After I've put Danny to bed that evening, I go down into the kitchen and make myself a cup of hot chocolate from Russell's special stash. I've just plunked myself onto a stool when my mobile vibrates and for a split second, before the ringtone kicks in, I actually think it's him. My palms sweat, but then comes the boom of the ominous notes of 'Ride of the Valkyries' and I am almost relieved.

'Hi, Susan...'

'Rosie, I don't know what the hell you're doing down there, but it's certainly not inspecting the hotel.'

Oh God, she's in one of her beauties tonight.

'What do you mean?' I ask, but I know exactly what she means. She wants answers. Answers that I have failed to give.

'Either you send me a detailed report justifying the bad reviews, or I'm going to have to send someone else down there to carry out the inspection. And while the inn will be investigated properly and fairly, you will be summarily dismissed, due to your overall insufficient performance.'

Dismissed? Is she kidding me? 'But there is no evidence against him,' I hiss as I spot a couple of the pink hen party girls squawking by in stilettos below the window, chased by two Neanderthal men of the stag party. 'Or against me. I'm doing the best I can, considering this isn't even in my job description.'

'On the contrary. You have been evasive, making up excuses to postpone your reports, and you depict a scenario that doesn't exist. I'm beginning to wonder why you're covering for him, and I have a very good idea – you're sleeping with him, aren't you?'

I gasp. 'What? Of course not...' No, of course I'm not sleeping with him, as much as I'd love to. I can think of hardly anything else, besides saving his butt, but I can't tell Susan that, can I?

'Then you're about to,' she says. '*Shoulda guessed.*'

I roll my eyes as if she could see me, but I'm hoping this injects some degree of indignity into my voice. And I am indignant, of course. I'm a serious pro at my regular job, at the end of the day.

'I most certainly am not sleeping with him. I'm simply looking for evidence before I accuse someone of being unprofessional. And up until now I've only seen a man who cares about his business and who works round the clock to make sure everything is okay.'

She snorts, and I want to pull her right through the

telephone wire and strangle her with it. 'That's it, I'm putting in a formal complaint against you. You're toast.'

'What?' I gasp. 'You can't fire me – this isn't even in my job description! I— Hello?' Before I can say *Season's Greetings*, she's slammed the phone down on me. The Sacker is gone, and soon, I suspect, I will be, too. Just in time for Christmas. And oh, what a sorry one it's going to be.

All I know is that Head Office has well and truly cornered me by giving me an impossible task to perform. I've done it by the book, sending in regular reports, but have not made any moves against Mitchell, or anyone else for that matter. And I don't know how I'm going to get out of this one. I'm trapped, and images of me clearing my desk – something I've been wanting to do since she became my supervisor – now terrify me. What am I going to do with a bad reference? What hotel is ever going to have me if they'll be checking with her? Where am I going to go? What am I going to do?

I certainly can't accept Mitchell's offer to stay on and work here for fear of him finding me out. Maybe I could really look into opening my own pottery shop somewhere else in Cornwall. Somewhere similar to Little Kettering, but far away enough to never bump into Mitchell. I certainly have enough stock, all in storage. Excluding my pregnant Black period, most of my wares are based on beach colours. Ever since I can remember I've been dreaming of Cornwall.

But there's one huge obstacle. I don't have any money anywhere. How am I going to set up a business, let alone a home, on the three hundred pounds in my bank account? And it doesn't look like I'm getting a Christmas bonus, either. On the contrary. I'm getting the Christmas boot, and not the kind Santa wears.

When my Skype app signals a call, I glance at my laptop screen, hoping it's Susan, calling to mitigate the situation somehow. But it's my mum. I can't talk to her right now. She always reads me like a book and she'll know something's up. But if I don't answer she'll only worry.

'Rosie? How are you, darling? How's Danny?'

Just the sound of her voice makes me want to give everything up and run back to the safety of my childhood home where no one will kick me out if I haven't done my duty. Home. I miss it so badly. I miss all the years I was loved unconditionally. When a hug from Dad or a kiss from Mum would make everything better.

I swallow. What the heck is happening to me? I'm an independent girl and always have been. I smile as if I mean it so my voice will project happiness. That's what they taught me in business school. Smile like you mean it.

'Hi, Mum. We're fine. Danny is having a *great* time.'

'Oh, how lovely! Has he made any little friends there yet?'

'Everybody here loves him, Mum.'

She chuckles. 'I'm glad. But your father and I are so annoyed about not seeing you this Christmas. It's absurd. Who makes a mother work during her holidays? Doesn't your company have a heart?'

Good question.

'We were thinking of coming down to you, darling.'

My heart lurches at the possibility. 'I'd really love that, Mum. But the whole town is completely booked.'

'Is it? It must be a very nice place, then.'

'Oh, it is. It's really beautiful.'

'Shame. Will you be stopping by before you go back to London?'

Stopping by? Moving in rather, if this keeps up. 'We'll see, Mum. Danny really misses you both, and I...' My voice cracks. Talking to her is becoming more and more difficult by the minute. And pretending to be happy is becoming impossible.

'Rosie? Are you all right, love?'

'I'm fine, Mum. Everything's fine.'

'You know, Rosie, your father and I are thinking of moving away from Birmingham.'

'Moving? But... what about all your friends?'

'You and Danny are more important than all our friends. We're not getting any younger, and we just want to see more of you. Is that something you would like?'

Like? Having my family with me, after all these stubbornly independent but lonely years? I can hardly control my tears of joy. 'Of course. But London, Mum? You always hated it.'

'You and Danny are worth the sacrifice, love.'

I mumble something about missing them and hang up before the tears come.

Imagine, having them worrying about me, their grown daughter, and at Christmas time, to boot? Imagine them having to move down, business and all, to London, which they absolutely loathe, just to reassure themselves Danny and I are doing okay! They should be slowing down now, not thinking even remotely of making such a huge move. They should be kicking back and relaxing, not worrying about me.

I know my parents. Ever since Mark left, they have been hoping (God knows why) he'd come back. What my parents don't understand is that, in order for me to get over him, I'd needed to exclude any possibility whatsoever of him coming back. Only then could I be okay. Even if still today the mere sight of his flowers sends me reeling back to the past.

But I need to be even stronger, especially now. I'm over Mark, and have been for years. But I can't allow a man, not even one like Mitchell, to change my life around again. I came here for a reason, and I'm going to do it. End of. I'm not going to feel guilty about it anymore, because it's killing me. Even if he is the loveliest, most intriguing man I've ever met. Because in less than two weeks, Danny and I will be sitting at home, on a night like this, and I'll be wondering what he's doing, after putting the whole thing behind me. That's what I tell myself. But the idea of him finding out who I really am, along with never seeing him again... is too much to bear. I will miss Mitchell, no doubt. I will be wanting him all day and all night, while the man barely knows I exist. Why am I so unlucky in love?

As I turn to rest my forehead against the window pane, looking out into the silent, black night, the snow begins to fall, light flakes gently drifting down at first, like twinkling stars against the light of the wrought-iron storm lamp hanging from the wooden awning. And then, as if sensing my pain, it begins to come down harder and harder, non-stop, until the lamplight is only a faint glimmer in the white darkness.

My mum's phone call, which should have made me feel better, only makes me more miserable, like I'm a constant source of worry for my parents. A burden. I know I'm lucky to have them in my life, but it seems to me that every time Danny and I suffer, they are suffering with me, and I just can't accept that.

I ditch my hot chocolate and instead raid the fridge for a bottle of wine, which I never touch because I can't hold my liquor. It literally makes me ill.

But tonight, who cares? It's not like I'm driving, which is a great thing at that, because I wouldn't even know where to go. If Head Office fire me with an accusation of covering up for, or worse, sleeping with a colleague, I'm dead. I'll end up as a seasonal worker, following the harvests across the land. Apples in Somerset, hops in Kent, potatoes in Ireland, whatever. What a mess my life is.

One glass won't hurt. It's not like I drink every day. I hardly drink at all. I simply don't have the time, or the inclination. Why would I leave Danny to go down the pub? Just to get shit-faced? For what? I don't feel the need to. In fact, my last tipple harks back to the summer holidays. Danny and I were in my parents' garden. The sun was warm, the wine was cool, my parents and family loved having us there, and we were happy. I felt protected, safe, surrounded by loving faces and familiar objects that had kept me company since I was a child. The opposite of now.

Now, everything is falling apart. My debt load is soaring, I can barely make ends meet, child support is non-existent as Mark has never legally acknowledged paternity of Danny. For all Mark cares, we could both be dead. I feel so, *so* sorry for Danny, who always makes the best of every situation, but I know I'm not enough for him. How can I be, with my lopsided parenting? Every boy needs a male figure. And I haven't got one. Every child needs financial security, and I haven't got that either.

Maybe I should just quit and go back to my parents after all and work in their coach company. Why not? Mum would take care of Danny while I'm at work. He'd be able to see his grandparents more often, and I wouldn't be so miserable. Because, as I pour what I think is now my third (or fourth?) glass, I realise I am just that. *Miserable*. A miserable, lonely loser. And I have only myself to blame.

Because if I'd been smarter, I would've known how to keep my man. I'd be a great mum, and would be able to spend more time and money on Danny. I wouldn't be so afraid of losing my job and I could generally thumb my nose at the world and its adversities. But I find, right now, that I can't.

Everyone, now and then, needs their own little, personal nervous breakdown, and I think that I'm just about to have mine. Just a quick one, though. I've got to be behind the reception desk in a few hours, looking all chirpy and optimistic. The exact opposite of what I feel right now. Because right about now, if I drive, say, a screwdriver through the middle of my forehead, I won't feel it, so piercing is the pain inside my heart. And before I know it, I'm quietly sobbing my eyes out in the huge, dark kitchen, stifling the sounds with my forearms.

'Rosie, what are you doing in the dark?'

I look up from the table, shielding my eyes against the bright light. Of all bloody people…

Mitchell bends down to me as I'm practically sprawled over the counter. 'Have you been drinking?'

'Jusht a couple glasses. Or maybe five. I losht count…'

'But you said you can't hold your liquor, that it makes you feel ill. Why would you…? Hey, hey, come *here*…' he whispers as I begin to sob again. Jesus, could I *be* any more pathetic? But I don't care if he sees me cry. It's not like I have this amazing image to preserve anymore. Soon he'll know why I'm really here and he'll hate my guts anyway.

He pulls me into his arms, his chest solid and warm. It's a great place for bawling. God, he must think I'm a real loser. Very probably, he's thinking of taking his job offer back.

He turns on the kettle and then comes back to sit on the stool next to me, stroking my back.

'Where'sh Danny?' I ask.

'I'm assuming right where you left him – safe and warm in his bed.'

'I'm shuch a horrible mother,' I groan.

'No, you're not, you silly sausage.'

'And a terrible girlfriend, too.'

'What?'

'It'sh true! I have no fashion shenshe. I embarrashed him in front of his colleaguesh.'

'Who?'

'Mark. That'sh why he left me.'

'Ah. The bloke who sent you the flowers and the chocolates? Danny's father?'

'Yuh,' I hiccupped. 'He left me because I washn't good enough for him.'

'He's a knob, that's why he left you,' Mitchell says hotly.

'He shaid I'd be a terrible mother and he wassshhh right.'

'He's so not right, Rosie. You're a fantastic mother and a gorgeous young woman. And now he wants you back.'

'For yearsh I hid from relationshipsh, dedicating myshelf to Danny. I never really looked for love, although I hoped it might happen one day,' I bleat on, unable to stop myself. 'And now, here you are, real, true love, and I can't have you.'

He stops and stares at me. And in the haze of my

drunkenness, I realise I've spoken too much. I used the bloody L-word, can you imagine that? And I've scared him off yet again. I've screwed it up. God, am I good at absolutely nothing?

'Bed…' I say, suddenly exhausted. 'I need… to sleep.' Before I ruin everything else, too.

And before I know it, Mitchell sweeps me up into his arms. And we're not in the kitchen anymore. I know that because I can see his wardrobe behind him. Unless it has followed us into the kitchen, we are in his (my) bedroom. Maybe I have fallen asleep again and he has taken me up the stairs. I try to open the other eye and ask him if I'm heavy, but he doesn't answer me. Instead, he is pulling my shoes off. I am lying spread-eagle on my – his – bed, and I smile in drunken anticipation. The moment is finally upon us. I am going to have sex with him and I can't wait.

Let the guilt come tomorrow, along with the stark reality of life. For now, I want a tiny slice of happiness, a happy memory to take back with me when I leave this place forever. I want to see the expression on his face, but I can barely distinguish his silhouette against the lamplight behind him.

He doesn't join me, though, doesn't come anywhere near me, except to kiss my forehead as he pulls the covers up to my chin. As he pulls away, the sense of loss is heartbreaking. It was now or never, because tomorrow I won't have the courage to act upon my desires. There's nothing I can do, nothing I can say, to make him stay.

'Goodnight, Rosie. Sweet dreams.'

12

Snow Angels

The next day is the day of the Mother of Hangovers. I don't remember what or how much I've drunk, but I do remember Mitchell seeing me in that state. And, oh Christ, did I actually say what I think I said? Did I tell him I love him? What the hell is wrong with me? It's not love. It's lust. Loneliness. And imagining myself with him is not helping dispel the enchantment. I want him more than ever now, just as I am about to lose it all.

So I lie low and hide out in the back office, hoping he won't venture out of what I consider to be neutral territory, i.e. the front desk, the lobby, or the restaurant. Actually, I'm hoping he'll stay away from the joint altogether. He must think I'm an absolute wreck. I only hope he can forget last night.

'Mornin', Rosie,' he greets me, leaning forward with his forearms on the counter, a huge grin on his face.

Oh God. Not only have I dreamed of him all night, I can't stop thinking about him. I actually conjure up these scenarios where we're cooking together, or walking hand in hand through a field, or… waking up together. Go figure. Me and my impossible dreams. He is way too good for me and I feel like a letch. The nicer he is, the more he pisses me off.

'Morning,' I almost snap back, my heart riddled with guilt, so I am really trying to stay concentrated on the day's work, all the while being acutely aware of the tendons and muscles in his forearms. They're huge. And his hands are always fiddling with something. Today it's my pen. When I can stand it no longer, I reach out and pluck it from between his fingers.

'I need that,' I say when he squints down at me curiously, the weight of his gaze unbearable. He's so close he can probably see my every single pore, dammit. And what kills me is that, when I shoot him a quick glance, his expression is halfway between teasing and beseeching. How does he manage to master that look, half puppy, half sex-god?

It's that simple. I can't control myself, so I turn away from him and the possibilities in his eyes and try to concentrate on getting some work done. That's why I'm here, that's what I'm going to do.

'Busy?' he asks.

'Focused,' I correct him.

'Thank God we have you, then.' He grins. 'Have you given my proposal any thought?' Mitchell asks and I want to scream at his poor choice of words. Proposal. Not that I expected a proposal from a bloke I've just met, of course.

Forget that he's kind, dependable, that Danny loves him to pieces and that he is a solid role model for him. Forget that whenever he walks into the room, my heart starts drumming some mad beat, that I can't think clearly and that I just want to throw myself into his arms.

'Rosie?' Mitchell's voice shakes me out of my dreams. 'Have you decided what to do?'

I shrug, my eyes on the carpet. Oh, to be able to look him in the eye. If he mentions what I said last night I swear I'll kill him.

He moves in closer, his eyes searching mine. 'What... are you leaning towards?'

Jumping onto your lap, I want to answer, but I simply cough. 'I'm... still thinking.'

'Well, you do that then, but don't take forever,' he says as he grabs his keys off the counter and, with a wink in my direction, turns and strides out of the lobby.

What the hell's happened to me, practically overnight? First, being much too busy trying to survive, I didn't even look at men – not even by mistake. And now? I've become a sex maniac. A sex maniac with a conscience, to boot.

And then I hear Laura chuckling as she comes in.

'What's so funny?'

'Don't worry, Rosie, you're not the only one who's gaga over him.'

Busted.

'Gaga over whom?' I say, trying to ignore the heat flooding my face as I continue to pretend to be busy.

Laura rolls her eyes and giggles. 'For the boss, of course! I heard some of the hen girls are angling at... well, you know. Bets are on who's going to land him first. My money's on you.'

Hen girls angling for a go at Mitchell? What did I expect? Already the girl from the hen party tried to approach him.

And that other one from the other night at the town hall after the movie, Abby. Everywhere I look there are women ogling him. I haven't got a cat's chance in hell.

'Me? Are you nuts? I'm not here for a turn, Laura.'

'Don't be fooled by the attitude, Rosie. Mitchell's a lovely chap.'

'He can be,' I reluctantly agree. 'If a bit cocky.'

Laura shrugs. 'I told you, that's his armour.'

'You think?'

'I know for a fact. He's always so self-deprecating, but in a charming way.'

I think about it. Not that I need to. He's taking up so much of my thoughts these days. When he doesn't piss me off royally.

Laura beams. 'It's so endearing, how one minute he'll look at you with those eyes and then transform to Mr Sex On A Stick on the turn of a dime.'

I shrug, not knowing what to say, because damn, I couldn't have said it better.

Laura bursts out into a laugh. 'Oh, come on, Rosie! You think I haven't noticed how you gawp at him?'

'I do not!'

'Yes, you do! And then you do that funny thing of putting on that face, like you've just sucked on a lemon, as soon as he looks your way... Exactly, *that* face there! You don't fool anyone.'

Oh, God, can she really tell? What am I going to do? I haven't come here to make a fool out of myself.

'Does Mitchell know about all these women shamelessly lusting after him?' I ask.

'No, I told you, the guy's clueless.'

'And yet, he flirts.'

'Only with you.'

I make a face. 'He does not.'

'Oh, so then what was that just now?' Laura asks, nodding to the spot on the counter where Mitchell had been leaning only a moment ago.

I shrug. 'How am I supposed to know? He's your boss.'

'If you play your cards right, he could be yours, too. He needs to hire someone. God knows he needs proper staff.'

That's a fact. Everything's so in tatters, it's a wonder the place manages to stay open at all. Luckily, the restaurant, the strongest point, is doing very well thanks to the locals and Russell's talent.

'What do you say, Rosie? Will you apply for a job here?'

'Why don't you? You've already started looking into proper training, haven't you? You'd be perfect.'

She makes a face. 'Me? I'd love to, but I'm nowhere near as good as you.'

'But, Laura, that's only because I've been doing it for years on end. You're an absolute natural. I can't think of how good you'd be if you took a course. Just think about it.'

'And you?' Laura asks. 'Will you settle here, in Little Kettering?'

I've been thinking about nothing else. Leaving London. To live in Cornwall. Sending Danny to the local primary school. Renting a pretty little cottage by the sea. That sounds like heaven. But not here. Not in Little Kettering, seeing Mitchell every day, and spending even more sleepless nights thinking of him, at least up until he susses me out. No thank you. I'd need a shrink by the end of the week.

'I don't know, Laura. Let's get you on your way, first – what do you think?'

At that, her smile brightens. 'If you think I can do it.'

'Hell, yes,' I answer, squeezing her arm.

After lunch, with the pretext that I'm looking pale and need some fresh air, Mitchell drags me outside to the huge field north of the inn where he and Danny are making a snowman with last night's freak snowstorm. A snowman. Mitchell, the official Grinch who hates Christmas, has taken it upon himself to play with my son. Whereas Danny's own dad has buggered off, presumably disappeared off the face of the earth. I sniff, pretending my eyes are stung by the cold. How can I not be touched by this? It's much more than we've ever had. Immensely more than we ever expected from a stranger whose life I was sent to destroy.

Although everything around us is covered in white, the sky is a clear blue and the sun is shining once again. There is no trace of pollution, nor litter, nor tyre-marked snowbanks. The grit doesn't settle on the crisp top layer of snow, turning everything to a faded grey like in the city where black and white means mostly black. Here, it's all quiet, pure and clean.

So, like one of Danny's playmates (I don't think I'll ever outgrow my inner child), I hunker down next to them and start packing the snow around the base to stabilise the legless, round-tummied character slowly taking shape. Mitchell and Danny are mirror images of red-cheeked, happy concentration, exhaling the cold air that seems to act like laughing gas on us. I must be losing it. Last night I was desperate, and now I have no idea how I feel. All I want to do is forget. And laugh, like I haven't done in years. And out here, in the cold, with Mitchell and Danny, there's no time for thinking. Just... *being*.

It's been a long time since Danny and I have had this kind of quality time, out in the open. I sit back on my haunches and take in the scenery. Above us, the trees are bare, glistening happily in the crystal-like snow bathed in the feeble sunlight. God, I wish these fairy-tale moments could last forever. Expand until they take a proper place in time and our memories, and not just fleeting flashes that are gone before I can frame them like little pictures in my heart. Which I can't. But I can at least take photos of this memorable, wonderful moment in our lives. One that, I just know, Danny will remember forever.

Just looking at him, rolling and patting snow with his little hands in the shadow of such a great man like Mitchell Fitzpatrick, makes me wish I could retrieve and flesh out these pictures and bring them to life on a crappy day at work and say to Danny, *Remember when we were in Cornwall? You were about to turn eight, and it snowed? And we were happy.* I wish that I could offer my little man more than just the *Remember Whens*.

I know Danny is easily content with the simple life I can barely afford him, but how long can it last? How long can I pretend a meagre meal of bubble and squeak is a cowboy's banquet? How long can I pretend that the two of us are perfectly fine on our own, and that he doesn't need a male role model if he is to grow up happy? And how do I tackle those male problems when he starts to grow into puberty?

Because he won't be eight forever, and will eventually see through me. I am the single mother who was dumped by his father, housing him in a two-bed flat in a noisy, violent city. How long can I keep pretending it's Shangri-La? And how long before he sees our life for what it is? And once he's understood what a loser I am, it'll be the end. He'll lose his respect for me. Maybe even grow to pity me, if not resent me.

And sitting back, watching Danny basking in Mitchell's approval, makes me all the more aware of what is lacking in my little boy's life. What Danny really needs is a family. A man to look up to and emulate. Someone to turn to for the answers Mummy doesn't have. If only I could've predicted the future back then. I'd have tried to make Mark happier, tried to not make him want to leave me. I never understood why I wasn't good enough for him, and why I suffered so much when he left, because all the time I knew he wasn't happy with me. I suffered, too, knowing I wasn't enough.

But I'd still have gone through all of it, just to see Danny crouching before his snowman here today, his baby blue eyes filled with wonder at the touch of snow, and with joy from a single smile from Mitchell.

And then, when the afternoon can't get any better, Mitchell gets the bright idea of tobogganing. All he has is a couple of sheets of plastic, but they're more than enough. I watch and clap my hands as, Mitchell in front, they push off the top of the tiny hillocks, arms in the air, laughing and shouting, Mitchell louder than Danny, all the way down. I watch them as they trudge back uphill over and over, Danny's cheeks bright red, his short little legs working double time to keep up with Mitchell's stride, which is very appealing by the way.

Oops, there I go again. One minute I'm all teary-eyed

proud of my little gent, and the next, I'm lusting after a man I've just met. I need to snap out of these morbid Emily Dickinson moments.

'You wimps,' I suddenly shout, hiking up what Mitchell has dubbed Horror Hill and which they've been avoiding all afternoon. 'Let me show you how it's done!'

'Rosie!' Mitchell calls, and I can hear the alarm in his voice. 'You can't be serious – not there! It's dangerous! Come back!'

'Ha!' I laugh. Dangerous. I've survived way worse.

'Rosie, no! There is solid rock under that hill! You'll get yourself killed! Stop!'

I spread my plastic sheet out and deposit my derrière on it, my legs neatly tucked under me, pushing off gingerly, hankering for the old, familiar feel of speed and freedom. As if, flying down the side of a hill, I can catch my childhood memories, when I was happy, and had a head full of dreams waiting to come true. Wait, did he just say… solid *rock*?

'Rosie!' he cries, but I've picked up speed now, my sheet of plastic encountering no friction whatsoever, and I realise I'm flying towards my death, because the second my body hits the rock, I'll be a *dead* body.

'Mum! Look at me!' Danny calls from the top of a tiny hill Mitchell has deemed safe for him to slide down on his own. With a wave, he pushes himself off, and we're both going down in opposite directions, soon to meet somewhere in the middle. Only he's already at his destination, while I'm still flying, gaining momentum and altitude as I go. And soon, I will be landing with a crash, and I'm only glad that Danny is too distracted to realise what's happening.

For a terribly long moment, I'm suspended in the air, with

brain freeze, the cold air and my screams burning my throat raw, as flashes of not my own childhood, but Danny's first years flit through my brain. But I'm not even terrified. It's like I'm watching this on TV, as a spectator, and that my body, my life, isn't even mine. And I realise what terrifies me. Forget about my death – I'm not capable of controlling my *life*.

And I think of Danny, and my parents having to drive all the way down with the horrible news of their daughter's self-inflicted passing, and Danny having to move to the Midlands with his grandparents because, lo and behold, his mum has once again messed up.

And then I land with a painful thud, flat on my back. Mitchell scrambles over to me and I watch them both, like in a dream, my head turned, because it's the only part I can manage to move.

'Rosie, are you all right?' Mitchell stops at a skid, immediately all over me (his timing stinks), while Danny is approaching, dragging his sheet of plastic behind him.

'Did you see that, Mum?' he cries.

'That was fantastic, darling,' I chime despite myself, because I know that not only is my body numb from the cold, but that I'm in big trouble.

I look at them, unable to move, and not even sure that I haven't broken my back.

'Can you move your feet?' Mitchell asks.

Check.

'Hands?'

Check. And then I burst out laughing. The feeling of elation, of freedom, is one that I haven't felt in a long time. For some wacky reason, I've never been happier in my life.

Mitchell's not sure whether I'm crying, or laughing from shock. His hands are running all over my body (not in front of the baby, dear), checking for broken bones. *Now*, with eleven layers of clothing separating my skin from his, he decides to frisk me?

'Jesus Christ, Rosie, you scared the crap outta me!' he finally cries, his hands on my arms as he's hanging over me, while Danny starts to pull on my neck.

'Can you get up?' Mitchell wants to know.

Can I? Probably. Do I want to, with this gorgeous, kind and sexy man looming over me, giving me his undivided attention? Nuh-uh. But I can't stay here forever, with my ass stuck to the ice, can I?

Doubt clouds Danny's adorable little face. 'Mum, are you okay?'

'Yooh…' I laugh. 'Let's do that again!'

'Not on your life, sister,' Mitchell exclaims, unsure whether I'm serious or not. 'I almost died of fear.'

'I'm fine.' I didn't hit my head or anything. Or did I? I can't remember. If only. It would be great to hit my head and forget a lot of things, and just live our lives from this moment on, forgetting about my little secret, his past, mine and everything else standing between us and a possible relationship.

Mitchell, now convinced I'm okay but just a tad bonkers, starts to chuckle, and soon, we're all rolling around in the snow, high on laughter. Maybe I should be reckless a little more often. It's great fun.

'Let's make angels!' Danny cries and darts off for a new, smooth patch of snow.

Mitchell turns to me and touches my cheek. 'I already have one.'

Angel. He called me his angel. Maybe he means his guardian angel, seeing that I'm trying to help him out? Yes, that's got to be it. Because I don't know that he would see me as his angel in the sense that I'd like it to be. Because I would. I would like there to be more between us. And it's the first time in eight years that I've actually thought of a bloke at all in that way.

But it's not just attraction towards Mitchell. I think almost any woman would be attracted to him. I think it's more of an affinity. Completely blotched by the reason I'm here, of course, but nonetheless an affinity of sorts.

In any case, apart from the time I spend with Danny, it's the best day I've ever had. Even compared, *especially* compared, actually, to my dates with Mark. Mitchell has managed to make me feel welcome, special and... and... understood. Mitchell acts as if he actually cares. Now I know I don't want to make the same mistake I did with Mark ages ago, but they are not the same man, and I am not the same person anymore.

13

A New Life by the Sea

After a few days of steady sunshine that had melted the snow and almost completely dried the underlying mud, Mitchell invites me for a walk along the coastal path. Despite all my resolutions to stay away from him, my heart skips a beat.

I have done all I can for today, having already sent in my next report to Susan until notice of my termination reaches me. What's keeping her so long? But I'm sticking to my guns, i.e. that currently, there is still no evidence to substantiate the suspicions of malfeasance on the part of Mitchell Fitzpatrick, and that I am instead looking into the feasibility of his being set up by someone who holds a grudge against him.

When my email to Susan gets an 'Out of the Office until further notice' notification email back, I know I have a few days off. She must have finally met someone and is hopefully shagging him senseless on some sun-drenched beach. Maybe that will mellow her a bit. Or maybe (wishful thinking, I know) Susan the Sacker has finally been sacked herself. In any case, I'm off the hook for a few days.

So I dash over to the stables to make sure that Jeremy is going to be fine with keeping Danny, but the two hardly acknowledge me as I go, Jeremy raising a hand in salute as Danny is absorbed in filing a horseshoe. They are both in their element, as usual, so I am free to go and discover what Mitchell's invitation might hold.

Am I seeing too much in this? Could he have any interest in me at all? Or is he simply trying to lure me away from his accounts? Or, worse, is he going to confess some theft to me and then chuck me over the cliff? To be sure, I let him lead.

I have avoided him these past few days, having been a bit all over the place emotionally. I didn't want him to see how much I really am attracted to him. Because even if he really is genuinely interested in me, we have absolutely no future together.

The weather has freakishly warmed up, and is now not Christmassy at all, even for southern England, with a gorgeously clear blue sky that seems one with the clear blue sea. It looks and smells like my memories of the Mediterranean and even the constant breeze seems to have died down. Everything looks perfect. Could it be the proverbial calm before the next storm?

Wheezing but trying to hide it behind casual-ish gulps of air, I follow him along the path as he points out this and that cove, and while he's not looking, I can't help but admire his leg muscles. After all, he is walking in front of me. I'd be blind (and dead) not to notice. After a good twenty minutes he stops, thank you God, looks about, and grins. 'This okay?'

There is a small family just over the hillock a few yards

away, but we're far enough not to be overheard by them. 'Sure,' I say, wondering why we are here.

'I'm starving now,' he says, unfurling his waterproof picnic plaid and pulling out some goodies. I should be starved, too, but am feeling queasy. If I didn't know better, I'd say I was pregnant, but I know it's only stress.

I take the piece of meat pie he's cut me and nibble on it absently, watching him down his own food with gusto. He has a nice way of eating, manly and polite.

The views up here are postcard perfect. If only life could be just as perfect. It strikes me that anyone passing us by at this very moment might even think we're a couple on holiday. And they'd probably also think how lucky I am to be with someone like Mitchell. Oh, if only they knew!

About half an hour later – food, wine and casual conversation all consumed – there's a strange silence hanging between us.

He glances at me from beneath those fan-like lashes, and then looks down at the patch of grass separating our hands. 'You have such little hands, Rosie,' he suddenly whispers as his face turns red under his light beard. Oh my God, is it still possible in this day and age to find a man who actually blushes?

Normally, I'd be the first one to break eye contact, but I can't. I can barely believe he's sitting next to me on this clifftop, our hands less than a foot apart. He's gently raking the grass with his long fingers as we both stop to watch. They are long and elegant, but incredibly strong (I've seen him lug barrels downstairs on his shoulder). I am tempted to reach out and touch his fingers with mine – even a pinkie would do – to make a complete fool of myself.

Luckily I still have a modicum of self-control. There is no way that I am going to make a first move ever again. Even if I have to give in to the idea that, no, I am not indifferent to this guy in the least. I can feel my longing in the space between us. And I can feel I'm not the only one. I can hear it in his deep voice that makes my stomach vibrate. And I can tell by the way his eyes flash and his face lights up when I walk into a room. Maybe it's just a… a thing, that will end when I go away. But for now, it's here.

But if that's not enough for him to tell me, then I could ruin it all in one single pinkie-touch. Send him running for the hills. I know he's still smarting from his previous relationship, and the thought of being rejected keeps me in my corner and has done so for the past eight years. Maybe I'm just not going to have The Relationship. Maybe all I got was Mark. He gave me Danny, which trumps any man any day. So maybe I should just count my blessings.

And even if I've been alone since forever, I wonder whether one year for Mitchell on his own is enough before opening his heart to someone new. And in any case, I'm just passing through. Which is lucky. Or not, I wonder?

'You cold?' he asks, looking up. It's like he's piercing my gaze now, with his eyes that are questioning, probing. I can't stand it any longer, so to avoid saying something cheesy like I usually would at this point, I just shake my head. And that's when he grasps my hands and puts them between his own huge ones. I nearly have a stroke for the surprise.

'I notice you never wear gloves,' he whispers, his eyes lifting to mine. 'Your hands are so cold.'

No, I definitely can't stand it anymore. I've never been this attracted to anyone.

In a parallel world, I watch myself whipping to my knees and throwing my arms around his neck, bringing him to me in a lung-crushing kiss. In that same parallel world, his mouth responds to mine like second nature, and before I know it, we're rolling around on the picnic throw, amidst the pasties, the meat pies, the tiny scotch eggs, cheese and Branston pickle. The packets of Quavers pop softly as they are flattened and explode under us, and the chocolate mousse is long forgotten, along with the family only a few yards away.

And then the real world returns, where he's talking to me, expecting an answer. What has he just said? My head is lost like a buoy in the enveloping sea of his voice. I can hear it but none of it is making any sense.

'... Rosie?'

Oh God, this happens to me all the time now around him. He must think I'm a real flake, incapable of remembering two words in sequence. Talk about goldfish memory capacity. I try to guess what he's said by the look on his face. He's smiling, rather shyly, so he can't have just asked me to sleep with him or anything so forward. (Need I say how disappointed I am at that?) I'm completely clueless. Might as well admit it.

'Run that by me again?' I whisper, and he grins.

He leans in, his eyes never leaving mine. Oh my God, this is finally it. Is he going to kiss me now? I feel like I'm going to fly, among the highest, purest clouds. And my forehead is still slightly damp from schlepping – that's Danny's favourite new word – all the way up here. My hair must be a mess and, I swear, if there's any Branston in my teeth I'll die of shame. I can hear my own heartbeat in my ears. But

I also hear music. Not daydreamers' fantasy music, but real music.

Damn. This has almost become a running joke now. Because it's my mobile phone, or more precisely Stevie Wonder singing 'You are the Sunshine of my Life'. Mitchell's face splits into a grin and I cringe in embarrassment for how apt the song is to the situation. But it's actually Danny's ringtone.

'Excuse me,' I whisper. Yes, I know what you're thinking, but my baby might need me. The one time I'd ever missed a call, he'd fallen off the swings.

'Mum! I just rode Mabel!' he shrieks.

'What?'

'The mare!'

Of course. The horse he has a crush on but that wasn't reciprocated so far. 'Oh, darling, that's wonderful!'

'Jeremy says I can ride her again tomorrow!'

'I'm so proud of you...'

'Will you tell Mitchell? He'll be proud of me, too!'

I look up. He can hear every word and his eyes are twinkling with amusement.

'Of course.'

'Okay. Bye, Mum!'

'See you later, darling.'

I hang up and look at Mitchell. 'That was—'

'I heard. Good news, isn't it?'

I nod, my lips still tingling, waiting for his mouth to resume its journey to mine.

But something's changed, like he's disappointed, and he's already up on his feet. 'We'd better get back, Rosie...'

'Oh,' I say. 'Sure.' What, not even one measly little snog,

in this, the most romantic place in the world? Well, thank you very much, Stevie Wonder...

In the jeep on the way back, we sit in total, painful silence. I don't know what exactly it is that I've done, but it's put him off me completely. It can't be the song. It's got to be the Branston, I just know it.

After we get back to the inn and Mitchell helps me down, I thank him for lunch and make a mad dash for my office, where Danny is waiting to tell me all about Mabel. Which is a relief, because I need to lose myself in my son. And work – happy, good, normal things – so I can try and forget the cock-up I've just made of the afternoon – and my self-esteem.

'She's a true darlin', Mum!' Danny says about Mabel. Do I detect a slight Irish accent?

Laura, who is working at Reception, looks up and winks at me. I roll my eyes and dedicate myself completely to Danny's account of the afternoon, but every now and then I notice Laura leaning back in her chair and smiling at me inquisitively. Am I that transparent?

A couple of hours later, she goes on her coffee break (with Alex), leaving me to watch Reception.

'Rosie...?' comes Mitchell's deep voice. Oh, God. Here it comes, The Uncomfortable Conversation.

'Yeah?' I say over my shoulder as he comes in to stand over my desk. I am trawling through TripAdvisor to concentrate on the few complaints on this site, but apart from Ms Lorna Greene who bemoans the lack of castor support cups and The Wanderer who didn't like the colour of the wood (remember them?), TripAdvisor is definitely not the source of the inn's downfall.

After the fool I've made of myself earlier, I'm lying low like a leper. And my teeth were Branston-free, by the way, in case you're still wondering about that. It must just have been one of those things. We just didn't click. Or rather, I clicked big time and scared him off. But maybe our almost-kiss did absolutely nothing for him.

Mitchell leans on the counter, lowering his voice. 'What's this I hear about a hotel inspector?'

I sit up in a jerk and stare at him. I can feel the blood draining from my face, and the life seeping out of my Will To Live reserve. Because now I'm dead. He's dead, Laura's dead, we're all dead.

Like a rabbit caught in headlights, I look up into his own narrowing eyes, and I'm hoping he can't see through me, but who am I kidding? The moment of truth is now upon us. What did I expect?

'A… h-hotel inspector…?' I manage.

'Yes, a hotel inspector, Rosie.'

Well, that solves my problem of how to tell him I'm a lying hound. But now? What can I say? 'Uhm…'

He leans on his elbows and peers further into my burning face. 'Gotcha!'

I stare at him, not understanding. Is he *joking*?

'Oh, Rosie, your face! Still, it's always better to stay on guard, don't you think? Head Office is not very happy with my inn at the moment.'

I swear I almost exhale bits of lung and heart as he ruffles my hair and picks up a folder, leaving me sitting there. Is he bloody *kidding* me? Nothing – *nothing* is worth having a heart attack for, of course – but to lose his confidence and friendship would've literally killed me. It's bad enough that he didn't want to kiss me. It doesn't help that he's ruffled my hair like he would Danny's.

It also doesn't help that all afternoon while Danny is at the stables with Jeremy that Mitchell doesn't look like he'll be leaving the immediate area around my desk anytime soon, as he is instead hanging around without any obvious reason. He's going through some files, but on the third round of reading them, I deduce he's bored stiff and simply trying to kill time while spying on me, to see if I'm earning my keep. He just won't go away, and finds all sorts of excuses to ask me questions, trying to catch me out on something or other. If he asks me where I work in London, I'll have to make up a name, and then if he looks it up, which he will, I'll just have to wing it. What else can I do?

'So…' he says, his voice deep and chocolatey. Just listening to him makes me want to throw my files into the air, crawl over the desk separating us, grab him by his sweater and… beg him to forgive my deceit.

'Yes, Mitchell?'

He eyes me directly, a serious look on his face. I can't tell if he's going to kiss me (highly unlikely, given his track record) or tell me off.

'So what's the deal?' he asks.

I blink. 'Deal?'

'Are you going to stay on and work for me or not?'

Here we are again. I have to give him an answer, eventually, before he takes back his offer. But if I'm not planning on accepting it, what does it even matter?

'I-I don't know, Mitchell. It's a great offer…'

'It is and I'd help you with everything else.'

'Everything else?'

He shrugs. 'Getting Danny a placing in the local primary, finding a place to live. You know.'

Just the idea of starting all over in this beautiful corner of the world makes me smile. But would it really be good for Danny after all? Tearing him away from his school and his friends? But then I tell myself, if it makes you happy, it can only be good for you. But Mitchell doesn't understand why I can't do it, not here, with him, as much as I'd love to. And I need to buy some time.

'I'll think about it, Mitchell. Thank you very much. I promise not to take too long to give you an answer.'

He smiles. 'Okay.'

If he's disappointed, it doesn't show. Maybe he's not perturbed in the least. Maybe it's all in my foggy head. I need someone to help me clear it, so when Laura disappears on her afternoon coffee break with Alex, I dial Liz's number.

'Hey, doll, what's up?' Her chirpy voice breezes through my phone alongside the tapping of her keyboard.

'I kind of screwed up,' I whisper, looking behind me in case someone walks by.

'What did you do, sleep with the boss?' she quips.

I cringe, and the typing stops.

'You didn't! Tell! Is he as good as he looks?'

'No, I didn't sleep with him, Liz! But… we did almost kiss.'

'Almost?'

'Well, Danny called me. He's the only thing that could stop me.'

'Wow. Looks like someone performed a miracle on you. You told me he was a real piece of work.'

'Yes… yes, I did. But in fairness, I didn't know him as much as I do now. He's hard-working and honest.'

She whistles. 'Wow, all that from an almost-kiss?'

I blush, but she's right. I really do sound biased. 'I don't know what to do, Liz. I really really like him.'

'Honey, it's great that there's finally a bloke who interests you after Mark. God knows it took you long enough to get over him the first time.'

'Yes, well, there's not going to be a second time.'

'Good, I'm glad to hear you say that. But sweetie, it's probably for the best if you don't settle on Mitchell Fitzpatrick either. Besides, you'll be home soon enough. Don't put yourself through anything with an expiration date.'

She's right, of course. But there's still that one tiny detail. 'He offered me a job.'

'Who, Fitzpatrick?'

'Yes, who do you think? He offered me his *own* job. Oh, God, if he found out…'

'Hold it, Rosie, hold it. You're getting in over yourself. First, focus. You went there to assess the situation and find out why the place has such a bad reputation, right?'

I huff. 'Yes.'

'Okay. In order to do so, you have to get to know him on a personal level. They go hand in hand.'

'Right.'

'But, and here's the thing. You can, if you want, seeing as he's such an Apollo, have a little tryst with him.'

'But you told me not to get involved…'

'I meant emotionally, Rosie. No strings attached.'

'But what about the job offer?'

'Oh, Rosie, was he even serious? He can barely keep his own job, let alone give a reference for you. Besides, what the hell are you and Danny going to do all alone in Cornwall?'

I don't have to think about that one. 'Be happy? Besides, he said he'd be there for us.'

'So did Mark, sweetie.'

That one shuts me up instantly.

She sighs. 'I know you're miserable, Rosie. That tosser ruined your life by dumping you all those years ago.'

'Yes, but he also gave me Danny. And I wouldn't – I couldn't – have it any other way. I'd do it again a thousand times, you know that, Liz.'

'Of course, hon, I know. Danny is the best thing that's ever happened to you. But you do need to also have some fun.'

'But I can't with Mitchell. I can't pretend I'm just a girl on holiday. I've come here to spy on him. I'm deceiving him. Guys like *Mark* deserve something like this to happen to them, but not Mitchell.'

'What do you mean?'

'The poor guy was dumped by his wife last Christmas.'

'Ah. Are you sure you want to get involved with a married man?'

'The divorce is being finalised.'

'He told you that?'

'Laura, his receptionist did.'

'So you two haven't even had that conversation yet? Jesus, Rosie, what exactly *does* he say to you?'

'Not much, really. Most of it is looks and innuendos,' I admit. 'But he's really nice to me. And Danny adores him.'

'Careful, Rosie, or you'll get seriously hurt again. Because you sound like it's the real deal for you. But is it the same for him?'

Terrific question. Does Mitchell have feelings for me that will extend beyond Christmas? 'I'll have to get back to you on that,' I answer.

'All right, hon. Be careful. And keep in touch.'

'I will, Liz,' I promise and ring off.

Is it? The same for him? The question keeps jumping around in my head. If it were to be the same for him, shouldn't he tell me so, before it's time for me to leave? A job offer is not a declaration of one's feelings. Or should I tell him about my own feelings? I'm completely out of practice and so rubbish at this.

Experience has taught me to never show my hand (or my heart, in this case), but all my girlfriends say that if I don't ask, I won't get, and that I should make things happen. But what if I presume too much? What if I let myself go to the idea that he might be interested for real, and then it turns out I only make a fool out of myself? And not only that: how on earth could I expect him to develop feelings for me, when I know I don't deserve them?

If this were a BBC Period Romance, it would be easy to make the proper, moral choice. I'd be someone really cool like Kate Winslet. I'd not worry about the consequences and quit my job, take Danny somewhere remote (as if Cornwall wasn't remote enough) and go and sit on a windswept cliff high above the raging sea, my knitted shawl wrapped around me, while I torment myself with the thought of him, lost to me forever for my one mistake of not revealing my identity to him.

And then, because it's the BBC (and Cornwall), he, in the form of someone dashing like Captain Poldark himself, would appear at my back and hold me, whispering words of comfort into my ear, hopefully along with some PG-14-rated stuff.

And then he'd take me back home, where we'd live happily ever after.

That night Danny and I climb up onto my bed for our bedtime chat.

'So how's it going?' I ask as I ruffle his hair.

'I love it here, Mum,' he says as he plays with my necklace. 'There's so much to do.'

I smile. What a world of difference. He's changed so much. This place is good for him. There is literally no trace of the pale city boy who arrived. In his stead is a confident, happy child who bounces out of bed in the morning, whereas I'd have to half-drag him to school in London.

'Mum, do we have to go back to London?' he asks.

'You like it that much, then?'

'Yeah…' he sighs.

I laugh. And wonder. Do we really have to go back? And if I lose my job, what is there to go back to? I've never worked in any other field. And I can't work for Mitchell, of course, because once Johnson Hotels fire you, you're out. Not to mention Mitchell's disappointment. I won't even be able to show my face in Little Kettering.

But again, the idea of opening my own pottery shop and giving pottery throwing lessons, albeit on the other side of the county, comes back to my mind.

I left Birmingham for London in search of work, and myself. But what if I have found myself here, in Cornwall? And as far as Mitchell goes, if I lived on the other side of the county, we wouldn't be bumping into each other, right? So, all in all, is leaving London for Cornwall such a crazy idea after all?

Danny slides off my bed and yawns. 'Okay. I'm sleepy now, Mum. Goodnight.' He kisses me and heads for his own room. I watch him go with a mixture of pride and nostalgia. It's incredible how well he's doing here. He's growing more and more confident each day. Maybe I need him more than he needs me.

And Mitchell? Maybe I even need Mitchell more than he needs me. Because there's no denying it. Something has shifted between us after that near-kiss experience and my drunken declaration of love. Only not in the way I'd hoped, i.e. the two of us being overwhelmed by a sudden passion and promising eternal love to each other. If anything, Mitchell seems more... distant.

Which is just as well. I'm not here for a Christmas romance. Or rather, that's not why I was sent here. Better to actually concentrate on the reason I *am* here. And make sure that, whatever happens, and whatever decision Head Office makes, he's protected. Even by me. Because the last thing I want is to harm him. I know I'd rather quit.

Now all I have to do is find the courage to change my life around.

The next morning I get up early and spend all morning sorting out invoices – paid ones, this time – and nod to

Laura as she comes in to relieve me for lunch, Danny at her side. Leaving my position behind my desk and taking Danny's hand in mine, we decide that a stroll into town is what we need.

I have no aim or agenda, so I'm content to let Danny lead the way and bring me to places Mitchell has taken him to, and meet the town folk, whom Danny is already acquainted with.

And I have to say that Little Kettering is the epitome of the quintessential corner of England – no flagship shops teeming with yobbos in hoodies and baggy jeans worn around the ankles slinking away from the CCTV cameras on the high streets or throwing up on public transport. Instead, fairy lights line the streets and bakeries and antique shops and tearooms are abundant. No fast-food joints here, thank God, but simple, old-fashioned food. It is all so lovely, it actually looks like a location set for a period drama.

There are two bus routes – used mainly by the elderly and schoolchildren. On the weekends the kids go into town to catch a movie or to spend their pocket money, while the elderly all chat amiably about the Good Old Days. Everyone is so laid-back it's refreshing. No one fighting over a seat, no one jabbing you in the ribs because you're taking up their breathing space on the Tube, and most of all, no one looking over their shoulders just in case.

'Look, Mum!' Danny cries, pointing towards the post office. 'Santa!'

I turn my head, and, sure enough, there he is – red suit, white beard and all, distributing presents. He is absolutely huge. And cheesy beyond hope. But the kids love him.

My own memories of Santa Claus are very vague, but

this guy is… how to describe him? Adorable wouldn't even begin to swing it. You can tell he's – get this – actually happy to be there, talking to the kiddies on his lap, promising all sorts of lovely presents – if they've been behaving, that is.

And then he beckons Danny over. 'You, over there, young man!' he bellows in our direction. 'Have you been good?'

Danny's face lights up when he realises Santa is addressing him. My little boy is so clever and mature that I sometimes forget how young he really is. And that he still, despite everything, believes in Santa. My nose starts to tingle and I look away, but only for a brief moment, because I want to see the sheer happiness on his face as he climbs up onto Santa's knees.

'So, what do you want for Christmas, young man?' he asks.

Danny thinks about it and cups his hands to deliver his secret wish into Santa's ear.

Santa stops, and scratches his beard. 'Is that so?'

Danny nods.

'Are you sure you wouldn't want something like a bicycle, or a toy tractor?'

Danny shakes his head. 'No, thank you, Santa. See what you can do, okay?'

Santa looks at him, and then his eyes rest on me. 'Yes, son. I'll see what I can do. What about your mum then?'

I can only imagine what Danny has asked for – a functioning father? His very own family, and I can't bloody give it to him for the life of me. And then I realise everyone has turned my way and is looking at me expectantly. Have I missed something?

'Come on, up you come,' Santa says.

I look behind me, just to make sure, and notice everyone still looking at me expectantly.

'Wha—? Me? No, no, no. Thanks anyway.'

'Come, now, love, there's a whole bunch o' kiddies awaitin'.'

I'm inclined to desist, but everyone is urging me on, so rather than be a party pooper, I make a fool of myself by leaning against Santa, embarrassed.

'Come on, love, don't be shy.'

'But I'm heavy,' I protest.

'Nonsense. You're as light as a fairy. Now, what can I get you this lovely Christmas?'

I huff. This is ridiculous. What can he get me? 'I just want Danny to be happy forever,' I whisper, thinking that not even Santa could grant Danny his wish.

14

An Early Christmas Gift

The next day I spend my lunch break in the village looking for gifts for Danny's Christmas birthday, but I also find something for Jeremy to thank him for taking care of Danny so well. Shopping is difficult for someone you don't know, but I suspect, as he is elderly and single, that he'll appreciate a hamper with fresh, good old-fashioned Cornish products, like proper, homemade pasties, authentic yarg, stargazy pie, hevva cake, saffron buns, Cornish Mead, etc. All real stuff, not the tourist package.

For Sally, who works long, hard shifts directing her staff and who could use some time to self-pamper, I choose some products like lavender-oil-based shower gel, some kiwi skin scrub, beauty creams, a loofah sponge and a gorgeous bath robe. Something to start her off with.

For Laura, I get the complete set of *Poldark* novels (she's obsessed) of which I've seen a paperback copy stashed under the front desk counter. These people have helped me out, taking care of my son, to me the most precious person in the world, so I'm hoping to get it right for them this Christmas.

And for Mitchell? What do I get him? How do you shop for a man you barely know and yet... care for? He's not much of a fashion follower, nor does he wear cologne or ties. Having been single for most of my life, I am positively rubbish at buying gifts for men. Especially a man I'm interested in. I have no idea. I've checked upstairs and he's already got the complete set of CDs of his favourite bands, and I don't know who else he likes. I settle on a DVD of *It's a Wonderful Life* for him, in memory of that night that was an almost-date. I hope he will at least get the irony of my gift.

I know I'm getting way ahead of myself, but if I could, I'd get him a brand-new life. A new job he loves, a new home, rather than a suite in an inn. And a future with me. Not that I'm saying that would be a good gift for him. It would be, for me, though.

As I'm debating this, I round the corner onto Little Kettering High Street, catching a glimpse of – you guessed it – Mitchell himself, coming straight at me. I don't know why, but I panic and duck into a pub, hoping he hasn't seen me.

In through the doors, the day plunges into the darkest of nights, and I blink, momentarily losing my bearings. I grope my way to a tiny table in the darkest corner, hoping he doesn't decide to stop in for a drink. But, of course, the door swings open and in he comes, strutting across the floor, like Ross Poldark on Trenwith land, and over to a table where the woman from the other night at the movies – Abby – is waiting for him with two pints of Guinness.

I hunker down into my seat, hoping he won't notice me as I watch him rest his elbows on the small table, studying the woman closely. She places a hand on his arm and is talking to him in dulcet tones.

Mitchell takes a sip of his beer and quietly surveys the rest of the patrons, so I sink lower into my seat and hide behind my menu, even if I know I've done nothing wrong. It's not that I've followed him in here or am spying on him. When the coast is clear and he is once again in deep conversation with her, I make my escape.

As I'm doing so, my mobile pings inside my pocket.

Rosie, I miss you. Call me. Mark. Xxx

As if. Four and a half hours away, assuming he hasn't moved back to his beloved Manchester, and almost ten years later of this on and off communication system, and he still manages to rattle me.

I am loath to put the Christmas presents under the tree, even for Danny's sake, because if any of our prized guests help themselves, Danny will be heartbroken, But I still want to give him – and the inn – some festive cheer, so I leave Laura at Reception and scout around in the supply storage room for some empty boxes – which I find in abundance. In the semi-darkness of the room, I start making mock presents with all the different kinds of wrapping paper I have left over and once I'm done, I haul them over to the tree. I stack them up neatly, the smallest ones on top. There. That looks very Christmassy.

'Can I add my pressies to yours?' comes a voice behind my back.

I turn, and there is Mitchell, on his haunches, with a bag full of gifts. 'What? Oh, sorry, these are fake,' I inform him, and his face falls. It's like Scrooge waking up elated on Christmas morning but instead finding out he's missed it after all.

'Oh. Well, in that case,' he says, retrieving his own packages, and disappears down the hall into his office.

'Again, that one could use a kick in the right direction,' Sally says with a smirk as she passes by.

'What do you mean?'

She wipes her face and gives me a Be Serious look.

'What?' I ask innocently.

'The whole village knows you two are going to end up together eventually. Seize the day – grab happiness by the horns. Go for it.'

'You're mistaken, Sally. I'll soon be leaving.'

'Yeah? Some great job awaiting you, too?'

I sigh. 'I wish. Susan, my boss, calls me Rosie Miss Nobody behind my back.'

Sally's mouth falls open. 'And you let her?'

I shrug. 'Calling her out would mean jeopardising someone else's job.'

'It would jeopardise hers. Good!'

I twist my mouth in resignation. I know Sally's right, but I don't want to rock the boat. Not if Danny and our livelihood is in it.

'You have got to stand up more for yourself, missy,' she scolds me gently.

'I know. I know I should be more assertive. I'm working on it.'

'You do that,' she says. 'And don't let Mitchell push

you around either. He's as good as gold but sometimes he doesn't know his own place.'

'Tell me about it.'

'But *your* place, Rosie, is here.'

I look up at her.

'Oh, come on, Rosie. Wouldn't it be your dream to settle in a breath-taking village like this? Out of that filthy city? And think about how happy Danny would be.'

I smile at her choice of words. Sally and I are so similar, she could be the sister I never had.

She pushes off with a groan, 'Gotta go. And remember – seize the day. I'm keeping my eye on you.'

I smile at her. She is truly lovely.

'Rosie, put on your worst clothes,' Mitchell says as he saunters up to the desk with a smile that warms not only my cockles, but my entire soul. This man is a mystery to me. One minute he's angry and the next he manages to cheer up completely.

'Shouldn't you be saying "Put on your best"?'

He shakes his head. 'Nope – the absolute worst you've got. My surprise is ready.'

I've had all night to wonder about it, and still I have no idea what to expect. And I'm still wondering what he was doing with Abby in that pub.

'What is it?' I ask again, warily, still not convinced he's not found me out. With him, you never know.

He grins. 'Not telling you. Be ready in ten minutes.'

'But the desk… Danny…'

'Laura can mind the desk, and Danny is coming with us, of course.'

Meaning it's child-friendly inasmuch that he isn't about to throw me off the cliff in front of Danny. Which is much more than I deserve, at the moment, so, good enough for me.

The surprise, I surmise as we are winding through the High Street in Little Kettering, is on the other side of town, and I'm not allowed to ask any questions, but Danny is tittering, holding his little hands in front of his mouth to stop from blurting out answers to my questions. I'm so not used to getting surprises that I can hardly contain myself.

'No clues, Danny,' Mitchell says with a grin. 'You promised, remember?'

Danny nods, his eyes twinkling with mischief. What on earth are these two plotting?

And then, at the end of the road, right before an iffy-looking garage, he brakes and they both slide out. I swear I feel like one of those guys in the mafia movies, just before they're sent to sleep with the fishes.

'Come on, Rosie,' he says gently, taking my hand, and I follow them through a tiny door.

The interior is dark and gloomy, but then Mitchell flicks a switch, and I gasp.

There are tables everywhere, and each and every one of them has red chunks or slabs on them. Fresh clay. There is a pottery wheel and... a kiln!

'How...?'

'Danny told me about your passion for throwing pottery.'

'Oh, my God...'

'You can come here whenever you want. I met with the owner today who let it to me for a few months with a renewable contract. You can have it for as long as you want.'

For as long as I want? What does this mean? Is his job offer independent of everything else? Of course it is. I saw the way he and Abby were looking at each other in the pub. If he feels nothing for me, as I now understand, how will I be able to stay on here?

I look between Mitchell and Danny, who are beside themselves with glee. Despite myself and my doubts and worries, I finger the clay, my hands already itching to get dirty.

'There's a makeshift kitchen with a kettle through here, and a fire while you wait for your goods to be…' he grins at his own joke '… fired.'

Fired. I wish he'd not use that word. He's being adorable and my conscience is killing me.

I look up to the neon lights hanging from the ceiling, in the hope that my tears will stay inside my eyes where they belong.

'Danny…?' Mitchell says. 'Why don't you go and switch the kettle on in the kitchen, mate? Be right there.'

Danny eyes us both, understands that something is up, and obeys.

At the sound of the door closing, Mitchell takes a step forward and weaves his fingers through mine.

'Thank you… for this…' I manage. 'It means so much to me. But I really don't deserve it, Mitchell…'

'Are you finally going to tell me your secret?' he whispers. 'I know it's eating you alive.'

It is, and I can't stand it any longer. And I burst into sudden, stupid tears.

He sighs. 'Why don't you just talk to me, Rosie? I promise you you'll feel much better afterwards.'

'Oh, I doubt that,' I hiccup, trying to suppress my sobs.

'Is it about Danny?' he prompts.

Is it? Sort of, if you consider that I won't be able to put any food in my baby's belly, unless I ruin Mitchell's life.

'Is he unwell?'

'No, he's perfectly healthy…'

'Are you unwell?'

I shake my head.

He pulls me in closer. 'Do you need money? I can help you, Rosie. Let me help.'

He has money to give. And he'd give it to me. All this makes the situation even worse. One, because he shouldn't be having any spare money anywhere, according to my calculations, and two, he shouldn't be so kindly offering it to me, the woman commissioned to destroy him.

'No, it's not that, Mitchell,' I moan. 'But thanks anyway, for offering…'

He's ducking to look into my eyes, his thumbs gently wiping my tears away. Oh, God, could he be any sweeter? Can I feel any more unworthy of his trust? How can I possibly accept his offer of a job, and of this place, knowing what's looming up ahead?

'Then how can I help you?'

I shrug. 'I don't need anything. I just need a break, that's all.'

'A break from work?'

'A break… from my life.'

'You don't have to help out during your own holidays, Rosie. As a matter of fact, why don't you stop worrying about the place? It'll be fine. And you can stay as long as you want.'

Oh, could he be any kinder? Could I deserve him any less?

'No,' I sniff, 'I'm fine. I want to help.'

'All right, then. Now how about putting this baby in motion? I'll go make a cuppa and bring Danny out to see his mum working miracles.'

'More like monsters.' I titter nervously. 'I haven't done anything in years.'

'So? It's like riding a bicycle, isn't it?'

I shrug. 'More like practice makes perfect.'

'Well, you sit yourself down here and start mucking around.'

'Okay,' I concede.

A moment later when they come back, I've already cut a small slab of clay off and am slowly adding water to it, hesitant and actually quite horrified seeing the trouble Mitchell has gone to just to organise this.

It's a good thing Danny is here, or I'd actually be daydreaming a *Ghost* scene repeat, Patrick Swayze's slippery fingers intertwining with Demi Moore's in one of the hottest Hollywood scenes ever. But Danny and Mitchell are in the clay guck up to their elbows, disregarding each and every one of my suggestions and laughing. Mitchell has his head thrown back while Danny is actually shrieking with delight as the table turns and the clay collapses onto itself. And I just know I am way luckier than Demi.

15

Ding Dong Merrily on High

When Mitchell saunters into the office on December 22nd, I can hardly contain myself, clapping my hands together. That's me. I have the most extraordinary ability to pick myself up. My shrink used to call it Reactive Depression. 'Are you ready for tonight?' I ask.

His eyes widen in surprise, but then his brow creases. 'For...?'

'The carolling.'

He looks at me, realising I'm not joking, and laughs. 'Oh, I won't be coming.'

'What? Why?'

He shrugs and slides me a wry glance. 'I can't sing to save myself.'

'It doesn't matter. It's the spirit that counts.'

'Besides, you don't want me around. I'm the closest thing to Scrooge that you'll ever meet. I don't do Christmas.'

Of course. Being dumped at Christmas Eve and all that.

We kind of linger, skirting around the subject, but it's not the right moment.

He coughs. 'So, what have you got planned for Danny's birthday tomorrow?'

'Presents. A cake.' And then I have a thought. Will it be enough? Should I organise something more special, something completely unforgettable to mark our time in Cornwall?

'What's that frown, Rosie? What is it?'

'Huh? Oh. I just want to make sure that his birthday will be memorable. I haven't been spending much time with him lately and I don't want him to feel abandoned or something.'

'He knows he's the love of your life,' Mitchell says softly before he coughs and adds, 'And... how is Danny with not spending Christmas with his...?' Mitchell asks.

'Dad? Mark's only seen him a few times, maybe ten, tops. My mum keeps hoping that one day he'll magically appear after all these years and... well, you know how mums are.'

Mitchell grins. 'For a few years. I'm an orphan.'

I can feel my face fall with a thud to the ground. And then I can't help but ask myself, did he grow up in an institution, or had he found a loving family? There are so many things I want to know about him.

What does one say in these cases? Sorry? Or, 'If they didn't want you, then you haven't missed much'? Damned if I know, so I keep my mouth shut, my eyes holding his until he breaks the silence with a chuckle.

'What?' I ask.

He shrugs, shaking his head as if to dismiss his thoughts. 'No, it's nothing.'

'Tell me.'

He looks up, and it's enough to glue me to my spot. 'I… was just wondering… how people meet. Or rather, *why* they meet. Is it fate, or does the universe not give a damn and things just happen haphazardly?'

'Why… do you ask?'

He takes a step towards me, now serious. 'Because… ever since you stepped into my inn… I can't stop thinking about one thing.'

I chuckle despite myself. I do that, when I'm nervous. Laugh like an idiot. 'About how "ruinous" I am?'

His brow furrows. 'What?'

'You told Danny that I was ruinous.'

Mitchell laughs. 'I actually said "luminous".'

'Luminous? Me? Oh!'

'Yes, you, luminous. And there's more, Rosie…'

'What's that…?'

But he doesn't respond, and as I watch, he takes my face in his hands and ducks to touch his lips to mine in the most tender of kisses.

Without thinking, I reach up and wrap my arms around his neck, and he deepens the kiss, pulling me up against his chest. Which is rock solid, wide and inviting, in case you're wondering.

Oh my God, I can't believe this is happening between us. Never had I ever thought that the grumpy Irishman would ever find his way to my lips. I can't even begin to describe the electrical charge zapping through me, causing my heart to skip, hop and sing.

When he pulls back (no, no, no!), he licks his bottom lip and grins, and for the first time, I notice that one of his front teeth is crooked. But, somehow, it only adds to his charm, because he isn't a picture-perfect magazine model with regular features, but a real live man with lovely, endearing flaws.

His eyebrows have a life of their own, dark and winged, and his eyes, which in the ray of sun streaming through the window, have these faint but adorable little smile wrinkles at the corners. And I learn that his hair, that mop of dark, loose curls, really is *tickle-me-soft* to the touch. He smells clean and fresh. And his kisses make my knees buckle.

As I brave a look up into his eyes, he grins down at me.

'Wow...' he breathes. 'You sure are somethin', Ms Anderson.'

I'm barely able to stand now, all the while trying to get my body back under control, because it is still singing like a live wire after that kiss. I want to jump around like I'm on a pogo stick, leap and bound over skyscrapers (not that there are any here, thank goodness), swing from vines (ditto) and belt out a Tarzan call at the top of my lungs. But instead I blush and mumble something along the lines of *So are you, Mr Fitzpatrick*. You'd think I'd come up with a better retort, but to be fair, come on, even you didn't see that one coming, did you?

But I need to anchor myself to reality. The smooch was parallel-universe amazing, but what about Abby? Are they an item? And how to find out without asking directly, which would make me look like an idiot at this stage?

'So,' I say, disentangling myself with great discipline from him when instead I wanted to climb onto his back and be his second skin forever. 'You'll come carolling, then?' If for nothing, I want to see if he brings Abby along.

'Will it make you happy?'

'Yes.'

He grins before he drops another delicious kiss onto my mouth. 'Then I'll come carolling.'

'Excellent. You'll love it, you'll see.' And so will I, unless he shows up with *her*.

I've planned the carolling evening to death, but an hour later, I'm an absolute wreck. The last thing I want to do is make a dog's dinner of it for everyone.

'Laura, have we got everything under control? The stew and stuff ready for tonight? They'll be freezing and starved when we get back.'

'Yep.'

'And the cheese and crackers and crudités while we're waiting for everyone to show up?'

'Yes.'

'Mints to soothe their poor throats?'

'Yeah. We're good on all fronts,' she answers as she scoops up her bag. 'See you later.'

'Bye. And thank you!' I call after her. Then I turn to Mitchell, rubbing my hands. 'I can't wait.'

He stops to watch me with a grin. 'You really are excited, aren't you, Rosie?'

'Like a five-year-old.'

'Awh, that's so sweet…'

'I can't even imagine Christmas without carols. It's like…'

He puts down his registers and moves to stand before me, taking my hands in his, a sexy grin playing at his lips. 'Like love without kisses?'

My cheeks go red-hot at the mere thought. 'Sort of.'

'Well, then if that's the case,' he murmurs, nuzzling the side of my face, raining tiny kisses on my skin, 'then I want in...'

'Hey, I forgot—' Laura's voice reaches my brain. She's come back, and I hadn't even noticed, lust-blasted as I am. 'Oops,' she whispers, tiptoeing out.

I push Mitchell away and he chuckles, pulling me back into his embrace. 'Look at you, my prim and proper lady. You're like one of those eighteenth-century heroines.'

I look up, confused. 'Doesn't it bother you?'

'Doesn't what bother me?'

I lift my hands to my surroundings. 'I work for you. Well, at least temporarily.'

He takes my hands once again, drawing me close. 'I wake up, knowing I'm going to see your face. I have breakfast with Danny every morning. What is there to bother me? Hmmm...?' he murmurs against my lips, and I can't even remember what the problem was in the first place.

The evening turns out to be much colder than expected, but everyone has turned up, including the three celebrities who live in the area, i.e. Nina Conte with her gorgeous husband (was it the Cornish air that attracted such beauty?) and three children, Chloe, Ben and baby Sadie. Chatting away and giggling with them are the Amore sisters, Natalia and Yolanda, respectively a journalist and a celebrity chef and mother of twin girls who are slightly older than Danny.

'Thanks for inviting us, Rosie, this is so lovely!' Nina Conte exclaims as her son Ben runs over to make friends with Danny, and under my ever-watchful gaze, they're off to help hand out carol sheets.

'Yes, absolutely,' Natalia Amore adds, her eyes round with delight. 'It looks magical!'

'Thank you both for being here,' I chime. I want to tell them how I've literally devoured their writing and how awesome I think they both are, but in all probability many people have already told them. 'You must be really busy.'

'On the contrary,' Natalia says. 'My sister Yolanda is always the one to sort Christmas out so I've got all the time in the world.'

'Well, then the two of you can come over to mine and sort me out, too,' Nina says. 'I haven't even started yet!'

'At least you have that gorgeous man to help you,' Natalia says, nodding towards an effectively striking man who is cradling their baby.

All are in a festive mood, all practising their scales. It seems like more than half the local population is here, each and every one carrying glow sticks, candles and flashlights as laughter and song soon fills the freezing air, little clouds of the revellers' breath dissolving above our heads.

Danny and I distribute the snacks as we wait for the stragglers to arrive, while Mitchell, rubbing his hands, mingles with the townspeople, hugging and laughing with a friend here and there. Although he's not one of them by birth, Mitchell fits in perfectly.

The road into town is festooned with bright Christmas fairy lights that weave in and out of the trees, creating one continuous dazzle of lights that reflect in the snow and on the icicles hanging from the frozen branches. It truly looks like the set of a Christmas movie.

'You're good for L.K., you know that?' Mitchell muses.

I can't help but grin. 'I think it's the other way around.'

'Rosie, are you still thinking about my offer? Will you accept the position of manager?'

And my spirits are dampened again. 'But... what about you? Is your... project...?'

He takes a sip of his brew. 'It's going well,' he says with a cheeky smile.

'Oh, good to know,' I say, fishing for more info, but a group of carollers have reached us, wrapping their arms around Mitchell who, with one last grin, lets himself be carried away by the throng.

He's got plans. Where is he going, then? Back to Ireland? And why would I even consider staying if he's going?

A loud booming voice covers the rest and everyone laughs. I look up to find the source. Mitchell was right. He can't carry a tune in a bucket, so when everyone starts teasing him, he shuts up and continues to do the catering instead, thank goodness.

Danny helps him, and every time Mitchell gives him a pat on the back or praise, my little boy simply glows, and I want to reach out and smack a grateful kiss onto Mitchell's sexy mouth in front of everyone. But I know that if I even start, they'll need a crowbar to get me off him.

And Abby? She did show up, but on another bloke's arm, and if my eyes didn't deceive me, there was quite a bit of snogging going on in the bathroom at The Trawler's Net, i.e. the pub in the centre of town. I suppose they preferred to make their own music.

★

After a fun night of carolling, the villagers return to the Old Bell Inn with us. Laura puts on a Christmas CD and everyone gets busy. Some set the table, others put huge pots of stew onto the Aga to heat, while others get the desserts and drinks ready. It's like one big happy family and, despite the fact that I'm only passing, I feel at home. More than I ever have in London.

The stew is delicious and nutritious, just what we need after an evening stamping our feet while belting out the very best (and the very worst) of our Christmas repertoire around the village.

I look up from my bowl of soup with a grin. Everyone is happy tonight, especially Danny, who is in Christmas heaven. Where else could we actually have this community spirit? Where else would the village vicar know your name and nickname?

The next morning, in a hurry as usual, on my way down I grab a Bakewell tart from atop Mitchell's fridge and shove it into my mouth. I could eat a horse today.

But on the staircase, my mouth registers a rotten taste – the worst I've ever experienced. I spit out what's left of the Bakewell (not much, at this point) and am shocked to find that it's green. Good God, what is he trying to do, kill me? I go back to the room and put them in the bin so Danny won't eat them and then go back downstairs.

As I am sitting in the dining room ploughing my way through a stack of pancakes (romance makes the heart grow fonder, but also hungrier) and eyeing the door waiting for Mitchell to show up any minute now, I suddenly feel ill. It has to be the bloody green Bakewell tart. I feel I'm actually going to be sick right in the middle of the dining room, so I clap a hand over my mouth as a few onlookers stare at me, horrified, and then at their breakfasts. Some actually get up as if a spit-firing dragon had just appeared on their table.

Shit, shit, shit. In one stroke I've just ruined the hotel's only saving grace! What to do? How to save the hotel from crumbling to pieces now?

As I'm desperately looking for a way to put it right, Russell rushes in, wiping his hands on a tea towel, a look of concern on his face as he stoops to me, a hand on my shoulder. 'Rosie, are you okay? What happened?'

The crushed look on his face, of confidence smashed to pieces, is the last thing I need. I can't let this man – or Mitchell – lose their reputation. And then I get an idea. A crazy one, I'll admit, but it's all I've got. I wipe my mouth and struggle to my feet, perspiration coating my face.

'Sorry, people,' I call out with a smile. 'My doctor warned me about morning sickness! And this food is just soooo good, I just can't seem to stop eating! It's amazing, isn't it?' I prompt. 'Please, folks, a round of applause for our incredibly talented Chef Russell Jones!'

And while Russell is bowing and grinning at centre stage, his reputation still intact, I make a surreptitious dash for the nearest exit. That was a close call.

But did I really say what I said? That I was pregnant? Jesus, the lengths I'll go to, just to save this place from tanking. Mitchell Fitzpatrick, you owe me big time.

I rush to the toilet downstairs and heave up the remnants of what I can now safely call Rotten Cake. Why the hell would Mitchell keep that stuff? I wash and wipe my face, now feeling slightly more settled. That was a close call.

It's still too early for Danny to wake, so I go through my stack of this week's bookings to make sure everyone has arrived and has been checked in properly, but Laura shoos me away. 'Go have some breakfast, I bet you haven't even eaten yet,' she says.

'Thanks, Laura, you are a shining superstar!' I call as I blow her kisses. In truth, I'm still feeling a bit iffy, and all I can think of is what a fantastic Christmas this will be, against all odds.

I'd like nothing better than to take Mitchell and Danny to spend Christmas with my parents in Birmingham, eat a traditional dinner, sit by a fire that belongs to a home and not an inn. But I know I'm getting ahead of myself and I'm not going to make the same mistake I did with Mark, when I'd assumed that when a man shows you a modicum of interest, he's actually *interested* in you. Not always true, and I'd learnt it the hard way.

But at least we've managed to make Christmas dinner at the Old Bell Inn a special one.

Everyone on staff is walking around cheerily stopping to chat to guests, which I always encourage. Nothing like a friendly face to talk to when you're away from home.

After dinner, Mitchell and I go for a stroll down to the village church, hand in hand, which in itself is a novelty as Mark never liked to hold hands.

But Mitchell? He is everything I always wanted. Who knew? And his respecting my indecision about the job without pressing me is even more testament to how honourable the man is. And I want to help him with his business more than ever. We also need to have some sort of chat about his numbers. And if it will help distract us both from this pull between us, there's no time like the present. But he beats me to it.

'Oh, before I forget. The first part of your Christmas present...' he says, pulling a small box out of his coat pocket. No, it's not that kind of box – I know what you're thinking! It's bigger than his fist. I stare at it, then at him. 'Open it,' he whispers. 'It's just a silly thing.'

I gently peel the shiny red paper back. It's a snowstorm. And inside, a replica of the Old Bell Inn. 'Oh my gosh, Mitchell...'

'May all your storms be bubble-sized.' He grins, leaning in for a kiss.

'Thank you. I'll keep it with me. Forever.'

'I know you will. Part two of my surprise will have to wait.'

'Oh?'

'What do you desire most in life, Rosie?' he says softly, wrapping an arm around my shoulder.

I shrug. 'For Danny to be happy, healthy. Grow well. For you to be happy.'

He stops, his eyes searching mine, with that mischievous grin on his face. 'And what about for yourself?'

Me? That's a good one. What do I want for myself? 'To be a good mother,' I answer, and he laughs.

'What about Rosie before Danny was born?'

He's right, I know. I'm a broken record as far as Danny is concerned, but to be honest, the idea of a personal life has never struck me – not until meeting Mitchell, that is. If I could wave a magic wand, I'd go back in time and not apply for my current job. And tell Susan to stuff it. But then I would never have met Mitchell.

'Well, the pottery studio is more than enough, to be honest,' I answer earnestly.

He smiles. 'The pottery studio does have a commercial licence. You could open your very own shop tomorrow, if you wanted to.'

'What? Here?'

'What's keeping you?'

'Well, first, I'd need to go back to my parents and fetch all my backlog. I haven't made anything in ages, and I'm not all that sure I haven't lost my mojo.'

'Of course you haven't. Once an artist, always an artist.'

What does all this mean? The fact that he has gone to all the trouble to sort this out indicates strong feelings on his behalf. Or am I reading too much into this?

I caress his face, wondering what I did to deserve all this. Years and years of pining over Mark, who never cared. And now? Karma really does exist, in its own twisted way. Because now that I've finally found The One, I can't have him.

Mitchell steps closer, his eyes glistening as he takes my hands, bringing them to his mouth. I make to move away, but he ducks to kiss me.

'I know, Rosie, that making life-changing decisions is tough. I'm here for you.'

Now *that* is heart-warming. That is exactly what I need to hear. Leaving my job isn't going to be easy, of course. 'There's a lot of uncertainty, ahead, for me,' I say.

He takes my hand and kisses it. 'I'll be with you every step of the way.'

'Thank you. Then I guess I accept your job offer.' And heaven help us all.

'That's not necessary, Rosie. I'll provide for you.'

Provide? I shiver at the thought. 'Oh, no, I couldn't! I've always supported myself, Mitchell. I can't have it any other way.'

He rests his forehead against mine, and takes my lips in a luscious kiss. 'We'll talk about that later. I think it's time we spoke to Danny, what do you think?'

I search his face. He means it. He really, really means it. This is monumental. Apart from Danny, when has anything this good ever happened to me? I can scarcely believe my luck.

'Uhm, can we wait a little while longer? Tomorrow is his birthday and I want it to be all about him.'

Mitchell grins and takes both my hands. 'Of course, Rosie. From now on, it's going to be all about family. And soon, you'll meet my own daughter, yes?'

I smile. 'I can't wait.'

'Neither can I,' he says, and leads me to his office where he continues to kiss me, and in a moment, something changes. We've shifted into a more urgent gear. Can it be he already wants to...? I know for a fact that I have been thinking of little else lately. Is it wrong to sleep with someone you barely know, even if the attraction is overwhelming?

I gasp and swallow at the same time. It's here, the moment I've been waiting for. And now I don't know how to act. I think of all the cool characters I've seen in movies or read about in books. How would Bridget Jones react? Either jump his bones or possibly puke with nerves – none of which are an option here.

But I don't have to think about it at all, because he's taken both my hands to his chest, where I can feel an incredible *boom-ba-boom* coming from his heart. So I'm not the only one, thank God. Only *he* manages to act upon his feelings and not sit there like a bump on a log. Me? I'm frozen, like a deer in headlights.

As I watch, caught midway between sheer lust and absolute stupor, he shifts so that his face is a couple of inches from mine again. I'm looking into his eyes, while his travel between mine and my mouth, back and forth, as if waiting for the right moment, like when you're playing skipping rope with your friends and it's your turn to jump in.

And me, looking like this! I swallow again, now in pure, heart-stopping panic. I should be cursing myself for not having reapplied my lip balm, because my lips must feel like sandpaper in this cold weather. That makes for some kiss.

But all the same, he doesn't back away in horror. If anything, he takes my chin in his hand and gently tilts his head to fit against mine again in what is the most... delicious kiss on earth or in heaven. It's got to be heaven, because I'm flying, soaring over the clifftops and enjoying it like nothing else.

'Rosie, sweetheart. I don't know if you've realised it yet but... I'd do anything to see you happy. *Anything...*'

Standing before him, on the abyss of something so monumental, it's as if I'm being swallowed whole, into this unfamiliar world of longing and reciprocated attraction. I'm unprepared, as I didn't expect this to happen. Not anymore, and certainly, not here, with Mitchell who, beyond any of my wildest hopes, is attracted to me just as much. And for a moment, just a moment, I hesitate.

'Do you want to wait? I'll understand, what with all that's going on,' he whispers against my mouth.

'No, no more waiting,' I whisper back, my hands on his slim hips, pulling him to me.

His hands are splayed across my back, holding me as if I was the most fragile, the most precious thing in the world, and he rests his forehead against mine, looking into my eyes, and he smiles. 'I've been dying to make love to you, Rosie…'

I smile back. 'Me, too, Mitchell.'

He lays me down gently, lifting my arms to kiss me everywhere, slowly, thoroughly, his lips hot on my skin, until, after almost nine long years, I can't wait another minute.

16

The Night Before Christmas

On the morning of Christmas Eve, I wake up in Danny's bed, cradling him.

This is such a different scenario compared to last night's. Mitchell and I made love, and I'm blown away by it. I never thought that I would actually ever have sex again with anyone, let alone with someone so... generous. It was all about me, whereas, when I was with Mark, it was never about me at all.

But Mitchell is tender, passionate and he even managed to make me laugh when instead I thought I'd be an absolute disaster. What a great night. I had no idea that pulling an all-nighter of sex could get me so galvanised and full of energy. I should be completely wiped out, but I'm not. I'm more energetic, and happier, than I have been in a long, long time.

Flashes of the previous night come back to me, and I find myself blushing and smiling at the same time. I remember everything very vividly; Mitchell's hot mouth searching mine, the warmth of his body as he held me, the raining of his kisses along my jawline... and so much more delicious stuff. I hug myself with a new-found glee, feeling like a teenager.

Mitchell. He is wonderful. Amazing. And, I'm scared to even think it, but I've never, in eight years, felt like this about anyone. Scratch that. Not even Mark made me feel this way, and I was pretty in love with him.

I still can't believe Mitchell and I have slept together, and that we are actually an item. After all, we've only known each other a couple of weeks. But they have been very intense weeks of constantly being stuck to each other's side for hours on end. And even when not on duty, Mitchell would always come looking for me and find an excuse to just chat. Of course, I'm going to take it slow, and not throw myself into it. But something deep inside tells me he's The One.

I realise, in retrospect, how obvious it must have been to everyone else that we were developing feelings for each other. How could anyone, in fact, have missed my blushing and gushing? Or the way Mitchell leans in, an ear-to-ear grin on his face as he whispers all sorts of nonsense in my ears that has me in a fit of giggles more often than not? It's the silliest I've ever been in my life... and the most fun I've ever had with a bloke.

In half an hour I'll see him again. His eyes will reflect our lovely secret. And maybe we can steal a kiss before anyone else surfaces.

As I dry my hair, I imagine happy moments with him, most of them taking place between the beach and a house we share, strewn with his artwork, my pottery, and Danny's and his daughter's toys.

Mitchell must have carried me back from the sofa in his office to my room as I was wiped out, so I'm grateful of his discretion. And the fact that he remembers Danny's birthday. There's a present on Danny's side of the bed, with a card. The envelope simply reads: *Happy Birthday to the best mate ever. Love, Mitchell.*

I stretch, a huge smile on my face. Today my little boy is eight years old. I've asked Maggie, Alex's mum from the local bakery, to bake him a huge, horse-shaped cake, and I got him loads of presents from various shops in town – mostly from Bigsby's Toy Shop. He will be *over the moon.*

In his little bed, Danny stirs, yawns and sits up, eyes already wide, my little angel. 'Good morning, darling! Happy birthday!' I chime, wrapping him up in a tight embrace. How many times will I ever be able to say that again? Every moment seems to flee and never return, so I cherish every single second with him.

He wraps his own little arms around me and kisses my cheek. 'Thanks, Mum!'

And then he notices Mitchell's presents. He reads the writing on the bag and grins. 'Can I open them in front of him, Mum?'

'Of course, love! We'll just call him to see if he's available.' I dial his number, feeling a rush of happiness. This day has started off in the best of ways.

'Good morning, Rosie,' Mitchell answers with a voice I've never heard. 'How are you, and how is Danny doing?'

I grin, feeling the heat as I blush. 'He wants to thank you for the presents, and open them when you're available.'

'I'm available now. See you in your room in a minute?'

Now that is a scenario I have imagined a thousand times.

'Sure.' I hang up. 'Get dressed, darling. Mitchell will be here in a minute.'

Danny nods, his own cheeks flushed with excitement. It's funny, the effect this man has on both of us. 'And can we have breakfast together?' he asks. 'With Mitchell?'

'Well, let's ask, shall we?' I answer as I get up to put the kettle on and heat a skillet for the bacon, and start beating some eggs for good measure. I pop in some toast as well and start setting the breakfast bar. It feels funny, setting the table for three. I have never done that before, and find myself reaching for the nicest mugs and plates. I could actually do this forever.

A knock on the door makes me jump, and Danny dashes to open it. 'Mitchell!' he cries and they high-five each other.

'Happy birthday, mate!' Mitchell exclaims, ruffling his hair. And to me, he simply smiles his special smile, just for me. It carries the solemnity of what is happening between us, but at the same time, the light-heartedness of the way we feel.

'Hi,' I say sheepishly. 'I'm making breakfast. Interested?'

'Hmm, thanks. I am rather peckish.' He takes the plates from me and continues to set the table while I turn down the heat.

'Scrambled okay?' I ask as he is smiling at Danny.

'Great, thanks.'

I put the bacon on the skillet, pour the eggs into a separate pan and start to stir as the toast pops up.

I turn to fish in the fridge for something – anything that will keep my face away from their eyes for the time that it takes me to stop bawling and surreptitiously wipe my eyes. They can't see me like this, a blubbering mess of happiness.

'Coffee or tea, Rosie?'

I start, and then clear my throat. 'Tea, please. But you don't have to do that.'

He drops a tea bag into the prettiest mug and waits, squeezing it out and putting it on a small dish, all the while studying my face. I can only hope my eyes aren't still moist.

'Catching a cold, Rosie?' he asks with an endearing twinkle in his eye. 'Your nose is red.'

'Oh, uhm, yes,' I say, grateful for the chance to sniffle without worrying anyone.

'This looks good, Rosie, thank you. Next time I'll cook breakfast for you two,' he says, eyeing Danny to see his reaction. Mitchell is so considerate of my son.

We all dig in, Danny munching happily on his toast, and Mitchell, who has the appetite of a horse, eats every single thing on his plate. I push my food around, trying to justify my right to happiness with the fact that I was here to spy on him, all the while losing my own argument.

'Not hungry?' he asks me.

'Uhm, not really, no.'

Mitchell finishes his coffee and I can't help but notice the strong hands cradling his mug.

'Danny, do you want to open your present now?'

'Can I?' he asks.

'Of course,' Mitchell and I answer in unison.

'It's a riding helmet! Mitchell, thank you!' he cries and throws himself at him. Mitchell grins and returns his hug.

'That's too much, Mitchell, thank you,' I whisper, and he grins and me and winks.

'Awh, mate, it's my pleasure. Did you look inside the helmet?' he asks.

Danny also looks at him and peers into the helmet. *'Search far and wide, but your next gift is near the hide.* Oh, wow, a treasure hunt?' Danny cries, positively bursting with happiness.

'Is that okay, Rosie? I never got a chance to ask you, what with all that happened last night,' he whispers and I splutter out my tea, barely missing my green jumper.

'Oh, uhm, of course. Thank you, Mitchell. It's a fantastic idea.'

'Can we go, Mum?' he asks.

I wipe my mouth and clear the table while Mitchell fills the sink with hot, soapy water. 'Let's leave these in to soak. We have more important things to do,' he says with a grin.

'Where are we going, Danny?' I ask him.

'Follow me!' he cries, reaching for his coat.

I wrap my jacket around my shoulders and we follow him downstairs and across the courtyard and down the lane to the stables.

Jeremy isn't there yet, or seems to have popped out, because except for the horses, the barn is empty. Danny walks around the tack room, tapping his chin in concentration, then turns to the saddles on the wall, lifting each one.

I eye Mitchell who purses his lips in an effort not to give himself away, but I can tell by the look in his eyes that Danny's very near. In fact, under the last saddle, there is a label that says 'This is the Property of Danny Anderson'.

My hand shoots to my mouth as I shake my head at Mitchell in disbelief, but he takes my hand.

'My very own saddle?' Danny croaks.

'You can't ride without a saddle, can you, Danny? Now look underneath it,' Mitchell says.

Danny obeys, finding a medium-sized package, which he tears open as if his life depended on it.

'Oh, wowee! Mum, look, it's a riding habit! Thanks, Mitchell!'

I start, my eyes swinging to Mitchell. It's too much. Those things are immensely expensive. I open my mouth to protest but he puts his hand on my shoulder.

'What does the label say?' Mitchell asks.

Danny peers inside and reads. '*Twirl, twirl, it's pinned on our second-favourite girl.*'

Their second-favourite girl? I wonder, but Danny marches straight to Mabel's stall and we follow him just in time to see him kiss her nose. 'Hello, lovely. Have you got something for me today?'

Mabel dips her old head, watching him with love-filled eyes as Danny reaches over her side where a bag is hanging. I eye Mitchell who is even more excited than my son. How can I accept all this on Danny's behalf? It is truly too generous. Mark has never given Danny anything, least of all his own time and affection.

Danny opens the bag containing a box, which he places on the nearby trestle table and we both gasp at the same time. 'Riding boots!' he cries, beside himself with joy, which makes two of us. Mitchell knows what Danny wants, and doesn't hesitate to give it him. But I am still incredibly overwhelmed by his generosity. I'm just not used to such gestures from anyone outside my family and Liz, whose gifts I still have hidden in my car.

'Mum, look!' he exclaims, pulling them out of the box. 'Thanks, Mitchell!'

'They should be your size, but we can change them if

not,' Mitchell informs me, then stops. 'Are you okay, Rosie? Did I overdo it?'

I look at Danny who is toeing off his sneakers to try the boots on. 'I just... we're not used to all this...'

Mitchell takes my hand and squeezes it gently in both of his. 'We need to have that conversation later, Rosie,' he whispers.

I look at him and his beautiful, kind face, and nod. Later. Now is not the time.

'Did you look under the boots?' Mitchell asks and I gasp. Surely not more?

Danny inspects his soles, where he finds a small note, and then looks at Mitchell. 'More?'

Mitchell grins and nods as Danny reads the note. '*Your final gift is attached to our number-one favourite girl.* Our favourite girl – that has to be Mum!'

'Me?' I blurt out, taken by surprise as Mitchell and Danny turn to me. 'But I-I haven't got anything stuck to me, have I?'

But Danny is already searching my jacket pockets, patting me down, until he gets to my inside pocket where there is an envelope.

'When did you slip that in?' I whisper as Danny tears it open.

Mitchell chuckles and whispers back, 'While you had your head stuck in the fridge, pretending not to cry.'

I stare at him and then tap his forearm. 'You schemer.'

'Never,' he says simply. 'I've no secrets. What you see is what you get.'

'Oh, wow!' Danny cries for the umpteenth time. 'Mum, he's given me Mabel!'

'Mitchell, thank you for everything, but a horse?' I say once we have saddled her and Jeremy has arrived to lead Danny out of the stall on Mabel's back and into the paddock.

'He and Mabel love each other,' he assures me. 'And I want him to enjoy her as long as she lives. And then, when she leaves us, to soften the blow, we'll get him a new pony.'

'But it's just too much!'

Mitchell leans on the fence, squinting up at the unusually warm December sun, then turns to look into my eyes. 'Okay. It's time for that conversation now, Rosie.'

I steal him a glance, not sure what to say, and he nods, taking my hand again.

'Danny deserves everything I can give him,' he whispers, his words only for me. 'And so do you.'

This is crazy. Unheard of. Is it supposed to be like that, the bloke an absolute sweetheart? I am so not used to his. My brain can't even conjure up the scenario. 'Mitchell, I—'

'I don't want to push anything on you, Rosie, but I have to be honest about how I feel about you. Both of you. Apart from Lola, you two are the best thing that's ever happened to me, and I want to take care of you. If you'll let me.'

I look up into his face, overwhelmed, as he frames my cheeks with his gentle fingers, and bends down to kiss me on the lips. His kiss is gentle, respectful, but at the same time demanding, his fingers now in my hair, his thumb on my chin, lifting my face.

'God, Rosie, I want you again, now, right on this fence,' he whispers, squeezing my hips.

I laugh, trying to compose myself. We are in public, after all, and my son is barely thirty feet away.

'Me, too, Mitchell,' I whisper back, a huge smile bending my face out of shape. 'But we're going to have to take it slow. I'm a little out of practice.'

Because I can't remember the last time my heart beat so loudly, out of control. Who knew we'd end up like this, snogging like there's no tomorrow?

'You and me both,' he chuckles, nuzzling my face, his arms around my hips. And then he pulls back to look into my face.

'You really are luminous, Rosie. You are so sweet and beautiful.'

'I am not,' I protest, then grin. 'Keep going anyway.'

He laughs. 'There's plenty where that came from. Don't forget, we Irish are poets. And lovers.'

I wrap my arms around his neck, getting more confident by the second on the strength of our night together. 'Is that so?'

His smile disappears. 'Jesus, Rosie, don't look at me like that. I'm barely hanging on as it is here.'

Wow. I have that effect on him. On what planet can things like this happen to me, Rosie Miss Nobody? But if this is what a real, kind relationship looks like, and if I can give my heart completely without fear of being hurt, then I'm in. All the way. For as long as it lasts.

When Danny is done with his lesson and brushing Mabel down, he saunters happily into the dining room where I have set a table with blue balloons tied to his chair. On the table nearby lay mine and Liz's gifts.

'Hold it there, missy, you forgot these!' comes a familiar voice at my back.

I turn to see Laura, Alex and Sally, along with Russell

and Annie and all the others, looking for all the world like the Holy Magi with their pile of colourful boxes. Danny slaps his cheeks in astonishment, his blue eyes shining with joy. He's never, not even back at my parents' home, seen all these friends, gifts and boisterousness around him, but he's in his element. Danny has no cousins as I'm an only child, but to look at him now, he is happy just as he is, surrounded by our new, wonderful friends who have taken us under their wing. It is so kind of them.

'That cold of yours getting worse, is it?' Mitchell chuckles into my ear, wrapping his arm around my shoulder in a gesture that doesn't escape Sally who nudges Laura who in turn grins.

I sniff and wipe my eyes again, laughing at my own ridiculousness.

Everyone gathers around my little boy to watch as he opens his gifts, each having so many nice things to say to him. He is definitely coming out of his London shell, my baby, and shows a confidence that not even he knew he had. We had to come to Cornwall to find ourselves... and everything else.

We all sit down to a mega lunch of all his favourite foods, which Russell has prepared. 'I'm only doing this for your kid,' he says as he brings in a huge tray of fried chicken and potato salad, Danny's favourites. 'And because the boss said so.'

Mitchell and Russell exchange glances and grin. It's a good day. The best we've ever had since Danny was born, actually.

After lunch, Annie wheels out the cake – a huge

horse-shaped dream of chocolate and vanilla fudge cream, made by Maggie, Alex's mother.

And that's when Danny leans over to me, arms outstretched, and kisses my cheek in front of absolutely everyone. Two weeks ago he wouldn't have wanted anyone to see me holding his hand to cross the street. 'Thank you, Mum, for all this, and for bringing me here.'

'Oh, my darling, you're very welcome,' is all I can say through my tight throat before he digs into his cake without a care in the world.

'I'm not surprised he said that, Rosie. He loves it here,' Mitchell says as we sit back and watch as Danny, Alex, Russell and, much to my surprise, even Jeremy all try to beat each other at the videogame Russell has bought Danny.

The girls are busy clearing the table from the food and rainbow of wrapping paper scattered around us. They have excluded me from the operations. 'You've done enough,' Sally says with a warning glance Mitchell's way. 'Now just sit down and… enjoy.'

'He is happy,' I sigh, as content as I can ever be.

'And it's all because of you,' he says.

'Me? You guys provided all the entertainment. I did nothing a mother wouldn't do.'

'No, Rosie. Not every mother would.'

I can't tell if he means Diane, or even his own biological mother who had died. But today is such a special day that I don't want to dampen anyone's spirits. Besides, what good is it to only think unhappy thoughts, when around you there is so much love and laughter? I, too, am happy here, and wonder what the future holds.

17

Merry Cornish Christmas

I get up early on Christmas morning to shower and wash my hair as quietly as I can so Danny can sleep longer, but after a few minutes he bounces out of bed, once again his new cheerful self. After a quick breakfast in the kitchenette, we call Liz, leaving my parents for later as they always get up late on Christmas morning. For a moment, I miss being there and having Christmas morning with them, but I am perfectly happy where I am right now.

Danny and I find Mitchell in his office, going through some files. There's no one around but essential cleaning staff on this wonderful, fantastic Christmas morning.

'Hey, Merry Christmas, mate,' he chimes, grabbing Danny's fist and pumping it in the air, then looks up at me with that *I know what you did yesterday* grin.

'Merry Christmas, sweetheart,' he whispers.

'Merry Christmas.' I smile back, so elated I might just about explode with happiness.

'Are you ready for the second part of my surprise?'

'Yes.' Whatever it is, I like it. Especially if it involves him and me. 'But I've already seen it all,' I quip, stifling a giggle.

'Silly.'

'Give me a hint.'

'Uh-uh.'

'Please?'

His eyes are glued to mine, and we've reached stalemate. He's not budging, the cad.

The front door opens and Laura bounces in. 'Merry Christmas!' she chimes and throws herself at us with hugs and kisses.

'Merry Christmas,' Mitchell says. 'What are you doing here? Didn't I give you the day off?'

'Yes, you did, Mr Scrooge. But I came by to drop off my pressies!'

Laura grins at me. 'Ladies first,' she produces a pretty gold and red package. It's a DVD on Cornwall.

'Oh, Laura, thank you,' I gush. And then my throat constricts at such kindness, but before the tears come, I reach down under my desk and thrust my own gift into her arms. 'Merry Christmas, Laura.'

She looks at the huge box, then back at me as she begins to unwrap. And then she gasps. 'Oh, my God, *Poldark*!' she cries, caressing the covers of the complete set of novels – all twelve of them. 'Thank you, Rosie!'

'No, Laura. Thank you. For your kindness, and your friendship.'

Laura's eyes moisten as she looks into mine, and reaches out for a great big hug.

'Listen, Laura, I'm taking Rosie and Danny on an errand,' Mitchell the Mood Killer says. 'We won't be gone long. Can you stay and watch the desk until we get back?'

'Mitchell,' I argue. 'Let the girl go, it's Christmas.'

'We won't be long,' he promises.

Laura looks from him to me, then back at him again as a huge smile lights up her face. 'Of *course*! Take your *time*!'

'Great,' Mitchell says. 'Danny, go upstairs and get your and your mum's coats. I'm going to start the jeep up. Meet you out front in two.'

Danny nods and dashes off, excited as can be.

Laura watches him go and then grabs my hands. 'Tell!'

I laugh. 'Tell what?'

'How was it?'

'How was what?'

She rolls her eyes, almost ready to shake the truth out of me. 'Don't give me any of that – it's as plain as the nose on your faces what you two are up to!'

'Laura, I think you're imagining things,' I lie, a smile twitching at my lips.

She raises her hands in a gesture of surrender. 'All right. I won't pry. But don't think you've fooled me. Or anyone else. Now go,' she says, pushing me away from Reception.

As far as surprises go, I have absolutely no idea what Mitchell's is – not even when we get into Mitchell's nice warm jeep and head down into town.

'Are you going to give me a clue?' I ask.

'Nope.'

'Is it something in town?'

He shakes his head, then slides me a mischievous glance. 'Something on the other side of town.'

I turn to Danny in the back seat. 'What do you know about this?'

He crosses his heart. 'Nothing, Mum, I swear.'

Mitchell grins at him in the rear-view mirror. 'Sorry, mate, I didn't tell you because this is a surprise for you, too.'

It only takes about ten minutes in all to traverse Little Kettering, and before I know it, we are just outside the opposite end of town, climbing a gentle, grassy hill.

'Where are we going?'

He licks his bottom lip and grins, but says nothing more.

I look at him, then look ahead as he pulls on the handbrake and comes around to open my door and help me down, like the best of gentlemen. I look around as my feet touch the ground. And I gasp.

I'm looking at what, at first, look like ruins, but then I realise it's a work in progress: a row of cottages high above the sea, just off the coastal path.

'This is Cove Cottages,' Mitchell chimes, taking my hand and propelling me up gently along with him as he bounds over to the open entrance of one of the houses where tradesmen are working.

'Yorrite, Mitchell?' one of them calls as he's lugging a cement bag.

'Lads, this is Rosie Anderson,' Mitchell says. 'And her son, Danny.'

Like in an AA meeting, they all turn and smile. 'Hi, Rosie. Hi, Danny.'

I smile back, still not entirely sure. Could it be what I'm thinking? How, if he has no money?

'You need to keep him away from here,' one of the men says as he walks by, his belly shaking as he laughs. 'He's working us into the ground – and on Christmas morning!'

Mitchell claps him on the back. 'Work, you? That'll be the day, Bernie. Besides, you're only here because your wives have kicked you out until dinnertime...' And then he turns to me and offers his arm. 'Just for the record, they're not actually working today. They just came to collect their stuff. Come on, let me give you the tour, Rosie.'

'Mum, look, a dog!'

'That's my Mac,' Bernie says. 'You want to play with him? Go on, he's good as gold, aren't ya, Mac?'

'Can I, Mum?' Danny asks me.

'Of course. But stay here out in the open. This is a building site.'

Danny hunkers down to pat the dog's sleek head, and grins. 'Hello, Mac, how are you, boy?'

'He'll be safe in the gardens, Rosie. Let me show you around.'

With one last glance in Danny's direction and his surroundings, I satisfy myself that he is within sight and safe before I follow Mitchell.

Each cottage is deceptively large, with views so unbelievably beautiful, the glistening sea peering in through the big, tall windows. Although still very much a building site at its initial stage, with a little imagination I can see it. The ground floor of each cottage is light and airy. And yet, it will be cosy and warm, begging for a happy couple holding hands by the fire... and a couple of kids. I can already see them, wearing warm woolly jumpers and playing board games, or watching a DVD while munching popcorn.

To the back, the gently rolling hills are blanketed in different shades of green under melting patches of snow. The quintessential English countryside at its best. When ready and furnished, it will be film-worthily perfect.

'Well? What do you think, Rosie?'

I look around, gobsmacked. 'Whose place is this?' I ask, but he just grins, the tip of his cheeky tongue peering through his teeth. I gasp. I was right. 'Is this your… are you…?'

He takes my hands. 'I'm doing it, Rosie. I'm opening my own holiday lets!'

On instinct, I throw my arms around him and pull him to me. 'Oh my God, Mitchell…!'

'No more audits, no more Head Office bloody breathing down my back. Just a small holiday rental gig with four self-catering cottages. I'll soon be my own boss!'

It couldn't be better news. This is what he wants. I'm so happy for him that he won't have to face Head Office. And then I realise that all my efforts to help him have been worth it. But now it's my job that's in actual danger, and I'm still pretty much in Susan's Bad Books until I can clear my position back at HO.

But it was bloody worth it, just to see the smile on Mitchell's face.

But there is always a but. I can't help but wonder: *How*, on his salary, did he manage to even find the deposit for this place, let alone make the mortgage payments?

'It's fantastic, Mitchell. When will it be ready?'

'I'm estimating another year or so. It will be years before I break even and start making a profit, but it's what I've always wanted.'

He's truly like a little boy on Christmas morning. 'I'm so happy for you, Mitchell!' I chime. Boy, I could really get used to this, having his beloved face inches from mine, ready to kiss whenever I want to. I'm on a clifftop in Cornwall with an extraordinary man. Can it get any more romantic?

18

The Christmas Confession

However, I mustn't forget- Christmas or not- that I've still got a job to do until further notice, so I switch on my laptop on and continue my perusal of all the reviews. I know the answer is in here somewhere.

As I'm scrolling down the rest of the comments, I get a new blog alert by Cummings And Goings:

'The most annoying, if not the worst, part of our stay at the Old Bell Inn is the hidden alarm clock in our room that kept going off every morning at three-thirty. Someone's idea of a practical joke. Well, it wasn't funny. It took us three days – our whole stay – to find it.'

I sit back and stare at the review.

And within the hour, I get another thirty alerts with the same message, bar a few lines here and there. Is there no end to the meanness? And against such a good man? Because he definitely is a good man. And he wants *me*! I sit back, the thought warming me through and through.

I'm so tormented but at the same time excited at the idea

of actually starting a new life in Cornwall, that my mind begins to form plans of all sorts as *his* face keeps popping into my mind. Mitchell, with his laughter, his broad shoulders and enveloping voice, played on a loop, unwilling to bugger off and leave me alone.

Now unable to concentrate, I move to Russell's kitchen to make myself my usual cup of hot chocolate. In half an hour it will be heaving with staff, so I'm relishing the quiet. Perched on a stool by the island, I watch the snow gently falling outside the window and nurse my hot mug.

'What are you doing in here, all on your own?' comes a voice from the door. The voice that makes my insides melt. Mitchell. Talk of the devil.

He comes to sit next to me, his wild but soft curls begging to be touched. And oh, God, don't even *look* at the patch of furry chest peeking out from his shirt.

'Enjoying the quiet before the kitchen storm,' I answer as he comes to stand next to me. 'What have you got there, hot chocolate?'

I nod, making to get up. 'There's some left…'

He touches my wrist. 'I'll get it.'

I watch as he moves about the kitchen with an assurance that comes from doing things on his own. And I wonder if his ex-wife had done nice little things for him, but I suspect she would have been more on the receiving end rather than the giving one.

It's like that, in some relationships: one gives and the other takes. I had given and given, while Mark had simply basked in the warmth of my love, letting me spoil him rotten, as if I should be grateful to even be in the same room with him.

'There's enough for a refill, you interested?' he asks and

I shake my head. I can barely breathe with him in the same room with me, let alone drink. God, how did this happen to me?

Mitchell comes and sits next to me with his mug. 'So...' he says, taking a sip and making an appreciative face.

Initially I'd dubbed him Mr Irish Charm, but only with the intent of sarcasm. Now that I'm getting to know him a bit better, I realise he's indeed very charming. And completely unaware of it, believe it or not. Doesn't he have a mirror? And can't he see the droves of women trailing in his wake?

'Regarding my job offer, I'll have the contracts drawn up.'

'Wait...'

He stops, his eyebrows shooting up in question. 'Why, what is it?'

I hesitate. This is too much – more than I deserve. The guy's willing to give me the job without even a proper trial period, based on his feelings for me. He's basically given me a knife so I can plunge it into his back. I just can't do it.

'Mitchell, thank you so much. You are too kind...'

He sighs. 'But...? Have you changed your mind? Don't you want to stay?'

It's not that. I want to stay, more than anything else in the world. But it's my deceiving him, my keeping back the truth about why I'm here in the first place, that is stopping me. So should I break the spell, and renounce this one moment of happiness that is being offered me? Even if I'll never see him again afterwards?

I look him in the eye. 'You hardly know me. You don't know me at all, as a matter of fact. For all you know I could...'

'What? Break my heart?' he takes my face in his hands. 'Rosie, call me hasty, call me reckless, but in the space of a couple of weeks I've learnt one thing. I love you.'

The inflection of tenderness in his voice makes me look up, and the look in his eyes touches me deeply.

He loves me? Like *I* love him, loves me? It's too good to be true. And also, it's way too complicated. 'But... but...' I stammer, 'You can't be serious – we've just met...'

Mitchell grins that cheeky grin. 'How long do I need to understand that your smile is the only one that I want to see every morning?'

Is that so? Wow. I can't believe that this is happening to me. 'But that *is* crazy, Mitchell,' I token-protest. Because I believe him. It's happened to me, too.

'And I want to take care of you, sweetheart. You don't have to worry about anything anymore.'

I swallow. 'I don't care about me. It's Danny that... he is crazy about you, too, and if something were ever to happen between you and me and it went pear-shaped,' and, dammit, my voice cracks. Just to be with him, squeezing my hand in this half-lit, strange kitchen so far from my own home, with my little boy safely sleeping upstairs in a warm bed that isn't even his, makes sense. In some weird way, it *feels* like home. Because Mitchell is here.

'Nothing's going to happen. Rosie. But I need you to feel like you can talk to me. About anything.'

I huff. If only I could.

I lower my head and Mitchell leans in, his lips barely a whisper on my lips. I can feel his breath warming my face, and then another breath as he inhales, his fingers lightly squeezing mine. I am also acutely aware of the heat his body is emanating, and the solidity of his pecs under my cheek.

I feel a sudden, falling tear, just the one, but it's enough. His eyes follow its movement and his thumb caresses my lower lip.

'C'mere …' he whispers, wrapping an arm around me, and pulling me to his chest, his other hand cradling my head. 'You're gonna be fine, you and Danny. You're doing an amazing job, trust me…'

I reach up, my mouth searching his, and he gently nibbles on my lower lip. As my legs melt, I sigh softly, leaning against his chest.

'Jesus, Rosie…' He swears, taking my face in his hands, his eyes caressing mine before he brings our mouths together again. 'I want to make love to you again so badly, but not in that crappy office…' he whispers.

'Me, too. But Danny's napping in your room…'

He chuckles under his breath, revealing white teeth. 'I'm the owner of a hotel and I can't get a lousy room.'

I grin. 'Wanna do it on the kitchen counter?'

He growls. 'Do not tempt me.'

'Where, then?'

'Jesus, Rosie… I'll take you anywhere you want. I just want to be with you.'

'Oh, Mitchell…' is all I can say. His hands on my shoulders are solid, anchoring me to the moment. And before I know what's what, he rests his forehead against mine, and his lips touch mine in yet another whisper of a kiss that nearly knocks me to my knees.

He caresses my face, his own expression now serious as he blushes. 'Rosie, I wanted to tell you… I'm keeping the last cottage for myself, and there's something I need to ask you…'

I nod, swallowing violently, unable to breathe, and he pulls away slightly, to check my reaction. In fear of mucking up this moment, I clutch at his shoulder blades, and he wraps me up in his arms and kisses me slowly and deeply. This man, kind and wholesome and good, is full of surprises. If only I deserved him.

And I realise I need to come clean. Now.

'Mitchell… there is something I need to tell you,' I venture. 'I'd rather not, because you'll think I've kept it from you on purpose. But, if we are really here, at this point, I have to be honest with you.'

He moves in and takes my hands. 'Tell me what's bothering you, Rosie.'

I take a deep, deep breath, holding on to his hands for what is possibly the last time ever. Because he will hate me. But I can't keep hiding the truth from him. He has become too important for me and I need to start this – or end this, as the case may be, in all honesty, come what may. But how?

'I lied,' I blurt out before I can stop myself, cringing at the confused expression on his face. 'I'm not a receptionist. I'm an assistant manager.'

He cocks his head and grins. 'I knew it. You are much too capable. You'd be perfect for the position of manager here.'

'Yeah, well, uhm…'

He takes my arm. 'But why didn't you tell me? Jesus, was I that unapproachable that you had to lie?'

'Yes. No. It's not your fault, Mitchell. But there's more.'

His eyebrows shoot up. 'I'm listening.'

Ohgodohgod. I've no choice but to tell the truth and all

the truth now. I inhale deeply and exhale in a rush. 'I work for Johnson Hotels.'

He blinks. 'Ri-ight…?'

'Head Office.'

'Ah. I get it now. You were sent to spy on me, so. You are here for an inspection,' he concludes, letting go of my hands.

I cringe. 'In truth, it's more of an investigation.'

His head snaps up. 'For what?'

'The bad reviews. But also, missing funds…' I cringe again as his eyes flash.

'And you thought I was skimming off the top? Jesus, Rosie, what do you think I am? How could you just come here and lie to me?'

'I had to,' I try to explain. 'I didn't want to, but everyone else was off on holiday and so they chose me.'

He's shaking his head, and the hurt in his eyes is like a dagger to my heart. 'We slept together, and I thought it meant something to you, too. Didn't it ever occur to you that honesty is a must in a relationship?'

'I wanted to tell you every day, Mitchell, but my job depended on it,' I try to explain, but he's shaking his head, moving away from me.

'All this time… you let me love you and all this time you were planning my downfall.'

This is surreal. All I wanted was for him not to hate me, and for us to separate unscathed. But I can see it's too late for that. How can he have not understood? I swallow what feels like a quarry full of boulders in my throat. 'Mitchell—'

'How does it feel, Rosie? How does it feel to take a man's heart in your hands and rip it to shreds? Does it make you feel good? Strong? Congratulations, you've completely killed my faith in womankind,' he hisses, rage altering every single one of his beautiful features. 'You came with the intention of ruining me.'

'I didn't!'

'No? Then what do inspectors do, exactly? I can't believe you were writing your little reports on me – which is, at the end of the day, fine – it's your job, and even jackals have to eat. But you...' His index is stabbing my heart, without even touching my chest. '*You* actually led me on, with your angelic looks and soft-spoken manner, making me think that you had feelings for me, when all the while you were thinking what an idiot I was to fall for you!'

I've hurt him badly and I can't stand it. I can't have him thinking I'd ever hurt him on purpose. 'No, Mitchell, you have to believe me – I never planned to harm you, not *ever...*'

He snorts and shakes his head, as if to himself, but when he looks up, there's murder in his eyes. 'And you know what the worst part is? That you used Danny, too. You used your own son, and the bond between us!'

'No...'

'You saw how fond I was of that little lad and you simply took advantage of the situation.'

'Oh, Mitchell, please don't be like this. You have to believe me. Do you really think I could ever set out to hurt you?'

'No. I didn't. And that's what kills me. Because I thought you were different. But now I realise that you're just like every other woman on the planet. You all want something. Even my ex-wife—' He cuts himself short, breathing hard. 'I'm a magnet for dishonest women. It's not your fault if I'm an idiot. It's mine. And it's a good thing I found out before it was too late.'

I want to tell him it's not true, but who am I kidding? It was in effect my task. That I didn't do a good job of it because I'm not cut out to do that to people, is something he'll never believe now. 'Goodbye, Rosie.'

Goodbye, just like that? Why is he treating me as if I had no scruples? I *tried* to tell him.

I open my mouth to protest again, to tell him that I never wanted to do it, but it doesn't even sound convincing inside my head. Nor would he ever believe that I was on his side even before I met him. And that *after* meeting him, I knew he had to be innocent. Yes, that does sound lame even to me, I know. But he should believe me, if he has any kind of feelings for me, shouldn't he? What can I say? So I close my mouth, because I can't come up with anything that will change his mind.

It's done. The inevitable has happened. Mitchell doesn't believe me and frankly, I can't blame him. We've only just met, and there is nothing there to indicate to him that I am trustworthy in the least. Not even *I* would believe me.

I want to say something, but the tears are already blurring my vision and I push my fists into my eyes as I brush past him and out of the office for the last time. There's nothing left for me to do, but to put aside my dreams of him, now and forever. Congratulations on losing a bloke once again, Rosie Anderson.

As I watch his retreating figure, I can literally feel the pieces of my heart breaking.

And then my bloody mobile rings. I have to answer it as it's Laura and she may need me.

'Rosie? There's someone here to see you.'

'*Me?* Who is it?'

'No idea. But he's pretty dishy, I can tell you that much.'

The only dishy bloke I know is Brad Peters from HO. He's Susan's henchman from HR and a real snake. He'll pat you on the back, even take you out to lunch, make you feel like he's your best friend and then bam – your P45 is served by dinnertime. And if it's him, Mitchell, Sally, Laura and everyone at the Old Bell Inn, including me, is buggered. I don't even want to think about the effect this will have on Mitchell. Heartbreak should never be served alongside a notification of dismissal.

You'd think Susan would wait at least until the day after Christmas. I wish that Mitchell's new place was already operational, and hope that he has the income to sustain him and his daughter so they can't harm him in any way.

What can I do but try to play it cool?

As far as I'm concerned, in the next ten minutes, I'll be unemployed as well. I can't work at the Old Bell Inn as it's one of Johnson Hotels' branches. Meaning I have to look elsewhere. Meaning I'm still in the shit because they'll want references, and judging by Susan's eternal love for me, I'm not getting any good ones from her. But that's not what's breaking my heart.

'Danny, you can go to the stables if you like, darling. I'll come and fetch you later, okay?'

'Okay, Mum,' he says and turns down the lane leading to the stables.

The last thing I want is for Danny to see me get sacked. I practically run through the main entrance. The man in the lobby is standing with his back to me, wearing a dark suit.

Even from behind I can tell he is fit. And speaking of fit, I think I'm just about to have one as he turns around. Because it's not Brad Peters come to fire all of us. That would have been a *blessing* in comparison.

'Hello, Rosie…' he says in his gravelly voice. The voice I'd yearned for over the past nine years: the voice of Danny's father.

19

A Not So Merry Christmas

I'm trying to sleep, but someone keeps tapping my cheek.
'Rosie...? Rosie, wake up!'

It's Laura, her face a huge question mark of worry. Kneeling on the floor on the other side of me is Mark. I've passed out from the shock, apparently. So I wasn't sleeping and it wasn't a nightmare after all. It is daytime and facing each other are my two worlds, past and present, colliding. And what a crash. An absolute train wreck. Jesus.

'You're okay,' Mark reassures me. 'You just had a little spell. Do you understand me, Rosie?'

I nod, but I'm really dizzy.

'How are you feeling?' he asks.

'Woozy...' I breathe, trying to sit up, but Mark pushes me back gently.

'Easy,' he whispers. 'You need to take it easy. I'll carry you to your room.'

*

Even as I lie on the bed, the room won't stop spinning. Mitchell is gone, and Mark is standing over me, unchanged, as if only a day, and not almost nine years, have elapsed. Time has left him completely unscathed. Still the same blue eyes with the Hugh Grant look, minus the playful demeanour. The same sandy blond hair, only cut shorter. The same designer suits in his uber-neat closet. And, above all, the same expensive aura that always clung to him.

'What are you doing here?' I whisper.

'I told you. I came to spend Christmas with you and Danny. I sent you a letter to let you know.'

'Why didn't you call?' I manage.

He shrugs. 'I did. I even left you a message, but you never answered.'

Oh God. I think I'm going to faint again. 'But… but that's absolutely crazy… after all these years… you can't just step in like this…'

'It's time for me to grow up, Rosie. Stop playing bachelor. The company's transferred me back to the UK. I want to buy a house fit for a family. For us.'

This is unbelievable. Mark coming back to me and wanting to be a father. This is everything I had always wanted. But now? Now that I have met Mitchell, and seen what real romance is supposed to be like, and the way men are supposed to treat their women? Now I see how it really should be. Only now it's too late. I've ruined everything with Mitchell.

I try to sit up, but my head begins to spin even more and Mark eases me back against the pillows.

'You're absolutely crazy,' I whisper.

'I know – I'm completely out of order. But… Christ, Rosie, I've been a real idiot. I want to change. For Danny. For us.'

There it is again – the 'us' word. What the hell is wrong with him?

'You can't do this. You can't just—'

'I know. I'm sorry.'

'Sorry?' I sit up slowly again, refusing his help. 'Do you realise how inadequate that sounds?'

Mark sits there, eyes on the floor, like a little schoolboy being chided. His usual trait.

I huff and rub my forehead. 'Jesus…'

'Rosie, I know you're angry and surprised and—'

'Angry?' I ape. 'I'm absolutely furious. How dare you come back like you've only been gone a day? After what you put me and Danny through?'

He remains silent.

How many times have I thought of what I'd say to him if he ever showed his face again? And now that he's here, it all comes out in an angry burst.

'Do you have… no, you can't *possibly* have any idea what it was like for me to give birth to our baby, knowing that you didn't even care enough to find out if it was a boy or a girl! Oh, but maybe I should be grateful that many years later you started texting me to ask how he was. And dropped by once in a blue moon, as if that would ever be enough for a little boy. And now you have the temerity to come here! How did you even find us?'

Mark's eyes shift. 'I called your mother.'

'My mum?' Of course. It's no secret that my mother dreams of a reconciliation between us and prays to that effect practically every night before she goes to bed. But how dare she actually interfere in my life like this? And how dare he even think I'd want to speak to him after all he's done to us? *Who* actually shows up like this after all this time?

'I know you've got lots of questions, Rosie. And I promise I'll try to answer them as honestly as possible.'

I rub my face as the room finally slows down. 'I have no questions for you, Mark. I have nothing for you, and neither does Danny. Now go back where you came from, and stay out of our lives.'

He hangs his head. 'You have every right to send me packing. Of course you do.'

I roll my eyes. This bloke is unbelievable.

'But please hear me out. I've booked a suite for a week. I wonder if I could persuade you and Danny to stay with me?'

'Stay with you? You must be out of your mind...'

He takes my hand. 'Please, Rosie. I know how much you must hate me. You and Danny will have your own room, of course. But I need to be with my son. I need for him to know that I love him...'

'Love him,' I say with a snort. 'You don't even *know* him.'

'Then give me a chance to get to know him, Rosie... please?'

'I don't get you! Why all the sudden interest?'

He hangs his head even lower, if possible. 'Can't a bloke redeem himself?'

'I don't know, Mark. Can he?'

He sighs. 'I deserve all your anger, I know I do. Every time I decided to call you, it seemed like it was too late, and every day that went by made it more and more difficult.'

'You should've thought of that sooner.'

'I'm not giving up, Rosie,' he assures me.

'And I'm not going to let you ruin my little boy's life!'

'I won't. I just want to get to know him. And make it up to you.'

'Ha,' I shoot back. 'You will never be able to make it up to us. Now please go away.'

Mark raises his hands. 'Okay. I'll let you rest. But I need you to at least consider the thought of letting me see him again. Rosie... I've been an absolute idiot, I know. But I need to make amends.'

He needs to make amends. What about Danny? What does he need? Does he need to be destabilised at the arrival of an almost-stranger who calls himself his father, when in truth they barely know each other? Up until now, my son was perfectly happy, coming out of his shell in this beautiful part of the country, in the company of truly genuine people, and now Mark wants to take all that away from him?

'Please, it's important to me.' One day, when I'm gone, I'll want him to know that I tried to make good on all my mistakes.'

'Oh, please, spare me your drama gambits and get out before Danny comes back and sees you. And never – ever – come near us again.'

Hours have gone by, and still no sign of Mitchell. Cups of tea and food have been sent up to me, but not by him. Not even a quick peek to check up on me. My calls and messages to him have gone unanswered. You'd think he'd at least send me a measly text back, but nothing.

I've been holed in here all day, with visits from Sally,

Laura, Jeremy and even Russell who has brought his special ginseng-based pick-me-up broth.

I don't want broth. It's Christmas, and I want to get up and out there, among my fellow workers and new friends, and mix and mingle and chat. And most of all, I want to see Danny and Mitchell. I get to my feet.

Danny has been popping in and out, all flushed and excited about a certain foal, and then about a coastal walk he's been promised by Laura and Alex. But not a word, not even from my little boy, about Mitchell.

Where the heck is he? I could be dead ten times over (even more, actually, as it only takes a second to die sometimes) and he doesn't give a toss. *And* it's Christmas Day, the worst I've ever had. So, shaking my ruffled feathers, I decide to mobilise my troops, i.e. Danny.

'Darling, can you please go downstairs and ask Mitchell to—'

'He's not here, Mum,' Danny answers as he's munching on a candy cane. 'He went down to the village. Said he had to meet someone.'

Someone who? Someone work-related? On Christmas Day?

20

The Ghost of Christmas Past

Just like old times, Adele's voice ringing in my head, I begin to brush my hair, feeling uber-sorry for myself. I'm 'Rollin' in the Deep' and 'Turning Tables' all over again. Adele is always there, waiting to pick me up, but this time she's got her work cut out for her as I have all sorts of miserable thoughts roiling around in my otherwise empty brain. And still no Mitchell. All this ignoring me is so awkward, so I've no choice but to vacate Mitchell's room. And move into Mark's suite. I'd much rather stick a fork in my eye, but where else can we go on Christmas Day so as not to ruin Danny's holiday?

'Mum, how long is my father staying?' he asks.

There go my efforts in trying to protect him. Mark must have seen him while I was sleeping. For the number of times he's spoken to him, I'm surprised Danny even recognises him. And I'm even more surprised Danny calls him that. The poor boy just wants to sound like every other kid.

'I don't know, sweetheart. But isn't it great that he came to see you?' At least I'm trying to put some oomph into my words, but they only come out as half-baked enthusiasm. I have to do this – look happy – for him.

'Oh, yeah, Mum. And he promised me we're going to live in a beautiful home with a huge garden as big as a football field.'

As big as his *lies*, he means. 'Honey,' I begin. 'You do realise that your father is here today but—'

'Oh, I know that, Mum. I prefer Mitchell any day.'

'Mitchell?'

'Mum, you can stop pretending, both of you. I know you are dating. And I'm grand with it.'

Grand – one of Mitchell's expressions. And there was me worried about how he'd take a new man in my life. It's too bad that the new man in my life is gone. The bond between them is undeniable. How am I going to dissolve it now, without breaking my son's heart?

'Mitchell's the coolest of the cool,' he says.

Before I can answer, a knock at the door makes me jump. Mitchell? Finally! I push the hair off my face, hoping he won't notice the pile of empty dessert plates on the bedside table next to me. I'll get him to listen to me, and explain everything properly, and maybe, now that he's calmed down, he'll believe me.

'Rosie?' Mark calls as he comes in and I struggle to hide the disappointment on my face. What the hell does he want, and why hasn't he hit the road yet?

He sits down on the edge of the bed and ruffles Danny's hair. 'Buddy boy, how about giving Mum and Dad a minute?'

Mum and Dad? Oh, this is so rich. Even Danny gets the irony of it and looks at him, then at me. I nod and he turns to go, shooting uncertain looks over his shoulder. For his benefit, I smile. But as soon as the door closes, my face becomes rigid. I can feel it, pulling in every direction, like a rubber mask.

'What are you still doing here?' is all I can say, because, unless he's invented a time machine to go back and undo his mistakes and the way he treated us, I don't trust him, and never will.

'Rosie, we need to talk in private.'

'I have nothing to say to you, Mark. Please leave my room.'

'Ah, yes... about that. It was very kind of the manager to give you his suite, but now he needs it back.'

Back? Mitchell wants his suite back?

'Get your things and put them in my spare room. Here's the key. Although I suspect he won't be back tonight,' Mark adds. 'I saw him get into a car with a gorgeous redhead. And a suitcase.'

21

The Ghost of Christmas Present

Now alone, I ponder the future. I don't want to need Mitchell anymore. Especially when he feels he has to go elsewhere to carry on with someone else. Whoever she is, she's just swooped in and taken him away. What can I do? Besides, it's not like I'm here for the long haul, is it?

It breaks my heart to think of Mitchell stepping aside so easily. But he can't have cared for me that much, can he, if he's already consoling himself with someone else? All I want to do is get up and run as far as I can. But I still have something to do.

I wipe the gushing tears away as, for one last time, I take in all of the familiar objects lying around – Mitchell's collection of *Band Of Brothers*, his Steve Miller Band CDs, his Scandi-noir books, and photos of his little Lola, the daughter I never even got a chance to meet.

Congratulations, Rosie, you beat your own record of falling in love and losing the bloke. I'll miss him so much – this place, my new friends, this kitchenette – I'll even miss the stash of Kit Kats and the bloody basket of stale Bakewell tarts. It all speaks of him, and the wonderful man that I thought he was. I'd thought that, were I to search the world far and wide, I would never, ever find anyone like him. How wrong I was.

And now it's over. I drag our trolleys off the bed, giving Mitchell's suite one last, longing glance. Just being surrounded by his stuff, reassured by the solidity of his presence, is like leaving the warmth of your own home. I miss him already. And I miss that special connection that we were slowly building and that is now gone forever.

And now Mark's arrival has only made it more complicated. He acts like we're still together, which would have pushed Mitchell away even further if he hadn't already metaphorically moved to the North Pole.

I only have one person to thank for this mess, so I call her.

'Hello, my darling! Merry Christmas!' she chimes.

I'm furious with her. I want to yell at her, but at the sound of her voice, I collapse. 'Oh, Mum, what did you do…?'

'Rosie…?'

'Why did you tell him I was here?'

'Oh, sweetheart, I thought that was what you wanted. I thought you were still in love with him…'

'Love?' I cry. 'He almost *destroyed* me, Mum! How could you even think…?'

'Listen to me, Rosie. You know I never stick my nose into your business. But this time, I must. Mark… is sorry. Can't you forgive him?'

'Forgive him? No, Mum. He's… he's hurt me too much. You *know* that.'

'Oh, my darling girl, this is not about you anymore. You

have a son to think of. Just think of what it would mean for Danny. He'd have a father, Rosie. And a beautiful house, a great life. He could go to great schools, go on unforgettable trips. Doesn't he deserve all that? Doesn't Mark *owe* him, and you?'

'I see you and Mark have had a long chat.'

She sighs. 'Sweetie, believe me, I understand your resentment. But you have to make this sacrifice for Danny. Why do you think your dad and I are still together?'

'What do you mean?'

'You think with your father it was all laughter and love?'

'What are you saying?'

'I'm saying that putting up with Mark is a small price to pay for your son's future.'

'You think?'

'Just follow my advice, darling. Let him back into your life.'

'Mum, I can't. I'm in love with someone else, and he was in love with me.'

Silence. 'Oh? Who is he?'

I groan. 'It doesn't matter. I don't stand a chance with him anymore.'

'Rosie, perhaps if you just—'

'I have to go, Mum,' I groan. 'Tell Dad Merry Christmas from me. I'm sorry we couldn't spend it with you.' And then, before the tears come, I hang up.

I'd hoped to spend the rest of Christmas with Danny and Mitchell, and have the best Christmas ever. But now, without Mitchell, I realise it truly is the worst.

*

It is the evening of Christmas Day, and on the outside I'm all happily exchanging gifts and good wishes, strolling around the village to see some familiar faces and to wish them well. But on the inside I'm falling apart. Danny is as happy as Larry because they all love him and he basks in the warmth around him. I truly don't know how I am going to be able to take him back to London.

We pop into Alex's village bakery/teashop called The Little Kettering Kettle, or just The Kettle, for short, for a rest and a snack. Apparently they are always open on Christmas day for what they call the Kettle Christmas. I'm not surprised to see Laura there, and I'm even less surprised to see Alex's arm around her neck.

'Rosie! Danny!' she calls as we step over the threshold. 'Come, sit!'

'Hi,' I make an effort to chirp as we take off our coats and scarves and sit on a bench by the largest window. 'So this is where the baking miracles happen!'

'Hey, Danny!' Alex chimes, ruffling his hair.

He used to hate it when people touched his hair, but now it seems he likes the affection. 'Fancy a hot chocolate with a nice slice of pie?'

Danny turns to me. 'Can I, Mum?'

'Of course, love. Make it two, please. But I'll have a coffee instead. Extra strong.'

Laura takes a look at me. 'Danny, why don't you go with Alex and choose something super-nice? Maybe you can even take him into the bakery out back and show him how they do their baking.'

Danny obediently slides off the bench and follows Alex

through the throng of cheerful patrons throwing hot teas and fancy Christmas desserts down their throats.

'So,' Laura says, studying me. 'You feeling better? You certainly caught us off guard. I didn't know you were still with Danny's dad.'

'I'm not,' I assure her. 'I hadn't seen him in quite a while.'

'You don't look very happy to see him.'

'I'm not, in fact.' Nor do I want to talk about my fiasco/mini-relationship with Mitchell. 'Tell me about you and Alex. Are you finally an item?'

Laura rolls her eyes. 'I guess so. He's a really great bloke underneath all that arrogance. Who knew?'

Yeah. They are full of surprises, aren't they? 'I'm happy for you, Laura.'

Our coffees and dessert arrive and with a thanks to Mel, the waitress at The Kettle, I wrap my hands around my mug and breathe in the deep, rich aroma, mixed with the scented wafts of the cinnamon apple pie that tickle my nose. Everything could be perfect, if Mitchell was mine. But right now, I'd even settle for him not avoiding me.

'And you? What's the deal with you and Mitchell?'

Danny is coming back with Alex, so I eye Laura who understands the topic is verboten. I'd like to tell her, of course, and to let her reassure me that it was all a misunderstanding, and that he'll forgive me. But I can't. I'm still, until Susan sends me an official email with the details of my termination, a Johnson employee, which entails discretion.

It's the one thing keeping me here, when all I want to do is pack my bags and move to the other side of the county, as far away from Mitchell as possible. Because it doesn't take rocket science to know that I've hurt him badly by betraying his confidence. He'd offered me a position in his inn, and in his heart. The former, I wasn't free to accept, and the latter, is no longer viable.

If he doesn't show his face anymore, then it truly is the end. I only hope that Danny won't be too disappointed. He is absolutely in awe of Mitchell. So am I, of course, but now I finally understand that it's not happening.

The only thing to do now is complete my task here, invent something or other that Danny will actually believe, smart little darling that he is, and move into Mark's room. But will that destabilise my son? Should I instead try my luck once again at another inn, assuming that I can find a room somewhere else? Or, I could send him back to my parents while I work out my last week here. That would get Danny out of it, but me? How am I going to be able to still look Mitchell in the eye, if he ever returns?

Guess what? Mitchell has returned, indeed, but that's only half of it. He's brought back the *gorgeous redhead* Mark had mentioned. He hasn't even tried to talk to me, or to look for me. In fact, he avoids Reception altogether.

The redhead is a younger woman – at least ten years younger. She looks like Catwoman in her tight leggings and boots, and only an oversized cardigan saves her from looking too provocative. Her eye make-up is heavy, but her lips are a natural, delicate colour which goes very well with her wild red hair. She looks, I have to admit, super amazing, with her Demelza image fitting perfectly with his Poldark swagger. I instinctively look down at my own tatty jeans. Some girls have got it. I don't.

I know it's the needy Rosie that I keep well locked up inside me, but how could I have mistaken those kisses, all that tenderness and our sense of closeness for anything much deeper? I thought that experience had taught me that men are men, and that whilst most women play their love moments over and over in their minds for weeks on end while floating on cloud nine, men just roll over and forget about it, ready to move on to their next prey.

And... she's managed to pull him in the blink of an eye. The minute *I* blink (well, faint, actually) he's off with someone else – someone, albeit, who hasn't been busy snooping behind his back like I have. Someone who is able to start a new, fresh relationship without any secrets. Someone who hasn't betrayed him before the relationship even begins. I know, it's not my fault – I didn't set out to deceive him from the start. It's Susan the Sacker's fault. But this is where we're at now. Mitchell has moved on without even so much as a glance behind him.

That evening, Danny, Mark and I have dinner together in one of the local restaurants in the village. Everyone around us is cheerful and festive, except for us. I can imagine what the Last Supper was like. Because it's excruciating.

'My, this looks delicious, thank you. Careful, Danny, it's hot,' I warn him as the waitress comes to our table with our roast Christmas turkey and all the trimmings.

Mark's doing his best to convince me to stay and to entertain Danny at the same time, who accepts his attention readily enough, although I can tell that they lack the chemistry Danny has with Mitchell. Who, incidentally, has just walked in through the door with Demelza on his arm.

He looks stunning in a pair of trousers that are not made of denim and what is actually a fitted sweater that makes him look ten years younger. If I hadn't slept with him, I would have never guessed what perfect musculature lies underneath his usually baggy sweaters.

It's obvious that she has had an influence on him and his choice of clothes. And in the space of a few hours, to boot. She, on the other hands, looks like a *Vogue* model meets medieval maiden in a long ruby velvet dress that accentuates all her perfect curves, her long red tresses billowing as she walks breezily to their table on the other side of the restaurant.

I watch them surreptitiously all throughout dinner as Mark is teaching Danny some magic tricks. She keeps laughing and beaming at Mitchell, feeding him pieces of her own food. God, it's so disgusting, the way she's clinging to him, that I want to look away. But for the life of me, I can't. It's like in those tragic car wrecks. You see it unfolding before your very eyes and as horrible as it is, you just can't look away.

I'm so angry with Mitchell for rubbing my nose in his new flirt. Who even does that? What are we, twelve years old? And besides, where has he been hiding her all this time? Evidently, as Laura had told me in the beginning, a whole posse of girls had their eyes on him, waiting for the right moment to swoop. And swoop they did.

And as I'm surreptitiously watching, what does he do? He reaches out and pulls her to him! Next he'll be snogging her right here, in front of the guests.

I want to get up, go over there and ask him if this is the

way he's trying to save his business, all the while I'm risking my very job to save his ass? What the hell is the matter with him? Really. My thoughts must have reached him, because he suddenly turns his head in my direction and our eyes meet. If I expected him to look away, I was wrong. He takes in the false little family portrait at my table and of course makes his own assumptions. Mummy and Daddy are back together. But it doesn't matter, because he's already found a diversion too.

She looks so into him, and he into her, that I just realise that all this time he's been lying to me. Because there's no way these two have just got together – not with the way he's looking at her. I can tell you right now that he's never ever looked at me like that. Serves me right. What did I expect from a Christmas flirt?

I look over at Mark, who keeps glancing at me, and I realise that he isn't going to go away without a proper conversation. If he's going to be living in the same country as us, let alone the same city, we might as well, at least, have a civilised rapport, if only for Danny's sake. For my part, I doubt Mark will ever change.

'I saw the way you were throwing daggers at the redhead,' Mark says as Danny does the rounds of the tables, delighting the villagers, his friends, with his magic tricks.

There is a distinct air of defiance in his voice. It's like he knows my feelings for Mitchell and he's challenging me to say something. Silly, silly man. You really don't know me at all, if you think I'm going to make a scene in front of everyone, my own son included.

Mark crosses his arms. 'Were you and that Irish bloke sleeping together?'

I start. 'I'm sorry, how is my life any of your business?'

'Does Danny know? And what about your job?'

'Mark, I hardly think you have any right to grill me about my private life after all these years when I don't even know where you've been.'

'I told you I've been in the States…'

'That's not what I meant. You left me. So don't even think of coming back here and dictating orders to me or Danny. You are a stranger to us, Mark. And you have no rights over us.'

'So you really are – sorry, *were* – sleeping with him. And now he's sleeping with her. Interesting.'

I'm clawing myself back from ugly memories that still burn like fresh scars on my skin. It nearly killed me the first time, but did it make me stronger? At this point, I don't think so, because I feel like I'm circling the drain all over again, grabbing at the rim of my own self-control. Control. I need to take control as much as I can again before Mark takes over in his usual style, and then I'll be nothing but a speck of dust in his personal ray of light.

The next day, I take Danny out for a breath of fresh air and away from Mark for a minute. Only we don't go into Little Kettering, but head in the opposite direction for the South West Coast towards the cliffs of Predannack. It is beautiful, and I take a deep breath before we continue. We go past a private farm, where the National Trust area begins, and climb over a stile and onto a very narrow path. Narrow and winding, dipping down and up, down and up, only to emerge on the verge of impervious cliffs, and when Danny skips off to explore, my heart nearly stops.

I want to shout after him to be careful, but I know it's just my motherly instinct. Of course he's not going to go flying off the cliff and crash down on the rocks below. The last thing I need to do is transmit a sense of insecurity to my son. He must grow up confident, and I'll be damned if I'm going to stem his curiosity and love of exploring.

Ten minutes later, we reach Predannack, and I spread a throw across the grass that is incredibly dry for such a cold day. Up here, the waves look frozen in time, barely moving. Although it's a sunny day, the cold is biting my cheeks. I wrap Danny's scarf closer around him. 'Are you not cold, my darling?' I ask him, and he shakes his head, his cheeks red with excitement.

I pull out our food supplies – homemade (well, inn-made) Cornish pasties, cheddar cheese, cream crackers, grapes, pears, a small carton of milk for Danny, a huge thermos of coffee for me, to go with the entire packet of chocolate biscuits I've accidentally dropped into the hamper.

When we're good and full, Danny puts his arms around my neck. 'Mum, can we go all the way to Soapy Cove? Mitchell says it's awesome!'

Mitchell, Mitchell, Mitchell. He's everywhere, even up here, with us. Is there no escaping him? All the same, I don't want us to leave Cornwall now. Danny loves it here, and so do I. It's all I ever wanted, for my son to be happy, grow up in a healthy, serene atmosphere. But at the moment, I have no choice but to go home.

Later, Danny is watching TV while I'm packing away things that we won't be needing during our last few days in Cornwall. It's heartbreaking to have to go, but at the moment, I don't have the means to make this move down here happen, let alone a job, and when everyone else finds out who I really am, they'll all want nothing to do with me.

As long as we're still in Cornwall, it's like I'm with Mitchell. Even if I moved to the other side of the county, there will always be a moment – a festival like Falmouth Week, a regatta, an evening of fireworks, when I'd bump into him again. And I wouldn't be able to stand it. How can you bear to find happiness, and then let it go? No, going back to London in the New Year is the best decision after all.

My mission is coming to an end, and if anything, we need to get back to see what my job scenario is. But I know that moving here is only a dream, and that once we get back to the Big Smoke and once again into the groove of things, reality will kick in, forcing me to see that a move here is impractical, what with no job to fall back on, let alone a house, and… let alone Mitchell who is gone forever.

Keeping my back to Danny, I let the tears fall. I'll wipe them away before turning around and facing my little boy, but just now, albeit for a few seconds, I need to let them flow. I need to grieve over the loss of the most wonderful man I've ever met.

'Are you really happy about going back?' Danny insists as I stifle a sob, swiping at my cheeks. 'Because you don't look it, Mum…'

I wipe my eyes and turn to him with an Oscar-winning smile. Or, at least, I should win one. Pretending to be happy when inside you're slowly dying is the hardest thing on earth. 'Of course I am, darling. I'm very happy to be going home.'

Perhaps it's for the best. If it's true that it is better to have loved and have lost than never to have loved at all. By now I've just about hummed all of Adele's sadder, deeper, gut-wrenching repertoire. Boy, does she know all about heartache. There isn't one line, one note she's written that I haven't felt straight through the heart.

Mitchell. Why did you leave me? Why didn't you stay long enough to hear me out? If only I could tell you how I feel about you, and explain what's really going on here.

'What do you think, Rosie? Rosie?'

I'm aware of Mark standing on the threshold all of a sudden, talking to me, and Danny's eyes on my face. How long has he been here? I didn't see him come in, nor did I hear anything he's said. And now they're both looking at me, waiting for an answer. How long have I been 'out'?

What do I think? About what? If I agree, I may be agreeing to him moving back in with us. If I don't...? God, I don't know what the hell he's talking about.

'Uhm... I'm not sure,' I say, scratching my head, scanning Danny's face. By the look of it, I can tell it's really important to him.

'Please, Mum, can we stay longer than just a few more days?'

'Darling, I'm sorry, but I have to get back to work in the new year.'

He lowers his head sadly.

'Oh, my darling, don't look so sad. Why don't you go and tell Mitchell we'll be leaving in a few days and thank him for everything?' Perhaps he'll come back with some news regarding Mitchell's whereabouts.

'Mitchell's not here,' Danny informs me. 'He's moved in with Penny.'

Penny. Her name is Penny, and I had to find out from my own son.

If there is still any doubt that Mitchell is over me, all I have to do is watch them at dinner again the next night. God, we are not dining at the hotel only to get away from having to see them together again, but it almost as if they're following us. You've replaced me, Mitchell. I get it. Enough.

And tonight, he looks, needless to say, absolutely dashing in a charcoal grey suit, a white shirt and no tie, his unruly hair pulled back in a stub of a ponytail, as he chats and laughs, occasionally scratching his beard, his dark eyes twinkling with sexiness. He truly has stunning features. But mostly, I *miss* him, his laughter, his kindness, his very heart. If he's seen me among the gazillion diners present, he's doing a fine job of avoiding me.

Mark makes a point of sitting next to Danny and keeping him entertained all evening with his usual bag of magic tricks. Yes, I remember how very good he was at them. Especially his disappearing act. I can't wait to get dinner over with and cry under the privacy of my duvet.

After dinner, we go back to Mark's suite where he drops a bomb on me.

'You want to *timeshare* my child?' I gasp.

'*Our* child, Rosie. You've been clear enough about your feelings for me, so I'm going to respect your wishes. And try to win you back in earnest. But in the meantime, I could spend, I don't know, every other weekend with him?'

So that's how he's planned to worm his way back into our lives. 'I don't think so.'

'Oh, come on, Rosie! Budge an inch, will you? Maybe I can have him for a couple of weeks in the summer and you could have him at Christmas and I could have him for his birthday, or vice-versa?'

I bristle. 'Christmas Eve *was* his birthday, Mark.'

He lowers his gaze. 'Oh.'

'You didn't even know that. You never even cared to find out when his birthday was, if not even to dedicate one fleeting thought to him once a year.'

'Look, Rosie, I really am sorry, but for how long must I grovel, when instead we could be planning his future together?'

'His future...?'

'Just think of all the things I could give him – a lovely home with his very own garden. He could practise all the sports he wanted to, go on all the expensive school trips. He wouldn't have to miss out on anything. He'd have financial security – a father figure. Just think about what he's missing out on, Rosie.'

As if I hadn't – for years on end. 'I'm sorry, Mark, but there's just no way I'm going to let you waltz back into his life, knowing you're going to leave when he least expects it.'

He lowers his head. 'Well, you're right to be mad at me, Rosie...' He steps forward and takes my hands. 'But this time I'm not going anywhere, I promise you. It's taken me a while, but I've... finally seen the light about you, Danny and me. I want to be able to play football with my son and all the things a proper father does. And I want to win you back, too. Let me in, Rosie, and I promise you won't be disappointed.'

'Mark...' is all I can say. His timing absolutely sucks. Years ago, I'd have given my right arm to hear that, but now? Now, for Danny's sake, it seems like my only option.

He kisses my hands. 'I've been a real idiot, Rosie. I treated you like a burden, because I didn't understand what a blessing a family could be. My own family was a disaster. I just assumed all families were like that. But now, I realise how much I've missed out on. Can the both of you ever forgive me? Because I'll spend the rest of my life making sure you do.'

Despite myself, and all he's put us through, tears come into my eyes. *Because* of all he's put us through. I know that I don't owe him anything. But I don't want my feelings to come between them. Not anymore. And he's right about one thing. I owe my son at least some good memories of his father.

'Give this little family a chance, Rosie.'

Mitchell, my dream of love, is gone. So are my dreams of moving to Cornwall and opening my pottery shop. There is no way I can support us without a job. And maybe it is right that Danny should enjoy his father, at my expense. I am the parent, so I'm the one who should be making the sacrifices, not my Danny.

'Rosie Anderson,' Susan booms through my mobile, sounding like my mother when I used her extension cord (and broke it) to build a swing on the fire escape at the age of six. But for once, I'm shocked to hear, The Sacker is happy. Evidently she did have a good time in Spain.

'I've got great news for you. I don't know how the hell you did it, but you're up for the position of manager.'

Which is not great news. Actually, it's bloody fantastic, because it means she won't be my line manager anymore. This also means no more aggravation, more money, a better flat. Mark could come and see his son without me feeling beholden to him for anything. And on my terms. I've never depended on anyone, and prefer it to remain like that.

'Thank you, Susan.' I am literally howling with joy on the inside, albeit a bit thrown by the fortunate turn of events. Only a few days ago she was looking to fire me, and now? I finally got the promotion I've been chasing for six years? Why now, when she has never been so negative about my work? What's brought this about?

'Your new position will become effective January 5th and you will be given one week to move into your new office.' I.e. hers. I wonder where she's going then? Hopefully away from Human Resources to found a whole new department, like Human Terrifiers or something.

'Oh, I won't need that long. It's just a couple of boxes across the corridor.'

Silence. Which makes the hair at the back of my neck stand on end.

'Your new office at the Old Bell Inn, Rosie…'

Huh? Is she kidding me?

'But… but what about Mitchell Fitzpatrick?' I stammer. She can't fire him without any proof! I should be the one to get the boot, not him.

'I'll get back to you later in an email with all the details. Don't do anything with Fitzpatrick until you receive my complete instructions.'

As if I'm about to prance off and tell Mitchell he's fired and that I'm taking his place.

'Susan—'

'Congratulations, Rosie. I'm just as surprised as you, believe me,' she says. Trust Susan to be so kind.

'No, Susan, I can't.'

'Can't do what?'

'Take Mitchell's place.'

'Why the hell not? It's not like you have a life in London.'

Gee, thanks for that, I want to say, but think better of it. She still is my boss, after all.

'I know I don't have to explain to you that in this company, either you move up or you move out.'

This is ridiculous. I can't do it, no matter what Susan says. Of course, I'd love to move to Cornwall, but not at the cost of Mitchell's job. It'll be at least a year before his cottages are ready, and I just can't do that to him, even if he won't talk to me anymore.

Besides, what the hell am I hoping for, Mitchell to magically and suddenly decide that he really wants me and not the redhead? Fat chance. Mitchell's gone from my life; he's slipped through it like a flash of lightning that has damaged everything in its path without even knowing.

If I ever was seriously considering moving to Cornwall and accepting Mitchell's job offer, it's all gone down the drain now: a new life in Cornwall with Mitchell and a better job. The prospect lasted but a few days, nothing more. Now all I've got is a weight in my heart, a brand-new ex-boyfriend who hates me, and an ex-boyfriend who's promising to erase all the pain he's caused us.

There's only one thing left for me to do.

So I go back to Mark's suite where he is sitting sleepily in an armchair.

'I'm willing to let you see more of Danny. For his sake.'

His eyes widen. 'You are? Oh, Rosie, I'm so happy, thank you!' He gets up and races to the dresser and, as I watch in horror, goes down on one knee, a ring in his hand. 'Will you marry me, Rosie?'

22

The Ghost of Christmas Future

I stare at him, and then at the ring, backing off in horror. 'What, are you crazy, Mark? Put that thing away. You can't possibly expect me to just… fall back to where I was almost nine years ago.'

He shifts on his knee and looks up at me, his face a mask of disappointment. 'I was hoping that we could put that behind us, for Danny's sake.'

I find myself nodding. 'Of course, Mark. I want Danny to have…' I swallow '…his father. But marriage? No.'

'I know it's sudden. You must think I'm pathetic. But think. We could be Mr and Mrs Wilkins.'

'Mark… marriage to someone you don't love is not the answer.' Let alone the fact that ever since Mitchell came into my life, I haven't given Mark a single thought.

'But that's the thing, Rosie. I've come to realise I do love you.'

I had been talking about me, actually.

'All these years away from you, being with other women and all, only made me realise that you are the sweetest, kindest, dearest girl I've ever met.'

I don't know about the kindest, but certainly the most gullible. My heart aches all over again to remember myself giving birth to Danny without him. And it aches even more to hear the words I'd so desperately needed all these years when it's simply too late. There is no more room for Mark in my heart. Only Mitchell.

'I want to make a will so when I'm old and gone, everything will go to you and Danny. I want him to have a legal father. And for you both to be protected and looked after. Do it for Danny. Give him a normal family.'

A normal family. For years I'd struggled, killing myself to give Danny just that, and now Mark says that we're not normal?

Could he be right? Could it be that only I don't see the truth – that we are not normal? Would marrying Mark and living with him make us normal? Is that really all it would take to make Danny's life normal and complete?

And then Danny's Christmas wish to Santa comes to my mind. I know he wants a family, and that I've fallen short of that. If I say yes, Danny's dreams will all come true. A father, a fantastic home, school trips abroad, a great school.

'Don't answer me now, Rosie. Just think about it.' He swallows, and looks me in the eye, his own moist. 'Just give me a chance to take care of you both. And maybe one day, you won't hate me so much...'

'Mark...' I can't seem to say anything else. What can I possibly say to a man who's broken my heart, made a few brief appearances every few years or so, and then comes back, wanting to make amends? I am not prepared for something as surreal as this.

'So, how are we going to do this?' he asks.

'Danny needs to get to know you better,' I say. But, even as I'm saying it, I wonder if it's the right thing to do at all. Mitchell was part of my plans. But I guess life is more than just having a man in it. Life is, I've learned the hard way, about making ends meet. Paying bills and raising your child with love and respect.

There is no room in my life for any man who's not Mitchell. For him, I'd have made an exception. Because he is exceptional. Or rather, he was, in my eyes. Now I know he's just a guy like every other. I don't need a man who will turn my life upside down completely. For now, especially now, I need a shot at security. I owe it to my son to give it a go.

So for Mark, I'll make room. For Danny's sake. Because he needs a father. But for myself, no one short of Mitchell will ever do. I'm out of the game for good.

The next morning I'm up early, with a headache the size of a cathedral. Danny is sleeping like an angel next to me. Coffee. I need coffee, before my head explodes.

But first, I have to finish what I came here for. I ease out of bed and slip into a pair of fresh jeans, ignoring my pasty face and brushing back my hair into a ponytail.

A few cups of strong brew and I'll be fit enough to give Mitchell's reviews one last look. Because I don't want to leave under a cloud, or just be the girl who lied to him. And because I'm still not convinced. Something, somewhere, is escaping my notice. I have to find what I'm looking for before I leave. I owe him that much, at least.

After shovelling two butter pastries down my throat and two cups of coffee, I adjourn to my place behind my soon-to-be-former desk and pull out my notes. Yes, there's definitely a financial hole concentrated in those twelve months. But my mind keeps straying to the blogs.

'Found it yet?' comes a voice from behind me, making me jump.

'Jesus, Laura, you scared the crap out of me,' I say, shielding the screen with my body as if I still had a secret to defend. Because it won't be long before Mitchell tells everyone.

'Oh, sorry, Rosie! I was on my way to breakfast. I just wanted to tell you that I'm going to really miss you guys when you go.'

'So will I,' I sigh. 'You've all made us so welcome, and Danny will be heartbroken when we leave.'

'Then don't. Accept Mitchell's job offer and stay. We'll help you with everything else – the house, the move. Alex has got a huge van.'

If only I could. But Laura doesn't know it's off the table now. And only I know the devastation he has left in my heart. In the space of a few days, he's healed my heart, opened it and broken it all over again, never to be fixed. This is not a patch-up job anymore. There are too many shards that have flown off in every direction. No one, least of all me, will ever find the pieces again. And this time I can't even try. I bite my lip. 'I can't.'

'I wish you could.'

'Besides, Mitchell's got his hands full now…'

Laura nods. 'Yes, Penny. She is a handful, but she does love him.'

As if you couldn't tell.

'And he…?'

'He's absolutely besotted with her, of course.'

Great. And she's telling me this now?

'Can I bring you some breakfast back from the dining hall?'

'No, thanks, Laura.'

'Okay, then.'

I still have loads of work to do, and if Mitchell doesn't like it, tough bananas. It's my job. I pour myself a cup of strong coffee and inhale the rich aroma. I thought I could get to know Mitchell a bit better. It didn't happen. I thought I'd have the guts to tell Susan what I think of her and Johnson Hotels. That didn't happen either. I thought I could look around here for a new start. Ditto.

And while I'm thinking of all my failures, the reminder of my biggest one, Demelza-Penny, suddenly appears on the door. I lower my eyes to my coffee, but I can see her striding towards me with that confidence that only a young, hot woman can have.

'Hey,' she says. I don't know if she's talking to the barmaid or to me, so I look up. She's smiling like the Cheshire cat. Good for her. I can only wish them the best, and that she doesn't eventually dump him like Diane did. 'You're Rosie, right?'

I nod.

She holds out her hand. 'Penny. Pleased to meet you.'

'Likewise,' I lie.

'Your little boy is lovely.'

'Thank you.'

'You're from London, right?'

'Yes.'

'And is that your husband, the man you were having dinner with the other night?'

For someone so engrossed in her own lover, she's asking me an awful lot of questions.

'Husband? No.'

'I didn't think so. You're single, right?'

By the way she's studying me, I can only assume she means, *Are you interested in Mitchell?* I can read her body language a mile off. It's what I'm good at. She wants to know what my expectations in being here are, and I suspect she's actually entertained by the idea that someone like me might have a hope in hell of being reciprocated by someone like him.

Now, I'm no shallow girl, but I know how many male – and some female – minds work. A girl like me, common and ordinary, is never going to attract someone like Mitchell for the long game, whereas someone like her, aka a complete and utter knockout, is going to turn his head a thousand times over.

Just look at her – the confidence of a young woman who has never had to fight for anything in her entire life, judging by the way men seem to fall all over her, much to Mitchell's annoyance. Because he's jealous, all right, no matter how much he chooses to hide it. Good thing I'll be out of here soon enough.

'Single? Not for long,' I lie.

Penny's eyebrows shoot up. 'Oh? I thought Mitchell mentioned you were on your own.'

The cheek. Of both of them. 'No.' I can feel my nose growing as I speak. I'm not good with lies. Actually, I'm absolute rubbish at them.

'Is that man your son's father then?'

'Yes.'

'So is he your partner or not?'

Jesus, what does she want from me? It's not like my presence here is a threat to her or anything. She must know the coast is clear and that I would never, could never, stand between them. I'm just not like that. Still, a woman can never be too sure about her man (experience has taught me that much).

'Yes.' Now, not only can I feel my nose growing, I can also feel a giggle forming in my throat. The idea of me and Mark is absolutely hilarious. At least it is now, after almost nine years. But I've put my foot in it now. Besides, I need to throw both Mitchell and this Penny gal off my scent. And it's working. She leans forward, obviously intrigued. Me and my big gob.

'What's he like?'

Like? I lean back. 'His name's Mark. We met at work.' And then I zip the lip, because I've almost blurted out the name of my company. See? I told you I'm no good at this.

'And Danny?' she asks. 'Do they get along?'

'Yes, luckily.'

'And yet, you and Mark don't *look* like an item. Are you may be interested in someone else?'

There we go. 'Oh. Absolutely not.'

'Oh. I thought you were interested in Mitchell.'

To hide the effect of the kick in the teeth she's just given me, I laugh. 'Mitchell Fitzpatrick? What nonsense.' I really do deserve that Oscar, by the way.

'Huh,' she says. I raise my head and she's looking at me like she doesn't believe me, her eyes never leaving mine, and I'm hoping I look convincing enough. Because if I don't, she'll go back to Mitchell and have a laugh. 'Mitchell tells me you were giving him some good tips. I wanted to thank you for that,' she says and I do a double take. 'We really appreciate your help.'

I nod. Wow. She sure has moved in fast. She's apparently taken every available vacancy in every aspect of his life – his accounts, his table, and his bed. I'm not just jealous. I'm bloody miserable. It serves me right.

Besides, it figures he wants someone who looks like Penny. If I wasn't jealous, I'd actually like her, although not as much as he seems to. But the memory of them, heads bowed together, whispering to each other and laughing at their private jokes throughout the evening, is killing me.

If I didn't think so highly of him, I'd think he's doing it on purpose just to hurt me, but who am I kidding? The chemistry between them is tangible. And to think he'd acted besotted with me only days before. I have to agree with the song – love stinks.

I think of them and want to kick myself in the ass. How the hell do I get myself into these situations? I swore I'd never, *ever again* lust after someone I can't have, and what do I do? Fall in love with the guy I'm supposed to be spying on and lie to him through my teeth. I push him away because of a sense of duty towards my boss who'd have me hanged, drawn and quartered in a heartbeat if she had her way.

And now, to top it all off, he comes up with a girlfriend. Why didn't he say so? Why do I always attract the two-timers and the dumpers? Just my bloody luck.

'I have to go now. Nice talking to you, Penny,' I say.

'And you,' she says. 'It would've been nice to get to know you better. Are you sure you won't accept that job and stay?'

I stop. Christ, does he tell her absolutely everything? And how is she even cool with it? Glad to know I don't represent the slightest peril to her designs on him. 'Oh. No, I'm opening my own pottery business and working from home.' As if. Boy, am I getting good at this or what?

'In London?'

'I'm not quite sure, yet,' I say. I smother a huff. Why is it so important for her to know? I am absolutely no threat to her whatsoever. Why won't she just let it go? Unbelievable. Why can't some women just enjoy their victories in silence, rather than rubbing my nose in it? 'Nice meeting you,' I repeat as I skulk off.

Later that evening, Danny and I cuddle a bit in the bed we are now sharing in Mark's suite. It is our usual end of the day ritual. In London it was a way to make sure we stayed in touch after a busy day. Here, it seems like the most natural thing in the world.

'Goodnight, darling,' I whisper, kissing his forehead.

'Night, Mum,' he whispers back, sleepily, his lids closing.

I tuck him in, thanking my lucky stars. Whatever happens, Danny and I have each other.

*

The next morning, I'm at my desk early, collecting my notes, trying to word my final report. But all I can think of is how tough it's going to be without Mitchell. Especially on Danny. Because this is not just about me. My little man has already fallen for Mitchell, despite the presence of his biological father on the premises. Danny has barely acknowledged him, truth be told. He only has eyes for Mitchell, much to Mark's annoyance. But then, you reap what you sow.

Despite myself, I start to list all of Mitchell's good qualities as a manager. Capable, hard-working. Even though I still don't know where he gets all that money, I'm convinced he's honest and that he hasn't stolen a single penny. But he isn't as honest on other matters. Like with my heart. Why didn't he tell me he had someone? That's men for you. They hack their way into your heart, despite your best resistance, and after they've torn your walls down, they simply... *evaporate*, leave you standing there, looking around you, wondering where they've gone. Leaving you amidst the ruins of your dreams. Congratulations, Rosie old girl. You have once again been had.

And yet, I can't hate him. I'm mad at him, sure I am. But to be honest, I'm mad at myself, because even now, the way he makes me feel has nothing to do with my evaluation, and yet, as I type away at my report, I can't help but think how all these qualities have made me stray from my job. I'm no professional, I now know.

To be fair, I've always known I can't just ruthlessly pick a hotel apart, close it down, and put someone out on the street. Especially over the Christmas holidays. I'm an assistant manager, not an inspector, or a heartless monster. I'll leave that kind of stuff to Susan.

But I'd still like to know who the culprit is. I'm sure that there is a solution to all this, my search for that one, elusive thing that is staring me right in the face, thumbing its nose at me.

'Please please please if u value ur life don't go their (sic),' one of the blogs starts. 'The only good thing was the food.' Oh, God.

And then my laptop suddenly crashes.

'No, no, no,' I plead, hitting Ctrl, Alt and Delete repeatedly, but nothing happens. The screen is black. It's dead, all dead. And so are we if I can't solve this. Of all times to bite the dust! 'Come on, don't do this to me now!'

'What's wrong?' Penny asks coming back to my desk.

'My computer just crashed.'

'Did you hit Ctrl, Alt and Delete?'

'Yes, yes, but it's not working. I need a decent computer.'

'I'm only using my tablet, so I can lend you mine if you want,' she suggests.

'Oh, you would? Thank you! I'm in the middle of something important.'

'Which is?'

'Someone's writing horrible things about the inn and I need to get to the bottom of this or else—' I bite my lip.

'Okay, I'll go get it for you.'

'Thanks, Penny.'

She studies me. 'You really care, don't you?'

What exactly I care about is not mentioned, and it's just as well. I have no time to get into any soul-searching conversations.

'Yes,' I whisper.

She smiles. 'I thought so.'

23

Cornish Homes by the Sea

Later that day, after Danny and I have had lunch, Mark pulls out his laptop. 'I've been looking at some houses, Rosie. Tell me what you think.'

Now, I know how much he owes us, but why do I still feel I'm selling myself out? Why do I feel like a scheming heel? Danny deserves to have the best. After all, Mark is his father, and his attention is long overdue. But I don't know where we'll be tomorrow, so how am I supposed to be choosing a house to live in with Mark, to boot, when all I can think of is Mitchell?

'Come over here and look at my shortlist.'

Biting my tongue, I do so. They are extremely expensive, upwards of eight hundred thousand pounds, starting from the smallest. I've always known he was rich, and it always bothered me that he'd never offered any financial support, even though I'd have never accepted it, of course.

But I still can't help but feel this is all wrong. It just doesn't feel... natural.

'But these houses are all in Cornwall,' I observe.

He grins at me, his eyes bright with happiness. 'And we both know how much you love Cornwall,' he answers.

'I – you want to live *here*?'

He takes my hand. 'Yes, I want us to live here. Is that all right, Rosie?'

I honestly don't know what to say. Of course I'm happy to live in Cornwall. Of course I want my son to have what he's entitled to. And I want Mark to do what's right. But somehow, it doesn't feel right at all. Mark is Danny's biological father, but is it right to accept all this, knowing that he might get itchy feet again? And to live under another the same roof with a man I don't love, possibly a stone's throw away from Mitchell? I am uneasy. I know what my parents would say, but to me it feels odd. I have been on my own for years, and to suddenly let him in... I just don't know. Not while Mitchell is in my heart.

'I'm glad you accepted to let me get to know him better. He's a lovely boy.'

Despite myself, I smile. 'Thank you.'

'And you're lovely too. I can't understand how I didn't see it. But I was an immature idiot, Rosie. All I cared about were my fast cars and my fast life. I didn't understand what a blessing it could be to have a child – a family. I do now, albeit too late.'

There is a pause, which becomes a lull. It's awkward, because, after all these years, I don't quite know what to say to him. He sees it too. He coughs and mercifully pulls his laptop closer to us.

'I like this one,' he says. 'It's on Rose Lane and has a huge garden for Danny to play football in. You love a kick-about, don't you, Danny?'

'Yes, sir,' Danny says as he forks apple pie and custard into his mouth.

'So, do you like it?' Mark asks. 'Would you live in it?'

I shrug. 'Danny, what do you think?'

'I love it, Mum!' he says, bright-eyed and rosy-cheeked, and I can't help but smile.

The two things I'd prayed for all these years – Mark acknowledging his son, and me finding love. If only I could have both. Life could be good. It should be great, even. Only it's a mess.

Stay, Mitchell had said. *Your place is here*. And I want nothing more than that. But now I'm trapped between the man I no longer love but who wants to make amends to us, and the man who I love with all my heart but who won't even look at me, let alone talk to me anymore.

That day I work late, all day without even a break for lunch, in hope, to be honest, of getting a glimpse of Mitchell. Am I truly not going to be seeing him at all before we leave? When I finally go up to our room, I find Danny and Mark huddled over his laptop.

'There you are!' Mark exclaims as I come in through the door of the suite, not quite knowing how to feel anymore. 'I've got good news for you. I've put in an offer on that house, the one in Rose Lane.' He smiles, spreading his arms wide as if to embrace the entire room.

Rose Lane. That's right in the middle of Little Kettering, no less. I sit down next to them. It's a gorgeous house, of course. Mark always had good taste. But to move in with him, I'm still not sure. Not at all, in fact. I can't live here now, not anymore, and bump into Mitchell every day. I need time out. I need to think before I act this time.

'And it would be very handy for your new job here as manager,' he adds.

I stare at him, then turn to Danny.

'Darling, it's past your bed time now. Go on ahead and I'll come and tuck you in.'

'Oh-kay…' he says, none too happy. He was enjoying the talk about his future home in Cornwall.

'How do you know I've been offered a position here?' I ask as soon as Danny closes the door to our bedroom. 'And don't say Danny told you because he doesn't even know.'

He falters. 'Rosie, how is that even important? The position is yours for the taking.'

'No, it's not, Mark. This is Mitchell's Fitzpatrick's job. And how do you even know any of this? You don't work for Johnson Hotels anymore. Not since you left for the States.'

He shrugs. 'I've been meaning to tell you. I got back in years ago by applying to the Florida branch.'

'What? You've been working for Johnson Hotels all these years and never told me?'

'Yeah. I've moved my way up.'

And then the clouds clear and it all becomes crystal clear to me. Of course. 'So it's you then! You're the one behind all this! You set out to get an honest man fired, just so I could have my dream job and accept to live here with you? Could you be any more manipulative?'

'I did it for us, Rosie. Besides, I didn't know the bloke would get fired. I assumed they'd move him up or something. It's not my fault he's going.'

'To think of all those horrible reviews you went out of your way to write! That's too low even for you!'

Mark eyes me. 'I don't know what you're on about. I just wanted some time with you and Danny. Only I knew you wouldn't agree to see me unless you had no choice. So when Susan mentioned she wanted to shuffle some people around, I asked her to give you the Cornwall job.'

The Cornwall job. How apt those words are, in every way.

'I know how much you love Cornwall, and that your dream has always been to run a quirky little inn like this one – and now you can! Rosie, I thought you'd be happy.'

'At the cost of Mitchell's job? You're trying to build your happiness on someone else's misery?'

'I'm just trying to help you, Rosie. I figured that if I could help your dreams come true, maybe you would consider taking me back. To where we were nine years ago. I know it's crazy, Rosie. But if we had something once, we can have it again, don't you think? I still love you.'

'But I don't love you anymore, Mark. How can you even think I ever would, after all you've put us through all these years, and even now, especially after this stunt you pulled on an innocent man? We're not moving to Cornwall with you, Mark.'

'But you said you said you'd always love me.'

I roll my eyes. 'That was years ago, provided it was *reciprocated*. Do you really not understand love at all? Did you really think that this was the right way to win me and Danny back?'

He frowns and gets to his feet. If it wasn't all so pathetic and sad, I'd laugh. But the good thing is, I can afford to laugh now. Nine years ago, not so much. Because I've changed. I'm stronger. Wiser.

But Mark hasn't changed one bit. He is his usual, manipulative self. He'll do anything to get his way – cheat, lie, whatever it takes.

'I'm back now, new and… and *reformed*…'

'Reformed? I don't see any difference at all in you, Mark. None whatsoever.'

'But I want what's best for you and Danny. I've moved up in the Johnson hierarchy. I'm an executive now, and I can provide for you both.'

'You can provide? By lying to us, manipulating and destroying people's lives? That's it, Mark. We're done here.' I pick up my phone and turn to go.

'Rosie, don't be your usual impulsive self. Stop and think. All you have to do is say yes and we'll be a family again.'

I whirl around, my blood boiling. 'Don't you understand that you can't use people like that? Wasn't what you did to me already enough? I was willing to make an effort – for Danny. But now, knowing how low you've stooped, that despite everything, you still can't be trusted? You haven't changed a bit.' For the second time in my life, Mark has let me down.

'But, Rosie, I was simply trying to rebuild our family.'

'We were *never* a family,' I cry out, louder than I intended. And then, I can see clearly. I know what I'm going to do now.

'Hi, Susan,' I say, trying to inject some sort of enthusiasm in my voice, meanwhile wishing her superiors would give her a side-move option, like maybe to the North Pole. Having said that, she'd probably scare the bejesus out of the elves and reduce them to pure slavery, and Santa to a whimpering mess. And the expression when hell freezes over? She's capable of that, too. Because that's what she does for a living. No, that's a lie. That's what she does for sheer pleasure.

'What the hell is going on there, Rosie?' she booms and I literally have to move my mobile away from my ear.

I swallow. 'What do you mean?'

'You're having a sordid affair with the manager. Really, Rosie, no wonder your reports are practically glowing. You have intentionally lied to me, and now I know why.'

'Hang on a minute. First of all, I'm not having a sordid affair with anyone.'

'Evidence tells me otherwise.'

A flame of indignity sparks in my gut. How dare she enter my personal sphere? What I do and whom I sleep with is entirely my business. And now too much is too much. I've had enough of her attitude. It's demeaning and I don't deserve it. 'Your evidence is wrong.'

'We are not at all pleased with your performance, Rosie. This changes everything. We're letting you go.'

Letting me go? After all these years of saving her ass? 'Are you seriously firing me on the sole suspicion of my having an affair with a colleague?'

'An investigated colleague,' she corrects me. 'That's it, you're both out.' And she hangs up.

I stifle a yelp. She can't do this, kick us all out onto the street! I rub my face, feeling absolutely helpless, and look up as Penny enters my line of vision. She is carrying her laptop, which she had promised to lend to me and which she now puts on the counter before me, a huge smile on her face that fades the minute I look up.

'God, you look terrible – are you okay?' she asks.

'I'm fine,' I snap. 'Sorry. Thanks for the computer,' I say as I fire it up.

'I can mind the desk for a few hours if you need a nap,' she volunteers. Why is she this nice to me? She really must be confident of her relationship with Mitchell. Unless – ah she doesn't know about us. That would explain it.

'I'm waiting for my dad. Is he here yet?' she asks.

'Your dad? I'm sorry, I have no idea,' I answer, pulling up the booking system. Maybe he could put her straight about the dangers of dating older men. 'Does he need checking in? I'll have a look. What's his name?'

She laughs. 'Awh, Rosie, not you, too?'

'Not me too, what?' I ask, my annoyance slightly rising. But I can't be mad at her. It's not her fault, really. Who could resist a guy like Mitchell?

'We get this all the time,' she goes on. 'Nobody believes he's my dad. Probably because he's so young and I call him by his name.'

'Well, then he and Mitchell must get along very well,' I say.

Penny throws her head back and gurgles with laughter, and then she steps forward to hug me. 'Rosie!' she cries. 'Mitchell *is* my dad!'

I stare at her. What is she on about? But then the words sink in. Mitchell is her dad? Not her sugar daddy or anything sordid, but her actual father? 'But… but… you're not Lola…' is all I can say.

She laughs. 'That's my childhood name. Penelope was too long for me to say when I was little so I used to call myself Lola.'

Penny. Penelope. Lola. And then I actually see it – the smile and the mannerisms. She is definitely Mitchell's daughter. She's not his girlfriend! He didn't go off with some other woman at the first hurdle. He's still single! And I am definitely still in love with him.

But... 'You don't even call him Dad,' I blurt out.

She shrugs. 'I stopped calling him that during my rebel years, and then it became a running joke.'

'Right,' I breathe out as I recover my British stiff upper lip and open her laptop.

Penny laughs. 'Anyway, you don't fool me one bit, Rosie. I know you're in love with him.'

Can I deny it? No, but I can change the subject, and fast.

'Right now, Penny, I'm more concerned about saving his job. Head Office is... What's *that*?' I gasp as an email warning flashes across the screen. It's quick, but I catch the name of the sender: susanhearst@gmail.com.

How can I have received an email from her if I haven't even logged onto my email account yet? I log on and check my emails, but there is no dismissal email there to speak of. If that email wasn't sent to me, there's only one solution, and still it doesn't make sense.

'Is there something wrong?' Penny asks, leaning in.

'Penny, can you tell me why Susan Hearst is emailing you?'

She stops in her tracks. 'Susan Hearst? She's my aunt.'

I can feel my eyes pop out of their sockets. 'Your aunt?'

'Yeah, she's my mum's sister. But she never emails me.'

The office is spinning and I grab the edge of my desk. 'Rosie, what is it?'

'I'm sorry, but I need to read that email, Penny. It's important.'

She looks at me for a moment, and then nods. 'Sure.'

She sits next to me while she logs onto her account. 'There's nothing here from her. I told you, she never writes me.'

'Penny, I know what I saw. Please, do whatever you have to do to pull that email up.'

She shakes her head. 'I don't know what… hang on. I just remembered I lent my mum my laptop last week. She must have forgotten to close her email account.'

'But surely it cuts out after a while?'

She starts tapping in her mother's email account and password, winking at me. 'She's tried to keep it a secret, but I'm my father's daughter.'

'Meaning?'

She grins. 'Meaning nothing escapes my notice.'

The page opens and Penny clicks on Diane's Inbox. There are plenty of emails from Susan, but my eye falls on one in particular.

Diane, I'm sending you the link of my latest post, which should bring Mitchell and the Old Bell Inn to its knees once and for all. Also, I've sent one of my assistant managers to inspect him and sack him. She's shit-scared of me, so consider it done. Mitchell is going down. Enjoy the money. It's all yours.

'Oh my bloody God,' Penny whispers, staring at me. 'My mum and my aunt were trying to ruin my dad?'

I had suspected since day one that Diane had something to do with the missing funds. But I had no idea that bloody Susan the Sacker was her sister. I had definitely not seen that one coming. So that's why Susan has it in for poor Mitchell.

There is no way I can ask Penny to spy on her own mum. Or is there? But I have to save Mitchell from an unjust accusation. I clear my throat. 'Are you and your mum close, Penny?'

She rolls her eyes. 'You must be joking. I think I remind her of Mitchell too much.'

'I don't mean to pry, but…?'

Penny hears my silent question and smiles at me. 'Mitchell wanted to open his own place here, while she wanted to move to London. She wanted a luxurious life and he didn't.'

And because she wanted the money, she doctored the hotel accounts instead. Jesus. It all fits. And, like I thought, Mitchell hasn't stolen a penny.

I know what I have to do next. Five minutes later, while Penny is out on Reception, and I'm still high on adrenaline, I call Susan.

'What is it you want, Rosie?'

'To tell you that I know what you did.'

'What are you on about?'

'Your sister wanted to get back at Mitchell for the end of the marriage. And the two of you orchestrated your revenge, although I suspect you were the brains behind it all.'

Silence on the other end, then: 'This is all nonsense,' she says.

'Nonsense? No, Susan. I've just had one question: Why is Susan so bent on ruining this man? And now I know. It was more than business for you. It was for your and your sister's own personal revenge. That's not very professional, is it, Susan?' I say in her own tone.

'You are rambling as usual, Rosie, and completely out of order.'

'I don't think so.'

'Just pack your little bags and get out of there. You are not allowed anywhere near a Johnson Hotel anymore. I already fired you.' The satisfaction in her voice is so deep and heartfelt, I can literally see her face. Smug. Smarmy. Arrogant. She had always wanted a reason to fire me, which she could never find. To her I may be Rosie Miss Nobody, but I'm also Rosie Miss Nobody's Fool.

I smile into the receiver, just so she can glean the satisfaction in my voice as I say, 'Too late, Susan. I had already sent you my notice and remonstrance prior to my call. And I also cc'd it to your direct superior, Brenda Watson, who will be thrilled to have a reason to get rid of you now. Shame on you, scheming and abetting your sister's theft to the detriment of a Johnson Hotel and its employees for your own benefit. You should check your inbox more often.'

Silence. Real, terrified silence I can smell all the way from here. 'You can't do that.'

'Oh, yes I can. Read the manual, Susan. Goodbye.'

'You didn't!' Penny laughs, smacking me in the shoulder.

I grin, despite myself. 'I hope you don't mind.'

'Mind? Both Mum and Aunt Susan had something like this coming forever.'

'Well, at least Mitchell is free.'

'And that's all that matters to you.'

I nod. 'Uh, yes.'

Penny smiles and takes my hands, lowering her voice. 'Just so you know, Rosie – I've never seen him like that around a woman. Please don't break his heart by leaving. Give him a chance. He deserves it.'

I can't believe Penny and I are having this conversation, after all the wrong conclusions I'd come to about her. But it's too late for anything now. He doesn't trust me anymore, and who can blame him?

'Penny, your dad and I…' I huff in frustration.

She grins. 'I think you're perfect for him. And I've always wanted a little brother.'

I have to fight to keep back the tears. 'Oh, Penny, it's so complicated. I have to go back to London now and sort our lives out.'

She reaches forward to hug me. 'I like having you here,' she whispers. 'Make sure you come back soon, Rosie.'

24

Say Goodbye to Christmas

Our Cornwall time is up and it's time to say goodbye. I feel like I have crammed a lifetime into one short bubble of absolute bliss with Mitchell. And then burst it with my own clumsy fingers.

'Mum, do we *have* to go back to London?' Danny whines as I alternate between wiping down Mark's kitchenette counter and my eyes, the latter surreptitiously. This is the last time I'll have to do this, because tomorrow we'll be gone from this place. To think that before we got here, Danny didn't want to come. For the past three weeks we've become an integral part of this little community. Little Kettering had let us into their small circle, making us feel wanted. And now, it's all over.

I take a deep breath. 'Yes, darling, we do.'

'Because of my father?'

'Oh, no, darling. We make our own decisions – just you and me, Danny.'

'Mum, can I tell you something, without you getting upset?'

I stop and set my tea towel aside to sit next to him at the breakfast bar. He rarely spoke like this to me, and I can see the difference that being here has made in him. 'Of course, love. You can always tell me anything you like.'

He purses his lips, like an adult weighing his words. 'I'm not all that keen on Dad, Mum. I don't even like calling him that. I know he is, but – I sort of, don't like him at all, really.'

'Oh, Danny,' I whisper, taking him into my arms. 'You don't have to call him anything at all. You don't even have to see him ever again if you don't want to.'

As a matter of fact, that is my plan, and now that I know my son feels the same, I'm much easier about making that decision on his behalf. I had worried I was being too manipulative or protective, and that I didn't have a right to deprive him of his only father figure, excluding my own dad, and now Mitchell.

'So why are we leaving so soon?' he wants to know.

There's no need to burden him about my quitting.

'Did you and Mitchell fight?'

Fight? You might call it that, the sudden death of what could've been a fantastic relationship with an equally fantastic guy. 'Of course not, darling…'

'But, Mum, I heard someone talking about it.'

Oh, great. We're now the object of staff gossip. How did this get so out of hand? And to think I only came here to try and get away from my usual problems. I guess problems have their own GPS system so they don't just go and get lost like we'd like them to, but actually return and multiply like rabbits on speed.

I'd actually like to throw myself on the sofa and bawl my eyes out while drinking myself into oblivion, but because I'm supposed to be a responsible adult, I have to Mother up and bear it.

'Darling,' I say, wrapping my arms around him. 'There is absolutely nothing wrong. So be happy and give Mummy a kiss, okay?'

Danny watches me, unsure, but finally hugs me, his little mouth on my cheek, and that's all I need for now.

An hour later, we're all packed. I want to be home before nightfall. Excluding Mitchell, we've said goodbye to everyone, dodging their *Awh*, *whys* and are now ready to go.

Only... I can't leave it like this between Mitchell and myself. Of course I can't bear to look him in the eye ever again, so instead I sit down and write him a letter. Who cares if he pins it on the corkboard at Reception for a laugh? Whatever makes him feel better. Because I can't stand the idea of having lost someone like him. I will never ever find another Mitchell, no matter how long I live or how many people I meet. It's just not going to happen. Mitchell was everything I ever wanted. It just won't get any better than him. And I've blown it.

Which is pretty much what I write down in the letter, only that by the time I'm done I can't read it because the words are all blurry for the tears in my eyes.

I try different versions and several drafts. But it's all a cheese-fest. I can't sound any more pathetic. I don't even read it again or check it for spelling mistakes because he can't think any worse of me anyway, right? So I fold it, put it in an envelope and put it on his dresser.

Danny is pulling at my sleeve. 'Can I go say goodbye to Sally, Mum? Her shift starts in a few minutes and I want to thank her.'

My little man – the manners of a gentleman. How the heck did I raise such a quality kid? I ruffle his hair. 'Of course, darling. Wait for me in the lobby.'

Well, that's me done. I've quit my job and I've lost my brand-new boyfriend. What else is there? How am I going to go back to London, back to our pint-sized flat, and find a nine-to-five, having briefly known happiness?

And Mitchell, how did I lose him so stupidly? Where did I go wrong?

This is one whole giant mess. I ruined everything by myself. I really am 'ruinous', as Danny said. And speaking of, my boy will be waiting for me in the lobby. I know he doesn't want to go, but things like this are part of growing up.

When I've pulled myself together, I wheel out my trolley, and with one last, oh-so-longing look, close the door behind me for the very last time. I will never be able to come back to this beautiful place. Ever.

Breathing deeply, I drag my trolley down the stairs, and make my way to Reception, but Danny isn't there, so I dial Sally.

'Sally, hi. Can you send me Danny, please? We have to go now.'

'I sent him over. He's waiting for you in the lounge.'

'Oh. Right. Sorry. Take care, Sally…'

'And you, luv,' she says, blowing me kiss noises. 'And

thank you so much for putting in a good word and doing the paperwork for me. The spa is only a few months away now, thanks to you. I would have never hoped for it if it hadn't been for you.'

'It was my pleasure, Sally. You deserve it. I know you will be a success.'

'Bless you, luv.'

'Take care, Sally. Bye…'

In the lounge, Danny's trolley is there. Only he's not with it.

'Laura?' I call, just as she's coming out from the back office. 'Where's Danny…?'

Laura blinks. 'He said he was going up to his room to get something he forgot…'

'But I've just been up there…'

An icy chill grips my heart as I eat up the stairs, two at a time, and dash down the hall to Mark's suite. It's empty. I run around from hall to lounge to lobby to Reception, out into the parking lot, and into the woods, the trees closing in on me as I'm trying not to panic.

But Danny is nowhere to be found.

25

The Christmas Nightmare

From the day I learnt about my pregnancy, it took over my life. Nothing was more important than the baby growing inside me. And Mark leaving me had actually made me stronger. Because I had to push aside my grief to prepare a good life for my baby.

And from the moment I looked down at his tiny wrinkled face, I was in love with only him. But it was a stronger, purer love than any I'd ever felt before. One that never ends. You can stop loving a boyfriend. But a child – you can never stop loving your baby.

And now that Mark has taken him, I swear to get him back safe if I have to die trying.

I rush back to reception just as it's starting to rain.

Laura gets to her feet, alarmed. 'What is it, Rosie?'

'Danny!' I shout as I dash past her.

Where the hell can he be? How did he even get past me? For years I've watched him like a hawk so he would come to no harm, and now...

And then Mitchell appears in the doorway of Reception, blocking my path, taking my elbows. 'What's wrong?'

Forget our differences. If anyone can help me, he can. I rake a hand across my head that feels like it's going to explode. 'Danny's gone!'

Mitchell's face turns grim. 'With this downpour the roads will be flooded soon. We'd better hurry.'

Not in the mood for arguing, and actually grateful for an ally, I follow him into his jeep where he pulls out his mobile phone and starts making calls as he shoves into first gear and we are off. I only hope he has an idea, because the thought of anything happening to Danny is killing me by the second.

'Laura?' he barks. 'Get on the phone with Alex and tell him to post a notice outside the bakery, and to spread the news. Tell his mum to get on the phone too. I want everyone on this, and every house and shop in and out of the village checked. No stones unturned. Get the Chief Constable on it as well. And the Coast Guard.'

'The *Coast* Guard?' I wail. 'Do you think he might have fallen off a *cliff*?'

'Of course not, it's standard procedure around here when someone goes missing. He's probably just went out for a walk and got caught in the storm.'

'He-he was supposed to be waiting for me in the lobby. His suitcase was there!' And then a thought makes me gasp.

'What?' Mitchell says. 'What is it?'

'Mark. We had an argument. He wanted to see more of Danny, and I...'

I can tell he has his own questions about that, but he, too, is deferring them to a better time. If there ever will be. Oh, my God, if anything happens to my baby…

'I told you, Rosie, Danny is probably just having a wander. Kids are like that, distracted and all. Now chin up. We'll find him.'

'I only hope he didn't overhear us. Mark wanted us to move back with him.'

In the darkness of the storm, Mitchell's face inside the dark cabin of his jeep is illuminated only by the occasional slash of light by oncoming cars. His eyes swing to mine for a brief moment, and in them I can see a mixture of feelings. But not hatred for me. That look is gone. Not that it matters anymore. Nothing will ever matter to me if something happens to Danny.

'Any idea where he could've gone?' he asks.

I shake my head. 'He doesn't know anything outside Little Kettering, except for the coastal paths. Oh my God, this is karma coming back to get me. Oh my God, my poor boy…!'

His hand comes down on mine and steadies them in my lap. His hand is warm and strong. 'Rosie, listen to me. He is fine. We'll find him in no time. But I need you to keep your cool, do you understand me?'

I nod. 'Yes. Sorry…'

'No apologising. He's fine. I can feel it, Rosie. Just concentrate on all the places he might be.' Again, his eyes swing to mine and in them, I can see a certainty I don't feel, but it's something to hang on to.

'He… he likes the coastal path. Only it's raining now…'

'I'll call my mate at the National Trust. Get him to spread

the word up there. But he's in no danger, Rosie. If you and Mark were arguing, he probably went after Mark to try and convince him to reason.'

I dial Mark's number. I can only hope he hasn't changed it since he last sent a message.

'He's not answering! I don't even know where he lives anymore...'

'We have his address on file from when he booked,' he says, turning his wipers on full throttle.

'Where are we going?'

'To the motorway. Then... we'll see.' And then he reaches for my hand. 'We'll find him, sweetie.'

When Laura calls to tell us that the address Mark gave doesn't exist, I call Liz, who sends me a text message with the information.

Mitchell pushes a button on his mobile. 'Kevin is Chief of Police. He's my best mate,' he explains to me. 'Yeah, Janie? Mitchell. Can you out me through to Kevin? It's an emergency.'

I watch him as he speaks, his face drawn, his jaw tense. And he's pale, all factors that indicate that he's as worried as me, even if he's trying to hide it.

'Kev—' Mitchell says into his phone. 'Danny Anderson, Rosie's son, is missing. We suspect his father has him – a certain Mark...' He looks at me expectantly.

'Wilkins,' I answer.

'Wilkins. A right piece of work. Yep, thanks, bye.'

Yes, he is a piece of work. He left me, then came back, only to lie to me. But... what if Mark actually didn't take him? We might be barking up the wrong tree and wasting precious time. Where could my baby be? He hasn't got any money except for his weekly allowance. Which, thinking about it, he never spends on anything. Could he have gone to my parents? It might be a long shot. But we have to try it.

'Mitchell, turn around.'

Without questioning me, he looks for the chance and slips into a private road where he does a U-turn, trying to avoid the water rushing off to the edge of the road. It is now brown with mud, and ankle-deep. 'Where am I going?' he finally asks.

'To Little Kettering train station.'

26

Mud and Joy

My mobile rings. It's my mother, of all people. How can I keep my cool? I swallow hard and wipe the tears from under my eyes. 'M-Mum…?'

'Rosie, are you and Danny okay? We heard about the floods.'

'I'm on the road to Truro.' I don't want to alarm her by asking her to call me back if Danny shows. The anguish would kill her. 'I have to go, but I'll call you back,' I say and hang up. I'm trembling and feel like throwing up. I've never been so cold in my whole life.

Mitchell reaches over and touches my forehead. His hand is warm and I want to lean into it for the rest of my life. If this brief contact can do this to me, imagine how different my life would be if he was still in it.

And that's when, up ahead, we become aware of a river of mud gushing down through the side streets, blocking us from progressing any further.

'We need to stop for a moment,' Mitchell says, pulling into a safe parking lot and turning off the ignition.

'No, Mitchell, please, we can't stop!'

He turns in his seat and takes me by the shoulders. 'Listen to me, Rosie. We are going to find him. But right now, we need to make a plan here rather than running around like headless chickens. We need to think. And we need to get out of the storm. If we get caught in the mud, we won't be able to keep looking. Right?'

I close my mouth. He's right. With a car stuck in the mud we'd be absolutely useless to Danny. Reluctantly, I nod.

'Good girl.'

He gets out into the rain, rounds the jeep and helps me down, holding his jacket over my head against the rain, his arm still around me as he closes the door, which is a good thing, because my legs are so weak I can barely stand.

It takes us a good two minutes to dodge the traffic as the river has now burst its banks, but we finally do make it across the road to a pub. It's pouring down so badly I can't even see what the sign says.

Inside, he sits me down and soon a mug of coffee is slid in front of me as I realise my feet are soaked inside my ankle boots. Mitchell sits opposite me and takes my hand, watching me like a hawk.

I look up, my eyes misty, but I refuse to cry. I need to be strong. 'He might try to go to my parents' place in Birmingham,' I offer. 'But if he doesn't…? Where can he be…?'

His jaw tightens in thought as he looks out the window, fumbling for an answer, and then his eyes widen in astonishment. 'Bloody hell!' he cries as he shoots to his feet and out the door.

I turn my head to look out the window and freeze. As I watch, the tarpaulin off the back of Mitchell's jeep is pushed aside, and a little head emerges, followed by a small body and a pair of little legs, testing the ground for purchase.

'Danny!' I cry, jumping to my wobbly legs and dashing out the door to the road, which is now knee-high in a raging river of mud.

'Danny!' Mitchell echoes me, pushing his hands out before him in a 'Stop' command. 'Don't cross the road, stay where you are!'

The patrons inside the pub rush to the windows to see what's going on. Mitchell is now wading across the river of mud, now mid-thigh-deep. If he loses his footling and slips, he'll be washed away.

Danny, who can't hear him over the sound of the raging, muddy waters, thinks it's a lot of fun and, smiling, waves back, looking left and right before he crosses the road, just like his mummy taught him. But now, of course, there are no cars to stop him.

'Danny!' Mitchell and I cry in unison. 'Stay where you are!'

Danny looks around him, surrounded by the fast-moving river of mud and his face now crumples in fear.

And then a loud roar to our left makes my head turn. A wall enclosing an adjacent field collapses under the weight of the mud rushing downhill, the boulders scattering before our feet, mixing with the mud that has risen to just below window level.

'Danny!' I cry, throwing myself out the door, people following me.

Mitchell has reached him and hefted him onto his hip, my little boy hanging on to him for dear life.

The pub, which is higher than the road, is the only safe place, but there is no way they can make it back as the mud is almost at Mitchell's waist now. The rush of mud is too forceful, even for him. Behind them, parked cars are bobbing like dinghies, being taken downstream. Any second Mitchell and Danny will be washed away.

'Stay there, Rosie!' Mitchell shouts as I'm trying to figure out a way to help them.

Behind me, the patrons of the pub are locking into a double human chain, from the front door, down the few steps and across the flooded road, where Mitchell is slowly but surely advancing on his own. He gets halfway across before he is met by the end of the chain. I'll never forget the look on his face as he consigns Danny to the men reaching out to him. He shouts something, and they nod, but it's too noisy for me to hear.

My son is passed from man to man, until he reaches my arms. I'm shaking so badly I'm afraid I'll drop him, but, supported by two men at my elbow, I carry him through the door.

Inside the pub, it's pandemonium. A large spot has been cleared just inside the door, and coats are thrown over Mitchell and Danny. I clutch at them, smothering my son with kisses.

'I'm sorry, Mum. Don't cry, Mum. I'm okay, see?'

'What were you *thinking*?' I bawl. 'Why did you run away?'

'I didn't. I just wanted to ask Mitchell to convince you to stay here.'

'Oh, sweetie,' I bawl again, grabbing him and holding him tight to my chest.

Mitchell, whose hair is plastered to his head, wraps his arms around us as the crowd claps and cheers.

27

Christmas is For Forgiving

An hour later, we're sitting in the pub in borrowed clothes, courtesy of the generous townspeople, and now nursing a hot drink each. The rain has stopped, the roads are slowly clearing, leaving mud streaks everywhere. It's not the most beautiful of Cornish scenes, granted, but I've got Danny, and Mitchell, everything I need, right here at my side.

We watch Danny slurping at his pudding and Mitchell smiles at me beseechingly.

'Rosie? I was a right toss—' his eyes swing to Danny '— uh, fool. Can you ever forgive me?'

I laugh. 'Forgive *you*? For what?'

'I had a word with Head Office. You lost your job... to protect mine. How could I have got you so wrong?'

How, indeed? But in all honesty, not even I would believe myself. It certainly doesn't look good, does it? Who in their right mind would believe that someone acting, albeit temporarily, as inspector, would actually risk their own job to protect someone who not only was a complete stranger, but also a complete jerk? I mean, who does that?

But I have Penny to thank as well. If it hadn't been for her taking my side, and Susan exposing herself by firing me, we would've probably never found out about her and Diane's scheme to steal from Mitchell who hadn't had the foresight to change his PINs. I guess, what comes around, goes around.

'I didn't mean for all this to get so bad...' I mumble. 'You certainly didn't deserve the boot. I knew the missing money wasn't your fault. You couldn't be a thief.'

'How did you know?'

I look up into his eyes and I see all that I love about him. 'I just knew.'

'Thank you for believing in me, Rosie. I love you so much!'

'I love you, too, Mitchell – more than I can say,' I breathe, melting against him.

'So now you, me and the kids can all be together?'

I laugh. 'I'd hardly call Penny a kid, would you?'

Mitchell pulls me into his arms. 'Silly. I meant the baby.'

I literally break free from his embrace in astonishment. 'Baby? What baby?'

He blinks. 'Your baby. Yours and... Mark's.'

'What? I'm not expecting any baby!'

His face is a mixture of disbelief and confusion. 'Not expecting a baby...? But Laura said...'

Laura? Where the hell would she get such an idea from?

Mitchell swallows, visibly embarrassed and his ears are rapidly turning beet red. 'She... said you told the guests in the dining room you were pregnant.'

Oh my God. The bloody expired Bakewell tarts have

finally come back to bite me on the ass. 'No! I was sick, but it was those damn cakes.'

He starts. 'What, the ones in the basket on top of the refrigerator? Those were out of date! They were to be returned but then I moved out of the suite so I never got round to it.'

'Oh…' I whisper. 'Then why were they sitting in your kitchen?'

'So I wouldn't forget to return them. What are you, the food inspector now, too?'

'Mitchell, I only said I was pregnant because I didn't want the guests to think it was the restaurant food!'

He looks at me, confused. 'So it wasn't morning sickness?'

'No!'

And suddenly we're laughing like nuts, falling into each other's arms in sheer glee. And then I stop. 'Wait, you would've taken me on even if I was pregnant with another man's *baby*?'

He takes my arms. 'Sweetheart, you're one to talk. You were defending an alleged thief. Besides, I'm already gaga over Danny, aren't I? Might as well take the vain mum on board, too,' he murmurs with a grin, two adorable dimples bracketing his lips. 'Would you chuck me back in the mud if I kissed you now, Rosie?'

And then, I gasp at the realisation. *Dimples?* I'd never noticed them before. In all the panic, I hadn't really *looked* at him. He's completely clean-shaven, and even his hair is cut short. Gone are his gorgeous curls. 'Oh, my God! What did you do?'

'I went into town this morning to get a makeover. You didn't even notice my new tailored suit. Oh, well, that's shot to shit – or mud – now. No worries.'

'You look… you look…'

'Civilised?'

Actually, he looks *awesome*. For the first time, I can see that under that beard he had been hiding quite the chiselled jaw, and the dimples give him a boyish aura.

'I figured that the next step of my life required a new look. Didn't want to keep lookin' like a yeti today of all days.'

'Why, what was today supposed to be?'

'Did you really mean it when you said this was love?'

'You know I did,' I whisper.

'Can you forgive me?'

In answer to my question, he wraps me in his arms and envelops me in a deep, deep kiss. I am barely aware of Danny and the crowd cheering us on in the background.

He turns and smiles as a police car pulls up, and in comes a tall, boyish-looking man.

'Ah, Kev, mate. These here are Danny and Rosie.'

'Ah, finally!' the policeman says, ruffling Danny's hair and taking my hand. 'I've been listening to him going on and on about you for days. Can understand why, now!'

'Hey, no flirting. Did you bring the goods?'

'Ah, that I did.'

'What goods?' I ask, looking from one to the other.

'Nana! Grandpa!' Danny cries, bolting up from the table and throwing himself at none other than my parents standing in the doorway.

'Oh, darling, look how you've grown!' my mum cries as my dad enwraps Danny in a bear hug, both covering him with kisses, looking around for me.

'Rosie!'

'M-Mum… Dad!' I stammer. 'What are you *doing* here?'

'We've been here since this morning, love.'

'Why didn't you call?'

'We didn't want to ruin the surprise.'

'Well, you certainly didn't. I'm...'

And then they catch sight of Mitchell, standing in a pair of trousers too short and too wide for him. The hand-me-down jacket is straining across his shoulders, and despite the fact his attempts at a make-over have gone awfully awry, my heart turns over just looking at him.

Mitchell stands. 'Mrs Anderson. Mr Anderson. Good to finally meet you in person.' He grins, reaching out to shake their hands, and, by the look in my mum's eyes as they roam over his gorgeous and kind face, I can tell that she's pretty much a goner. Even Dad doesn't seem too displeased. Hang on, what...?

'What did you just say?' I repeat, searching his face. 'Meet you in person? What's going on?'

Mitchell smiles, his hand reaching out to caress my face. 'I figured I needed to call in my troops.'

'*You* called them?'

'Actually, Danny called them. I merely spoke to them to say hi. And we got to talking. About why you would go back to Mark when, in effect, you love *me*.'

I stare down at my borrowed Uggs. Of course, I can't deny it, can I?

'I'm sorry for pushing you towards Mark, love,' my mother says. 'I had no idea when you called. But this young man here has a heart of gold and he loves you dearly!'

And then, as Mum and Dad are watching, Mitchell sinks to his knees and pulls out a small box from his pocket. 'Rosalind Anderson, will you marry me?'

Epilogue

It might be a short walk to the altar on Dad's arm, but it's a tricky one, as the South West Coastal Path is anything but flat.

A gazebo has been erected just on the edge of Predannack Wollas, and walkers smile and nod at us as they saunter by, amused by this original setting. What better place to get married on this gorgeous summer's day?

Mitchell waits at the makeshift altar, more handsome and happier than I've ever seen him. But also, so nervous he looks like he's about faint.

I'm feeling pretty iffy too, and as I walk on unsteady legs, my eyes caress the sea of faces of the people who mean so much to me. Mum is in the front row, of course, sniffing, trying not to blow her nose or cry.

My aunt Milly is doing both, and so is Liz, my maid of honour, dazzling in fuchsia as she dabs at the edges of her eyes with a lacquered pinkie. There's also Sally who's done my make-up, and Laura, on Alex's arm. Next to them is Penny who is guiding Danny, our ring boy, so he won't hold up the rings at the wrong moment, and Jeremy, who has provided a horse and cart for one bumpy ride home, but it's all in good fun.

Russell has provided a major spread back at the Old Bell Inn, which Penny has taken over exclusively, while Mitchell's Cove Cottages will be family orientated with a children's park complete with ponies. Sally will be opening her own spa in September and I have just opened a pottery shop called Bits and Pieces. We've all achieved a lot in the space of six months.

Susan Hearst has been dismissed and, were it not for Johnson Hotel's decision to keep it quiet, she and her sister Diane would be in a pretty pickle.

Mark has disappeared off the face of the earth once again, and that's perfectly fine.

We have everyone we need here with us, including all my carollers, i.e. most of the village, who send us knowing grins. Somehow, they knew all along, when I had no clue. And I never thought I could ever be this happy.

I watch Mitchell as I near him, all the while musing on how strange this all feels. I have been kissed by the magic of Christmas love, after having been on my own for longer than I can remember.

Because I'm still not very experienced in relationships and dynamics within a couple, I don't know what is the right thing to say, or when to say it, or if some things are actually better left unsaid. In fact, there is a lot I still need to learn about love. But I do know that Mitchell has a heart of gold, and is untainted by all the ugliness in the world.

I know he values the simple, good things in life, like a Sunday roast and a beer after a nice long walk, high above the cliffs. I know the feeling of his arms around me at the end of a long day, and the look of love in his eyes. Danny loves him, too, and his love is totally reciprocated. They already have their 'sacred' time together to do their 'bloke stuff' and there couldn't be any more joy in my heart. I also know that Penny will be an important part in our lives, and am looking forward to that.

But I still have a million questions, like: *Is Mark ever going to come back and bother us?*

Will I sell enough vases to earn my keep? And what side of the bed will I sleep on in the new cottage? But I guess we'll just have to figure it all out. One Christmas at a time. Together.

Acknowledgements

Many thanks go first of all to my amazing Where-would-I-be-without-you editor, Rhea Kurien who made all this happen in the first place, and to all the lovely people at Aria and Head Of Zeus.

To my various tribes who support me unconditionally – my mum, family and friends, in particular my dear friend Phyllis Aquilina who shouts from the rooftops about my every book! I think she falls in love with my new male character every time!

And speaking of, thanks to my co-Aidan Turner fans on FB who write me to tell me how much they enjoy my books. That is so kind of you all and I truly appreciate your continuous support!

Also, many, many thanks to my writer buddies, in particular Holly Martin, author of the most gorgeous, feel-good and uplifting romances, and to the Queen of Crime, novelist Angela Marsons who has read and thumbs-upped more than one of my synopses! You ladies rock!

A special thanks goes to my FGM Elisabeth Jennings, romance writer extraordinaire and godmother of the Matera Women's Fiction Festival who told me to never stop writing.

And finally, to my DH and rock in the storm Nick for being there for me 24/7.

About the Author

NANCY BARONE is literally all over the place, in body and heart. She's an Italian-Canadian author of romantic comedy who lives in a farmhouse close to the Mediterranean sea but returns to the UK every time she can.

In her spare time she manages to work as an English teacher in a tiny Sicilian fishing village, and join her British husband on long walks with their dogs on the beach, all the while savouring Mayan chocolate and ricotta ice cream.

She also has the gall to classify her visit to Cornwall as 'research' for her novels.

Nancy loves to receive your messages – drop her a line anywhere here:

Website - www.nancybarone.com

Twitter account - NancyNBW

Facebook - Author Nancy Barone

Hello from Aria

We hope you enjoyed this book! If you did, let us know – we'd love to hear from you.

We are Aria, a dynamic fiction imprint from award-winning publishers Head of Zeus. At heart, we're committed to publishing fantastic commercial fiction – from romance to sagas to historical fiction. Visit us online and discover a community of like-minded fiction fans!

You can find us at:
www.ariafiction.com

� @ariafiction
🐦 @Aria_Fiction
📷 @ariafiction

🅐